TOM

DAVE FREER

TOM by Dave Freer copyright © 2016
Print edition published by Magic Isle Press, November 2016
Cover art:
© Skypixel, © Mentona
Cover design: Joe Freer
Interior art
© Irina Iarovaia
© Svetlana Alyuk
Proofreading: Periwinkle Proofs

ISBN: 0-9925490-3-5
ISBN-13: 978-0-9925490-3-9

DEDICATION

To Legolas, Batman, Robin and Duchess, our cat-family past and present.

CONTENTS

ACKNOWLEDGMENTS

Not even a mine of useless information like myself can know quite enough for such an improbable book. I need to thank Dr Nikhil Rao for advice on how not to kill your characters (but almost). Dr Shira Tomboulian for more medical advice for them, Brian Holcomb for his wisdom on the subject of suitable firearms, our vet John O'Dell for telling me a great deal more than I needed to know about the reproduction of cats, and Sharyn Lilley for the worst pun in the book.

Two of the chapters in this book have appeared in somewhat altered form, long ago, as short stories – and if I hadn't had a tight deadline and needed inspiration to write that second one, I might not have remembered what fun – as a character to write – Tom was, so thank you, Edwina Harvey.

As always my deepest thanks go to Barbara, my darling wife, who in addition to putting up with me for a lot of years, is also my firstest first reader, to whose skills both I and the readers owe a great deal. My thanks too, to my friends Melissa Siah, Najmul Hasan, and Sharyn Lilley for reading this for their input on their fields of expertise. Any errors are mine, not theirs.

The underlying inspiration for those stories, and this book, comes from four feline overlords who do not care if I mention them or not. Unless I don't thank them profusely, that is…

Legolas, Batman, Duchess and Robin… thank you for providing me with such a wealth of feline observational experience. Without you there would have been no book… and I would have lost, oddly, a great deal of joy in your service. I would have opened many less doors, and had far more bed to sleep on. I'd have sneezed less, and stepped on fewer mouse-entrails. But I have loved you dearly, my cat-masters

CHAPTER 1

THE CAT WHO CHANGED

"**M**rorw?" Tom eyed the chipped bowl with suspicion, despite the enchanting smell wafting from it, and his extreme hunger. It had been a hard winter for a half-grown cat. Pickings from humans could be good. So could kickings. It was the first time he'd come hunting up on the craggy mountainside. The cold teeth of winter and hunger had forced him to hunt some distance away from the barn he called home. So far it had produced not so much as a skinny field-mouse.

And now this scrawny human outside the old rotting stone tower was offering him something that smelled like it had to be food for the cat-gods.

He'd once stolen something that had smelled just like it from the pampered pussy that lived with an old woman on the edge of the village. The wolfed mouthfuls, in between hissing at the fat fluff-ball, had been worth being chased by the old woman and her broom.

"Here kitty. Have some nice fish," said the human.

The words didn't make a lot of sense to Tom. He knew some human, of course. Not as much as those cats that had successfully domesticated one, but he understood words like "scat!" and "get lost!"

It was the tone that worried him.

It was... peculiar.

Anything odd was a warning sign for a cat who lived by his wits.

Still, the food in the bowl smelled so good, and he was very hungry. Tom could smell any hint of a taint far better than any human. And this old bag of bones in the star-and-moon spangled robe would never be able to run as fast as him. There was no sign of any visible trap. Cautiously, tail waving he advanced step by step towards the fish.

Not all traps are steel cages or jaws. The scratched circles on the ground had meant nothing to Tom, anyway. Cats are somewhat more immune to magic than humans, but not completely so. It's just different for cats.

✨✨✨❦❦❦

Tom woke. Not instantly, alert and ready to run, as he usually did. A feral kitten that didn't, was soon dead. Instead Tom awoke... clumsily. In bits, as it were, but knowing that something was very, very wrong. He did what any cat would do under the circumstances – he sprang to his feet, in one single bound, claws out, ears back, hissing defiance, ready to flee.

Well, that was what he set out to do. What he actually did was to go from lying down to falling over in many separate disasters, starting with his front legs betraying him and him landing with his chin on the floor. He failed to stick his claws out. His ears refused to do what they should, his hiss was more of 'squark', fit for a bird! His hind legs were just too big and clumsy...

Only his tail felt right. And it felt 'right' by being dead straight up, with the hair on it fluffed, as it did when things were really, really, bad.

It happened to be true, too. Twisting awkwardly and peering at it, Tom could see his tail, tabby, fluffed and straight. That part of him was right and what it should be. The rest of him was not. His fur had fallen out. And his body was just obscenely wrong. "Wrong, wrong, wrong!" he yowled.

That sounded wrong too.

A human mouth was just terrible to howl out of. No better than a human body for springing and fleeing.

He still did his panicky, angry best.

It didn't help him get out of the stone-walled room. He head-butted the wooden door, but that didn't help, it just hurt his head. The noise he was making had just about the same effect. So, after a few minutes, he did what any sensible cat would do: lay down and thought about it, while giving himself a wash. His tongue couldn't reach the bits of him that badly needed that washing. What a stupid, useless body this was. He came up with no other answers right then, but a great many questions.

A while later the door opened. Tom spun to his feet... well, he fell over trying to do that, rediscovering that he was not a cat any more.

It was the scrawny old human, in his dirty star-and-moon spangled robe. He spoke... but what he said was not 'Scat!' or 'Damned cat!' or even 'I'll kill yer, yer little fleabag!'. As Tom wasn't sure what he meant, he decided on trying a cautious mew, while keeping a sharp eye out for the first chance to escape.

All that happened was that the human made the same noises again. And Tom gave him the same reply. The human shook his head and muttered to himself. Then he scratched his beard, and raised his stick. Tom did his best to retreat. He knew what sticks meant, even if he had no idea what the human meant. The stone-walled corner of the room limited his ability to flee. But the old human merely touched him with his stick, while rattling off a string of words...

And then he said: "I have work for you to do, idle boy. Stop lying around, dress yourself and get down to the kitchen!"

Amazing! The old human had just touched him with that stick and now the human spoke perfect cat...And then it came to Tom that there weren't even words in cat for 'dress yourself.' He tried to meow plaintively, in shock at this new horror. It came out as "Mwhaat's happened to me?" which was not what he set out to say, even if it was what he wanted to know.

He got an answer. "I need a new famulus. You're it."

Tom knew he shouldn't have understood what a 'famulus' was. But he did, even if the idea of him, a cat, being an attendant, a servant... was nearly as horrifying as finding himself in this body. "Let me go! I'm a cat," he protested, despite the fact that having looked at himself, he obviously wasn't.

The old human snorted. "You're a boy, now. I left your tail on though. That'll stop you running off. They'll kill you out there if they see it. Now, get on with it, boy. I want my supper, and there's pots needing to be scrubbed." And with that he turned and walked out of the room.

No matter what the human said, Tom was desperate to escape. Even though his mind was still whirling with all this newness and horror, that idea was still his uppermost thought. He looked at the doorway, at the retreating back of the human, as the door swung closed. The latch clicked. Tom stared at it in horror. To a cat that was confinement. And then it came to him slowly... It wasn't to a human. He'd seen them open doors.

He didn't have to like the idea of being in a human body, just to use it. So he tried pretending he was lunging for a bird and stood up on his hind legs.

It wasn't quite as easy as they made it look, but Tom was not good at admitting he couldn't do things. So he tried again, and again, until he more or less got the hang of it. Of course it was nothing on being a cat, but he could reach, now, as far as he could have leaped before. Having managed to stand on two legs... A cat will always seize the main chance, and right now that was the door-handle.

It took him a little while to succeed at making it work. He couldn't just stick his claws into it, because what he had now really didn't classify as 'claws'. On the other hand the stumpy fifth digit... well, that did make holding things easier. It was a necessary compensation for not having decent claws, Tom supposed.

The latch clicked and Tom was free.

To a certain degree of the word 'free', anyway.

He was free in a long, dank, dim stone corridor, lit by a few candles that flickered in iron wall-sconces. The strange things humans dangled on their walls hung there, supporting cobwebs. Tom did his best to creep along the passage, not knowing where out was, painfully aware that humans are just not built to creep as silently as cats, and humans who have only just discovered how to walk on their hind legs, less so.

The floor was cold, and so was he without fur.

He was, as far as his new human senses could be stretched, listening and looking very carefully for any sign of danger. And then he saw one, in a silvery framed hole into another passage.

It was a human. A young one, a male by the look of it, its bare skin pallid, its eyes wide beneath a shock of tangled head-fur, its tabby-striped tail moving in cautious curves. Tom froze.

So did the human.

Tom stood, motionless, staring at the human.

The human did exactly the same thing.

Eventually, Tom knew he was going to have to lose this competition. His new human eyes were just not as good as cat eyes. He just had to blink. So he did... and so did the human.

It occurred to Tom, that, although he'd seen naked humans before, down at the pool on the river, none of them had had such a fine tail. He waved his own... and so did the human. The word 'mirror' – which he had not previously known, or begun to understand, came to his mind. He tested what the idea implied, by moving his head. The reflection also moved.

Somehow a pool of still water had been trapped and pressed up against this wall! Tom could not resist looking at himself.

It was, for a cat, not an appealing sight. Despite the desperate circumstances, Tom tried several poses in this odd skinny human body... and was suddenly aware that the other cat boy in the mirror was about to receive a belt from behind from the scrawny old human.

It took a wallop from that old human's staff for him to work out that that applied to him as well, not just the reflection. He turned to flee, but Tom and his new human body were still not getting on quite correctly. His frantic leap bounced him against the far wall and left him in a heap on the floor. Tom got several more whacks from the staff as he cowered there. "I told you to put clothes on and get to the kitchen, boy," said the old man, crossly.

"M...clothes. Kitchen. I don't know," whimpered Tom, trying to watch for and dodge the next blow.

It didn't come. "Hmph. I hadn't thought of that," said the old man irascibly. "More wastage of my precious time! Well, get up, boy. I will show you only once."

Cautiously, Tom got to his feet, wishing he could trust them to help him run.

"Back to your room. There's one of your predecessor's robes there. You'll have to look after it. I'm not made of money, you know."

The room he had escaped, now that Tom was looking for something more than a way out... still had very little extra to see. A straw pallet, an old blanket – Tom had been on one once – and a three-legged stool, on top of which there lay a bundle of cloth. The old man pointed at it with his stick. "Your robe. Put it on."

Tom was still not too sure what to do with the human front-paws, but they did manage to pick the bundle up. A piece of rope fell to the floor.

He held the robe and looked at it in puzzlement.

"Put your arms through the arm holes and put the rope around your waist," said the man with an irritable sigh. "Really, if anyone had said it would be this much trouble… Get on with it!"

So Tom did his best. It was enough to provoke a snort of what might have been amusement from the old man. "That's both back-to-front, and upside-down."

Tom tried again. It was… odd having something that moved against his skin, but it was warmer, even if it did smell faintly of cheese. Tom knew that smell from the dairy which was close to the barn where Tom had lived. Tying ropes was a whole new mystery, that eventually his master lost patience with, and did it for him, before chasing him down the long passage, past his reflection, and through to another room.

He did not recognize all of the smells in the kitchen, but quite a few of them were rank, nasty and reeked of decay. Others were appetising… in that a smell of rat was that, to Tom. The old man pointed him at piles of crockery and pots on a long bench next to another door. "As you can't dress yourself, you probably can't cook either. Well, you will have to learn. Now clean those."

Tom looked at the piles of dishes, plates and pots in horror.

This human tongue was going to be completely useless for the job.

And then a huge black mass of bird-feathers flung itself at his face, claws out, shrieking: "Nevermore!"

Tom ducked just in time, but the raven's trailing claw left a parting through his hair.

※※※※※※※※

Tom learned. The first thing he learned was that escape from the tower was not going to be easy. Well, he learned that after 'how you actually wash pots' and 'humans are not as good at catching rats with teeth and claws as cats are.'

He finally succeeded in catching a big black rat. He fought the temptation to let it go and catch it again a few times, instead of just eating it. It would help to deal with the fact that the mouthfuls of fish were a long time ago. For some reason the thought of crunching the rat's skull was making him feel slightly queasy instead of hungry.

And then the old man returned to the kitchen, fortunately, not with his raven.

"A rat!" he exclaimed. "Excellent, boy! Just what I was needing for my latest experiment!" The old man looked at the scrabbling, chittering, squeaking creature Tom had, pinched hard, by the neck. "Follow me. You are not to touch anything in my laboratory unless I tell you to!"

Tom had already tried running away and been unsuccessful... Three times so far. He'd tried not doing what he was told, and learned that it caused pain and bruises. So he followed the old man out of the huge gloomy kitchen, and up a staircase. Stairs were new to his human body. He nearly dropped the rat, while coping with them.

The door at the top of the stairs was heavy, and studded with metal. The old man went in, muttering. Tom learned, later, that he wasn't just muttering, that those odd words meant something.

The room within was noisome –and not just in that it stank of strange and nasty chemical reeks, but there were also many little noises, hissing, bubbling and strange strangled sounding gurgles. A huge iron candelabra, hung from the roof, full of rows of candles, their solidified yellow wax hanging down in long dribbles. The walls were lined with benches or cabinets, and cages. The benches and central table were full of strange metal and glass apparatus, from whence some of the sounds and smells came. Some of the other sounds and smells came from the raven. It sat watching him, head askance, from a perch on the top of a bust of a beautiful woman. She was beautiful even if she wasn't a cat, Tom was surprised to realize. The raven wasn't beautiful. It looked ready for murder, but then ravens always do.

The old man walked over to a strange contraption in the far corner. It had a glass wheel hanging over it, which was slowly rotating, emitting puffs of sulphurous smoke. It dangled over a seething bath of grey glutinous quivering stuff, through which little blue lightnings seemed to crawl. The old man pointed a bony finger at a wide funnel attached to edge of the device. "Put it in there."

Tom was rather upset by this. It was his rat! He'd caught it. But something in that tone said: 'catch yourself another rat.'

So he dropped it into the funnel. And then he ducked fast, faster than the old man, because he still had some cat-reflexes.

The grey goop in the bath erupted with an explosive woomph! It wasn't grey anymore but burning. The suspended wheel spun so fast it shook itself loose and crashed into the wall in a shower of glass. The old man danced around stomping on burning bits, swearing in a way that filled Tom with a degree of admiration and awe. Cats instinctively understand the value and power of cursing and swearing.

Tom was less admiring about the smell of roasted rat... although it made him hungry, which was odd.

Eventually, the magician stopped swearing, and turned on Tom. "I'll need another rat," he snarled. "And get a broom and clean this mess up."

Tom was still new to the job of being a human famulus. "It took me ages to catch that rat. It was my dinner!"

He got a clout on the ear that was so unexpected he didn't even manage to dodge. But it did obviously set a train of thought going in the old man. "You'll have to eat bread and cheese. I need the rats. But I could use some food too. I hadn't thought of it for a while. Humph. I will have to arrange for you to learn to cook."

Tom stood wary, ready to duck any more blows, and ready to run again. He would have run a good few heartbeats back, if he'd still been a cat. But his new human thinking said it would be a really bad idea. Best to run when he wasn't being watched. Especially by the raven in the corner, which had him transfixed with one unblinking eye.

"Nevermore!" it said... and flew over to the human's shoulder, where it perched, and clacked its dagger-like beak, viciously.

The old man scowled and tipped his head away. "Get off. We'd better go and feed the foul fowl," he said to Tom. "Another job for you, boy. Last time I forgot to feed it, it took a bite out of my ear."

※※※※※※※※※

In a castle far away, a princess wept. She did that when she was livid with fury. She clenched her fists in rage. A helpless rage, which made it worse.

Princess Alamaya was neither pampered nor indulged.

She didn't have a wicked stepmother, but had to make do with a wicked Uncle, if by 'wicked' one meant conscientious and over-protective. Someone had plainly forgotten to tell Duke Karst, the Prince Regent, that he should be trying to secure the throne of Ambyria for his own revolting son. His son was revolting, Alamaya thought. All babies were. Plump, pink and making people go braindead and coo over them.

Even her, and she was disgusted at herself for doing it. He just had such tiny fingers and toes.

She wished desperately that her fairy Godmother would come to her rescue. Or even just visit. The old hag at least wasn't safe. Or nice. Or planning to marry her off suitably to protect the Royal House of Corvin. Godmother liked to drink too much and make rude suggestions to the footmen, or anyone else who was male and not running fast enough.

Alamaya just didn't see the sense of the latest edicts for her protection.

If she were cursed, and if her enemies were trying to kill her, she might as well have a good time first.

CHAPTER 2

THE HAUNTED SKULL OF THE KITCHENS

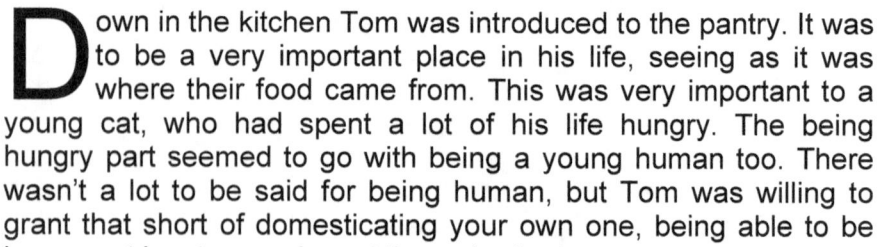

Down in the kitchen Tom was introduced to the pantry. It was to be a very important place in his life, seeing as it was where their food came from. This was very important to a young cat, who had spent a lot of his life hungry. The being hungry part seemed to go with being a young human too. There wasn't a lot to be said for being human, but Tom was willing to grant that short of domesticating your own one, being able to be human, at least around meal times, had advantages.

The old man sat down at the bench next to the table. "You haven't made much progress, boy. Not even lit a fire yet, let alone cleaned the place up. Get the bread and cheese. I'll have a mug of ale."

"I don't know where to get anything, old man," said Tom, still rather sullen at the thought of the rat.

He got an impatient cuff, which, this time, he managed to dodge. "Hmph. Show a bit more respect, boy. I am Master Hargarthius. You will call me that. Or Master." He creaked to his feet. "It's cold in here. I suppose you've never lit a fire before either. Follow me." He led Tom to a heavy, tight-fitting bolted door, which opened into a side-room, shelved from floor to just beneath the roof. "You must never ever quite close this door when are in the pantry. It does not open from the inside."

With the door only open a crack, it was dim in the pantry, and the old man leaned his stick against the wall, fumbled in his robe and produced a jar with virulent green squirming things inside it. He opened the lid, and then dug around inside his robe some more, until he came up with a small pair of tongs. He reached into the jar, and snapped up a writhing green thing – it looked like a fat, damp, angry mottled green lizard with a paddle-tail. Tom leaned in, curious. He'd eaten quite a few lizards. And a few more lizard-tails.

If he'd been a cat, still, he'd have had his whiskers singed as this creature's steaming tail suddenly flared into flame. As it was, he just staggered back and Master Hargarthius thrust the burning creature into a lamp-wick. The lamp lit up a rather chaotic little room. The shelves were full of bottles, bags and jars, and the floor-space crowded with sacks, a couple of barrels, and several tin canisters.

"Hmph!" That seemed to be Master Hargarthius's favourite noise. "I'd forgotten your predecessor indulged in a little looting before his... flight." That was followed by a nasty chuckle. "I do hope he enjoyed making the food last! You'll have to tidy up this mess. I hope he tried some magic in here. It would have served the filching chawbacon lackwit right."

Tom felt something nuzzle his elbow, and jumped back. It was, Tom recognised from his one lucky venture into the cool room behind the dairy, on the farm that he'd been born on, a cheese. It smelled like cheese. It looked like cheese. But it was moving. Moving towards him...

Master Hargarthius saw what Tom had retreated from, and snatched up his stick and hit it. Then he stomped on the still burning lizardy thing as the flame licked at a sack. "Malfecium! What a waste of a perfectly good salamander!" said Master Hargarthius crossly. "Be warned by that creature, boy. You must never try a spell of any kind in here. Magic works... differently in

11

here. You never know what might happen. I made that mistake once."

The cheese, Tom noticed, had somehow retreated right back along the long shelf, and was now hiding behind a large jar of something cloudy.

Master Hargarthius paid it no mind, but instead took a couple of items off another shelf and handed them to Tom, and took a mug from a hook, and drew some frothy beer from a barrel. "Go on. To the table. Get some plates. And you're not to drink my beer and you're to keep the pantry shut at all times, when you're not actually in it, to keep the vermin out."

So Tom did as he was bid. He got another clout for bringing a dirty plate, as the old man hacked slabs off the coarse loaf with a long glittering knife he drew from somewhere in his robe. The raven swooped down and snatched the first piece, and retreated to the corner of the mantel above the cold fireplace to tear it apart and eat it.

Tom was a little doubtful about the bread part. Cheese... maybe. To a cat it seemed wrong. But he was hungry enough to try the food, and to the human mouth it tasted very good indeed. He ate eagerly and greedily once he'd started – to the point that even the old man noticed. "Were you a wolf or a cat?" he asked dryly. "There is more. Don't lick the plate."

Tom had another slab of the bread, and more of the soft cheese. He realized that his captivity – which still absolutely had to be escaped – at least meant he would get food. He looked curiously at the beer the old man was drinking. It didn't smell cat-attractive, but then he'd changed his mind about both the bread and the cheese. He was still too wary to push asking for it, though, even if food and beer appeared to have had a mellowing effect on the old man, and on the raven, sitting on the mantel-shelf, cracking its beak and picking at crumbs.

"I think," said Master Hargarthius, rubbing the crumbs deeper into his beard, perhaps to save for later, "That you need a teacher, boy. I don't have the patience or the desire to instruct you properly, and you don't know enough to be useful. Wait here."

Instinct said to Tom that this would be a very good time to run. Besides instinct, cats don't take kindly to the concept of 'instruction'. It was like taking orders: All very well for humans and dogs... But the raven was watching him, unblinking. And even if it wasn't, Tom wasn't too sure where he could run to. There was no smell of outdoors, and the several doors could lead anywhere.

So he waited. He was to regret that, in the next few weeks. Not that running would have helped, but at least then the old man or the raven might have killed him outright.

That would have been better than enduring the skull of Mrs Drellson. Anything had to be better than the skull of Mrs Drellson.

Master Hargarthius returned and put down on the table... a skull. It still had a few wisps of hair attached to it, and the jaw had been wired on. Unfortunately it hadn't been wired shut. For a moment the skull just sat there. It was bone. Tom had seen bones before, even skulls. He was not particularly impressed or perturbed. And then Master Hargarthius tapped the skull with his staff, while muttering again.

The remaining snaggly teeth clacked together, and the skull of Mrs Drellson said, in the kind of thin, screechy voice that seemed to go right through Tom's head, without bothering to go via his ears. "Why is this kitchen such an awful mess? Answer me!"

Master Hargarthius pointed a bony finger at the skull. "Boy. This is Mrs Drellson. Mrs Drellson was the housekeeper here... once. She'll see that you learn what you have to do." He got up and walked out, while the black skull sockets stared at Tom.

As soon as the old man was through the door, the skull spoke again. "Well. Don't just sit there! There's work to be done! On your feet. Up, up, up!"

Mrs Drellson never stopped talking... except when Master Hargarthius was in the room. Even as the re-animated dead, the old housekeeper of Estethius's Tower of Art and Magic (which, she insisted, was what this place should be called) was wary of the magician. She called him 'Old Grumptious' contemptuously enough when he wasn't on hand to hear her. And she was horrified by the state of her old domain, the kitchens. There were several of them, it turned out, all, bar this one, were long unused and dusty and filled with rusty implements. Soon they were also full of the sound of Mrs Drellson's shrill voice echoing around the vaulted ceilings, as she drove Tom to dust and scour and polish and clean. The rats hated it, and so did Tom, and not just because it drove all the rats away.

Tom had wanted to run away from the first. After Mrs Drellson came into his life, he wanted to do so, desperately. But it wasn't possible, as he very soon established. And, dead or not, Mrs Drellson could make a cat-boy's life very unpleasant indeed.

Later, Tom worked out that if he'd been human by birth and experience, the levitating, talking skull – a skull that could send out little green whips of pain to torment him— would have frightened him witless. But as he had had no experience of being human, he assumed that every human household had something similar to her. He had wondered why humans were so needlessly industrious before he met the skull of Mrs Drellson. When he finally found out that work was normal in all human homes, even though they did not have levitating undead skulls driving the famulus to work, he was mystified about it all over again. Humans were a strange thing for a cat to be transformed into. Strange and very unpleasant.

By the time he went to his stone cell-room that night – and she chased him all the way – Tom was too tired to care. But the kitchen at least was a warmer place. Only part of that was due to his running about. Some warmth was due to the fire he had learned to kindle in the hearth.

It was all a learning process. Tom learned a great deal that he didn't want to know, including that "I licked myself as best as I can" was not an adequate answer to "You stink. Have you washed, boy?"

Immersing himself in water was just un-natural. And humans did stink. Every cat knew that. They were obviously used to it, so just didn't notice. Perhaps they couldn't smell as well as a disembodied talking skull, which made him wash by sitting in a tin bath half full of water, and washing his body not with his tongue as nature intended but with water, soap, and a cloth.

"That's not good for you!" he complained, when she told him to do so.

"And why would I care what's good for you, boy!" cackled the skull. "You're in the wrong place for good. Now wash. Or else!"

So, shivering in front of the kitchen fire, Tom had washed, watched by the empty skull-eyes, to make sure he did not neglect any spots – or wash any spots for too long. It was a horrible experience, and the skull seemed set on making him repeat it regularly.

Maybe Mrs Drellson's skull thought the water would numb his mind. But it didn't. He learned. He learned to start her boasting too. She told him a great deal more about his prison, that way. He also learned a little more about the human who had captured him.

"Oh, old Grumptious is a bad, bad magician," Mrs Drellson's skull informed him. "Nothing like as bad as Lord Estethius, of course," said the skull, proudly. "Lord Estethius was pure untrammelled evil. He always had at least fifteen house-slaves for me. And that was not including the magical servants."

Tom was not sure how a skull managed to sniff in disdain. "And he was always having somebody suitably whipped. Or turned out in the winter snow for dire-wolves to hunt. Old Grumptious has let the standards slip."

Gradually Tom worked out that it wasn't just the standards that Master Hargarthius had let slip, but some of the walls too. The tower was old and made of stone, part of it quarried into the mountain itself, part of it built stone on stone, back when this had been the wild country, full of dire-wolves and worse. Mrs Drellson's skull disapproved of the state of the tower. She said it had been bigger once. She disapproved of the wild-lands too. They'd been properly wild when she was a girl, unlike the inferior wildness of these degenerate times. Actually, it was hard to find anything she did approve of. But she disapproved most of the raven and of the cheese that lurked in back of the pantry. It seemed the skull was actually afraid of both, which Tom learned to use to his advantage.

They weren't his idea of great friends, or allies, either, but a cat-boy had to use what a cat-boy could find. He also began to learn what magic was, and that it was not something all humans had. It could be very useful to a cat. Or very dangerous. One could end up as a human... with a tail.

There were some visitors to the magician's rotting old tower. The first one took Tom a few seconds to recognize. He seemed a lot smaller than the vast human who had thrown things at a feral kitten he was chasing, at least when seen through human eyes. He looked as terrified as Tom had been, then. Tom wondered what he'd been stealing.

He plainly had whatever it was in the sack he was carrying. Tom, who had answered the Master's irascible bellowed order to come to the study, waited for Master Hargarthius to kick him, or better still, hit the man with his staff. Tom had learned to fear that staff.

Instead Master Hargarthius grumpily told Tom to take the sack to kitchen.

The man clutched the sack. "Not until I gets my money," he said in a voice of fearful defiance. "No money, no goods, Mister."

"Hmph," snorted Master Hargarthius. But he fumbled under his robe, and came out with a leather pouch. Tom saw the look of naked greed on the visitor's face, but the Master did not notice. He was busy counting out little clinking bits, which Tom's mind said were coins. They did not smell tasty.

The Master handed them to the man, who put down the sack and examined each coin and transferred them one-by-one into the other hand. He shoved them in a pocket, and nodded, grudgingly. "He can take the sack."

Tom reached down and took hold of it, and turned...

The visitor screamed. "He's got a tail! Monster! Demon!"

Tom nearly dropped the sack, getting away from the demon monster... before he realized that it was him. He turned slightly, looking back at the man, who was gibbering against the outer door. He thought he'd tell the village man he was a cat... but Master Hargarthius was laughing, and waved him away. Walking down the passage with the heavy, smoky-smelling sack, Tom had a bit more time to think about it. 'Monster' he understood. 'Demon'... that was more complicated. Whichever human the words in Tom's head had come from hadn't really understood demons. But he had been powerfully afraid of them. That made Tom strut a bit.

"Where have you been you lazy good-for-nothing boy?" screeched the skull of Mrs Drellson as he pushed open the kitchen door.

"I'm a demon monster," he informed the skull. "I have a tail."

It didn't have the same effect on the skull as it had had on the man from the village. The skull just cackled. Then it said: "And I'll burn that tail off slowly if you don't work harder and faster, you worthless hobgobbin."

Tom wasn't sure what a hobgobbin was either. However, he was fond of his tail. It was all that was left of him, in a way. He made haste into the kitchen.

"What have you got there?" demanded the skull, empty orbs fixed on the sack. "What nasty dirty rubbish are you dragging into my clean kitchen?"

"I don't know. Master Hargarthius told me carry it down here." Immediately he'd said it, Tom regretted it. If he'd thought quicker, he could have got her to order him to throw the sack out... but she'd have found a way to blame him, most likely. She did that. She was quicker at it than Tom. Maybe she had had more practice.

"Well. Put it safely somewhere then," she said. "The fire needs more wood. And fill the rack next to it, while you're at it."

So Tom hauled wood, until Master Hargarthius came down. "I thought there'd be slices of ham cooking by now," he said with his usual grumpiness. "Gold-plated ham, at what it cost me."

Tom found out, thus, that that was what he had carried to the kitchen: Ham, more of the heavy, solid bread, and more soft cheese. That was good. Better than braving the cheese that lurked in the far corner of the pantry, anyway.

The ham, once he'd learned not to burn it, or his mouth, was good too.

That was not something Tom found true of the second visitor to the tower.

☙☙☙☙❧❧❧❧

"The Princess must die," hissed one voice.

"She's going to. You need to learn patience," said the other, coolly.

The problem with a bespelled rat as a spy, was that it remained a rat. It wasn't, for all that she drove it, going to go beyond the arras. She could not see the conspirators. And her vessel heard as a rat hears, which was entirely different to how a human hears, she'd found. The witch could not work out just whose voices they were, from what she heard with the rat-ears.

"How do you know for certain?" asked the first. The listening witch was almost sure that that was a woman speaking. "It's only demon-gossip. They lie."

"So do humans, and yet one can learn to discern the truth from them."

Then the rat-ears heard another sound. A cat's footfall is not loud to a human, but to a rat... so it fled.

The witch sighed. So they knew about the demon. She'd have to use it, and soon, to get what she needed.

CHAPTER 3

IN WHICH THERE IS A DEMON

————————▶ • ◀————————

Tom had nearly finished another day, down in the bowels of the kitchens, when he was summonsed into the presence of the second visitor. Well, Master Hargarthius bellowed for food and drink, for him and his guest... and he actually sounded pleased.

Mrs Drellson's skull had the time of her... afterlife, telling Tom what to do, where to find the good silver, and making him polish crystal wine glasses and run down to the cellar – something he hadn't known existed, to fetch wine. And then run back down again, for a different bottle, one slightly less than three centuries past its prime.

Mrs Drellson's skull had revelled in entertaining the nervous nobility, gentry and other magicians for her master. The skull seemed to hope that time had come again. "Oh you should have seen them, all trying to be polite, trying to guess which dish was poisoned and how." The skull laughed scornfully. "Poison's always in the cabbage, if it's in anything. It can hide the smells of poisons, best. Now get on with it. The good sausage, I told you. Hmph. It's not what I'd call an adequate feast."

It still looked that way to Tom as he carried the heavy platter up the stairs to the Master's study. Some of the items arranged in the little bowls smelled decidedly odd, and cat-unpleasant. The wine however... that had a lovely scent, reminiscent of something. It made him feel combative, and was a little distracting. It took Tom a while to work out what it was rather like: The scent with which male cats mark their territory. So humans drank that? How odd.

He was still rather deep in this distracting thought when he took the platter in to the room, where his master was standing talking to the visitor. The master was pointing to a complicated diagram on the wall with his staff. The visitor wore bright coloured clothes, and his collar was trimmed with martin-fur – that was different enough – but what was really strange... well, he wouldn't have commented if it hadn't been for smell of the wine. That had temporarily distracted him from the reality of his place here in the tower, where asking questions meant dodging a cuff on the ear.

So he just asked the visitor, unthinking. "Why haven't you got a shadow?"

At which point a lot of things happened, very fast.

Even very fast for a cat.

The stranger stopped looking human, unless humans were able to suddenly transform into fluid, flame-like creatures, and no-one had told Tom about it. It dived out of its now-burning clothes and reached for Master Hargarthius. Then it shrieked and flung itself at the high window. But Master Hargarthius, muttering furiously, lifted his staff and... the staff grew, and the magician used it to scratch a line on the floor, completing a pattern there.

The fluid flame fell to the floor, and Tom dodged back, dropping the platter, scattering food, breaking the plates and shattering the wine bottle. He looked at the result in horror. Now he was in for it. He looked for the best route to flee.

But the door had closed itself. The air in the room was thick and smelled of lightning and cat...wine, and somehow the atmosphere tasted metallic. Tom settled for backing up against the wall, the one that had a bookcase against it, and was solid books. He wished he could back right into them. Some of them did seem to be nuzzling against his back, but right now he wasn't prepared to turn around and find out just how a leather-bound book could do that. What was happening in the middle of the room was too worrying.

It involved a strange and malevolent creature... who had always been strange and malevolent, and usually cross and hitting Tom. He was now fighting with a ball of flame that sometimes became a tiger, or a warrior, or an enormous striking serpent. Master Hargarthius did to it just what he always did to Tom, only quite a lot harder... With added lightning. "Avaunt, Demon," he yelled. "Avaunt, I command you!"

Tom wasn't entirely sure what avaunting was, or how he was supposed to do it, when it occurred to him that maybe the stranger was actually also a demon, and that, for a change, Master Hargarthius was not actually yelling at him. No wonder the man from the village had been afraid of demons! Tom rather liked the tiger, and wondered when he would get to being able to turn himself into that. It didn't seem to be helping the demon though. Under the rain of blows it had contracted to being a mere ball of flame.

"Quick boy," yelled Master Hargarthius, "Get me a containment vessel!"

Tom knew by now that saying 'what?' would be a mistake. But he had no idea what his master wanted. So he scrambled to find the only containment vessel he could think of, close to hand, the large chamber-pot the magician kept under the corner of his desk, which it was Tom's unenviable duty to empty.

Fortunately, it was not in need of emptying just then. Tom rushed forward with the florally painted pot and held out to the master.

"Not that you idiot... oh, well. It'll have to do. Put it down. You'll need to walk widdershins, seven times, saying 'Melba Aristo Otsira Ablem', forty-nine times, while I keep him here."

Tom's counting skills hadn't moved a long way past 'one, two, many,' before he had been trapped into this human body. But between his master and Mrs Drellson's skull and their requirements for various numbers of things he had learned the elements of arithmetic. That could work for the seven part. He had enough fingers for that. The forty-nine part... well, at least he had some idea what 'widdershins' meant. He had thought it involved the spoiled, white, fluff-ball cat in the village who had a human that other humans called 'widder' and it was always winding its way between her shins.

Fortunately for Tom's survival it appeared that Master Hargarthius could both count and keep demons entrapped at the same time... "Another three, fool boy," he yelled when Tom would have stopped. Tom looked inwards, warily, at the end of the three final repetitions. He was amazed to see a golden cone above the chamber-pot, gradually sinking into it. This might seem quite normal for the chamber-pot, but none of it missed. Then the Master stopped his muttering and the room was silent, except for the faint rocking of the chamber-pot on some shards of broken glass.

Master Hargarthius exhaled and tottered over to his chair and flopped into it, wiping his brow. "That was too close for comfort."

Tom had to agree with him. It had all been far too close for his comfort. He would much rather have been anywhere else, even the kitchen. And there, shattered on the floor were the precious crystal glasses, the wine bottle, and several plates and bowls that the skull of Mrs Drellson was going to have the fur singed off his tail for breaking, if he was lucky. He was trying hard to think of options, preferably for escape.

Then, to his utter surprise, Master Hargarthius looked at him. "Well spotted, boy. Maybe they're right, cats are less affected by enchantment and demonic manipulation than humans. Get a broom and clean up this mess, and get back to the kitchen. I'll have some beer. Hmm. Maybe I can use you more in my spell-work, and give you a little training in magic."

And then Master Hargarthius got up and picked up the chamber pot. Himself. Not even telling Tom to do it. That was very strange indeed. Tom walked to the door, still trying to make sense of it all, on his way to fetch the brush and dustpan, and to receive the inevitable yelling at by the skull.

The door wouldn't open.

Tom kept trying. Eventually the magician noticed and laughed. There was something very affronting to a cat-boy's dignity in being laughed at, but it was better than being hit.

"I'll have to unseal it, boy." He put the chamber-pot on the desk – something Tom had been walloped for doing – and came over to the door, and started muttering again. This time Tom was close enough to hear his words, and to watch the passes Master Hargarthius made with his hand. Tom stashed the memory away very carefully in his mind. It could be useful someday. He had to wonder if it opened other doors... like the front door. The door to the outside world, where a cat might not have to be the slave to an old curmudgeon who hit him, and attracted dangerous creatures.

On the other hand it was also a world where – if the village-man was like the rest of them, they might take his tail as an indication that Tom was a dangerous creature. Tom was strutting down the passage to fetch the dust-pan enjoying this idea, revelling in the dream of chasing the villagers off and eating all their fish, when it occurred to him that he'd seen the village men shoot a wolf, that they also considered a dangerous creature, full of arrows. He could wear his tail under his robe... but it was so uncomfortable, Tom couldn't keep it there for too long.

That was why he'd pulled apart the stitches on the back-seam of the robe to make a hole, to let his tail enjoy its freedom, instead of being crammed down inside the robe. It was far better than lifting the robe over his tail. The weight of the fabric was a constant irritation to his tail, and doing it that way it let the cold breeze in.

Tom had decided, reluctantly, that escape would have to wait a little longer. Perhaps until he'd learned a bit of magic himself. He quite fancied being able to turn himself into a tiger. There was a bigger, older tom-cat in the village that Tom would like to pay a visit to, in that form. And a few other girl cats might be more impressed with him, then. As a cat, Tom had just been at the stage of realizing that he was a tom-cat. That, it seemed, hadn't entirely changed, when he became human. The thought of girl-cats distracted him from the fear of Mrs Drellson's skull, until she screeched at him.

"Do they want more wine? They always want more wine. And take that blasted raven away. It has been flying around the kitchen, like a thing demented, which it is of course. But it is driving me mad."

Tom managed to avoid saying 'which you already are, of course' and said: "Er no. There was a demon. Things got broken." It was a hopeful slither out of 'I dropped the platter, and everything got broken'. Tom had learned by now that a direct lie to either the Master or the skull tended to end badly. But perhaps an indirect approach might work better? Like stalking a bird while pretending you hadn't actually seen it.

And it seemed that this was the case, or she could have been distracted by the mention of the demon. "A demon!" the skull chittered its snaggly teeth in what Tom had learned was delight, usually at Tom's suffering. "What order?!"

"It didn't order anything. I was told to fetch the master some beer, and I need a brush and dustpan to clean up the mess."

"Fool-of-a-boy!" He got a trickle of her green-lightning pain – but nothing compared to what he'd been expecting. "What was its rank?"

"I don't know. It smelled pretty bad. The air tasted like tin."

"For a magician's famulus you are a most terrifyingly ignorant boy," said the skull of Mrs Drellson. Tom got the feeling that if it could have rolled its eyes, it would have. "Get the beer and the dust-pan and get on with it, before we have Old Grumptious down here boasting about how he defeated a demon. Esthetius used to have half a dozen captive, in my day."

Tom had only thought of himself being very well-informed, for a cat, before. It did rather depend on where you looked at things from, and Tom still wasn't quite ready to look at anything from a human point of view. It seemed quite inadequate, despite being, Tom reluctantly had to admit to himself, more complex than the way a cat would have seen things. That didn't have to mean it was better, did it? "Well, I think he's got this one captive too. It's in the chamber pot."

"That'd give someone a nasty surprise in the middle of the night," said the skull, with more teeth chittering. "Get a move on, boy."

So Tom did.

The Raven fluttered up the passage ahead of him.

Inevitably it said 'Nevermore' as it flew.

ॐॐॐॐॐॐ

Princess Alamaya had held high hopes of the magic classes she had cajoled her Uncle into allowing her to be given. They had at least offered the possibility of escape.

She should have guessed that he wouldn't allow her to be taught anything useful. And the laboratory was a horrible old dump, full of ancient equipment from the time of the Enchantress Saliana, who had used this room in her disappeared grandfather's time. Its shelves groaned with the nasty chemicals and potions of yesteryear. It was dusty, tedious and hard work.

It was true that transforming – albeit temporarily – obnoxious and unprotected people into green frogs was not entirely useless. But the transformation spell didn't work on yourself. And anyway, what use to her was becoming a frog?

※※※※※※※※

Within the protective cone of silence that the conclave of plotters always employed, Malalia said, unctuously, "Magic use provides us with all sorts of possible ways of getting rid of her."

"She will die. It's not really necessary at this stage for us to intervene. It's not so much a question of how she dies, but when it will be most convenient for us," her Master replied, steepling his long fingers. "Possibly the biggest mistake Esthetius made was that he wanted to be the visible ruler. I am content with power, for now. And there are still a number of magic workers who are not suitably committed to organised magic. Old reactionaries, who are not ready to go with the new ways."

"How can they not see that our ways are much better, much better for the people?" Malalia asked.

He shrugged. "They will see sense or be dealt with."

CHAPTER 4

THE OPENING SPELL

——▶•◀——

If there was one sure thing about being a cat-almost-completely-transformed-to-human famulus to Master Hargarthius that Tom had established; it was that nothing was sure. Well, that and the fact that Master Hargarthius and the skull of Mrs Drellson had it in for him. He would have said that was true of the cheese that lurked on the third shelf of the pantry, and the raven, too, but Tom had discovered that they could be bought off. Or at least distracted with suitable bribes. Tom decided everything else was uncertain, and was out to get him at least some of the time.

The demon in the chamber pot was an entirely different matter. It didn't just want to kill Tom sometimes. It had it in for everybody, all of the time. That, as Tom learned over the next few weeks, was normal for demons, not just ones trapped in a pale blue chamber-pot, painted with rather garish pansies. Its power was constrained by the magics that bound it, but it still managed a little local malevolence. The pansies changed colour, and, subtly, shape, from time to time.

Tom found his 'promotion' from pure kitchen and house slave, merely under the lash of the skull of Mrs Drellson, to being permitted in the laboratory to be sworn at, to have pointy and hard objects thrown at him... and to assist, and in theory, to learn some small magical skill, was a mixed blessing. Mostly it wasn't a blessing. But he was learning more, both of magic, and of humans and their world, which was not quite the same as the world cats bestrode.

Humans had other ideas about who ruled it, for starters. Tom was coming to the conclusion that the human world was actually bigger and more complex than the cat world. And while it was perfectly obvious that humans didn't run it, or at least not as far as the cats were concerned, they did have 'rulers' like Dukes and Kings, who thought they did, and magicians who thought they should.

In the process they could make things very unpleasant for cats, and more so for cat boys. Tom had only the human part of his memory to rely on but he gathered that Dukes were powerful, and inevitably evil, and that Kings were even more powerful. Tom was still a bit hazy about the precise meaning of evil. However, Dukes who wanted to be Kings, and Barons who wanted to be Dukes, and Knights who wanted to be Barons... provided money to magicians like his master, to help them reach their goals. Master Hargarthius had been deceived into thinking that the Demon was a Duke, and one that he was acquiring from another magician, as a dissatisfied customer. Magicians disputed ownership of these providers of money with other magicians. The demon had been a competitor's attempt to put Master Hargarthius out of business, permanently.

Or that was at least how Tom had worked it out, so far. It was in all, a puzzling business that no-one explained much of, to him. Magicians such as Master Hargarthius spent a lot of time experimenting with things they weren't good at, and reading. Tom had already tried a fair amount of experimenting with things he wasn't good at, at least not immediately. Reading was still something of a mystery, but Tom was determined to work at it.

A great many answers seemed to lie in the books. Except – in some of the books – it didn't so much 'lie', as actively try to get out. Those ones were padlocked, and in some cases, were chained to the shelf.

Tom was still trying to work out exactly how this reading was supposed to work, and trying to grasp 'magic'. It could be very useful, it seemed. And quite dangerous... but then he'd been a fast cat and was a lot quicker as a human than Master Hargarthius was. He wasn't so sure about the raven, or the Magician's staff. Those could both move with a great deal of speed, all by themselves.

There was a great deal for him to think about while doing the many chores that fell to his lot. That was a good thing, because most of the chores were very tedious. As a cat he objected to chores. Cats did not do such tasks, they were for dogs, horses, donkeys or humans. As a boy, and a famulus, he found he had little choice about doing them. Whether it was cleaning up after the raven – or scrubbing floors (a pointless exercise, someone was bound to walk on them again) there was always something that the skull of Mrs Drellson felt he ought to be doing, every waking second. The one advantage about being called to the laboratory was that Master Hargarthius sometimes forgot he was there. It was like watching a mouse-hole. Tom kept quiet and thought... and he watched. Of course sometimes he ducked and ran too.

And then he swept up the results.

Tom finally discovered the back door. It was carefully hidden... from the outside. From the inside it was just another door that did not open. There were quite a lot of those. Tom naturally wanted to know what was behind all of them.

He regularly tried the door-handles, just in case... This was not always a good idea, as he found out when the one door revealed a bed with a snoring Master Hargarthius in it. But most of them stayed obstinately closed and tantalisingly mysterious to Tom.

Then, one day, he thought of trying the opening spell.

He did his best to remember it precisely. He was fairly good at that. He recited it, complete with the passes of the hand.

The door... grew long wooden fangs, a mouth... and snapped at his reaching hand. Then, as Tom watched from where he had thrown himself back against the opposite wall, the mouth yawned theatrically, and then faded back into the woodwork. Tom wasn't that easily fooled. He'd played games like that himself! But he did try the opening spell again, this time trying something that he'd possibly heard wrong, differently.

The door stayed shut.

Cross, and still somewhat shaken, he decided to kick it, sneakily and quickly in case the wooden mouth was just waiting its chance. It might have been, but the door swung open anyway, bringing an un-mistakable scent of outdoors and an icy cold wind blowing in... along with a flurry of snow.

That snow was enough to temper Tom's immediate instinct to flee. He'd always thought the inside of the tower bitterly cold, except for the kitchen, where it was his task to keep the fire going... but the kitchen had the skull of Mrs Drellson to make sure that Tom never just curled up in front of it. So instead of running out, and then running as far and fast as his legs could carry him, he just looked. Tasted the air of freedom, and thought about it.

Besides, he had the uncomfortable feeling something was watching him.

Turning around cautiously, Tom realized that he was wrong about something watching him.

It was two somethings who were watching him, silently. From a perch on a wall-sconce the raven looked at him, head askance, beady eye as unblinking as a cat. And back in the dimness of the passage, betrayed only by the green glowing eye sockets, the skull hovered. Staring at him. Waiting to see what he would do.

Tom closed the door, forgetting the mouth and teeth he had conjured. Fortunately, it seemed they'd also forgotten him. He remembered the teeth suddenly and pulled his hand away.

The raven shook its head, and said, again, all that it ever said. "Nevermore." It was a mournful comment at the best of times, and right now it sounded despairing. It fluttered away up the passage, as silent as it could be when it chose to be quiet.

That left Tom alone to face the wrath of the skull of Mrs Drellson.

Maybe he should have run into the snow.

But this time the skull did not inflict the lash of pain on Tom. She just said in a tone that might almost have been sad: "You can never escape a magician, boy. It's not as easy as just running out of the door."

"But, but what about the other famuluses?" Master Hargarthius had mentioned Tom's predecessors often enough. Some of them had come to unpleasant ends in those mentions. But not all... his immediate predecessor had fled on a magic carpet, with the contents of the pantry and certain other treasures, Tom knew, from Master Hargarthius's irritated comments about him. "And all the servants. The housemaids that you used to boss around."

"Magicians live a lot longer than we do," she said tersely. "And they have ways of making sure escape isn't worth it. He'll have some of your cat-hair, somewhere, in a little jar. That's enough for the likes of him to put a terrible fate on you, but Estethius was worse."

According to her, Estethius, the previous master of the tower, was always worse. And better too, better at having wealth, servants and at nastiness. The skull seemed rather proud of that. Tom did wonder at times how anyone could be worse than Master Hargarthius. Old Grumptious – as he and Mrs Drellson's skull called Hargarthius when he wasn't around – had a fierce temper, and could certainly be as irritable as a spring-time viper. But the part about the hair, all tied too well with the nasty comments the magician made from time-to-time. Hair, skin, finger-nails, blood, even tears all had magical properties. The magician was very careful about what happened to his own.

Tom had to face that most un-catlike of things again: not doing precisely as he wished. He'd have to find out more, much more.

And a magic carpet probably would not be enough. Tom liked carpets. They were much warmer under his cold feet than stone flags. He liked to dig his toes into them. He wasn't sure, just yet, how magic carpets worked, but he'd heard the master curse the loss a good few times. It had been supposed to come back of its own accord, but hadn't ever returned, not with or without the famulus.

The skull was in an unusually generous mood when he got back to the kitchen, after looking out at the snow. She set him to polishing brass and then the silver, in front of the fire. "It's bitter out in the snow," was all she said, before lapsing into almost silence – just the occasional snap to tell him to polish something better, or to put a bit more elbow-grease into it. He'd looked long and hard for that elbow-grease in the pantry. He concluded it must be on the shelf patrolled by the cheese. Polishing was rather like washing oneself is for a cat. A task that left the mind free to think about things. He dared a question, eventually. "Do all the closed doors have teeth?"

The skull cackled. "You need to get your cadences better, boy. Magic's more than just words. Most humans can't do it at all."

Tom thought about that, for a while. If most couldn't... it must mean he was better than most. That was a bit of satisfaction derived from it all. Unfortunately, the warmth and comfort were far too good to last. Old Grumptious awoke and bellowed for coffee. It was something that the Skull disapproved of in particular. "New-fangled foreign rubbish. That wicked witch Emerelda brought the trees for it back from who-knows-where. Small beer was good enough for Master Estethius. Get the milk, boy."

Now, the milk was one of the mysteries of the magician's tower that Tom had not understood. He knew where this kind of milk came from, by the smell. He rather liked it.

But there was no cow, and no dairy maid in the pantry, nor any obvious connection to one. Yet there was always milk in a wooden jug set in the back corner of the pantry. Sometimes it was still warm.

Tom went across to the pantry, his thoughts somewhat distracted as to whether he could get away with stealing more than a mouthful of milk – which, as long as he remembered to wipe his upper lip, and make sure that he was out of the line of the skull of Mrs Drellson's sight, he had mastered quite well. He always almost closed the door, so she couldn't see in. As he picked up the jug, after glancing behind him, she yelled, nearly making him drop the jug as he lifted it to his lips. But she was yelling. "Bring honeycakes", not "stop that, you revolting boy".

With a sigh he put the jug on the shelf and reached down the sweet honey cake canister. On turning back, to pick it up in the other hand, he realized to his horror that he'd set the milk jug down on the cheese's shelf... and the cheese had moved from its dusty hiding place among the old pickle jars to right up against the jug.

He snatched it away, slopping some of the milk onto the shelf.

"What's taking you so long?" demanded the Skull. "You're drinking the milk again, aren't you, boy? Don't make me come in there..."

"No," protested Tom. "It's this cheese. It's..." He swallowed, unable to quite deal with what the cheese actually was up to. It was lapping the milk with a little blue-veined tongue.

"Oh. You be careful of that thing. The old master's nasty jokes will be the death of us."

Tom didn't point out that it was a bit too late for her, but retreated from the pantry, pushing the bolt across with his elbow as best he could without spilling any more milk.

"Put the jug down and do it properly," said the skull sternly. "We don't want that dratted thing sneaking out of there."

So Tom did. He'd noticed before that the skull of Mrs Drellson was nervous about the cheese. Well, so was he. Cheese should not have a tongue of its own. He wondered if he'd imagined it. But there was a milk ring on the floor, which he'd have to clean as soon as possible, before Mrs Drellson's Skull's empty haunted orbits noticed it. He had spilt milk, that was for certain. He'd check it later. It might be useful anyway. "I'll have to close the door while I'm in there," he said. "I had to push it back with the milk jug. It was trying to climb out."

The Skull's snaggly teeth chittered in agreement. "But you can't close the door completely, no. Not ever! Take a wedge with you, in future." And then she started yelling at him to get a move on. So he did, heating milk, brewing coffee, carrying the bitter-smelling brew to Master Hargarthius, propped up in bed still with his nightcap on. Tom noticed it wasn't the same door he was called to as the one he'd looked in, once and found the Master asleep behind. Perhaps Master Hargarthius moved bedrooms. Perhaps there was more than one door. Perhaps the doors moved. It seemed to Tom that could be possible too.

But he noticed, when he finally got back to the pantry with what was left of the milk, that the shelf where he'd spilt milk was dry. There was no sign of milk ever having been there. So Tom took a chance and poured another splash onto it, and the cheese came oozing from its hiding place with quite remarkable speed. Tom didn't have time to watch it, but it definitely drank milk. Tom was a little vague on cheese-making but he was sure that the cheese didn't normally help itself to milk.

He had to spend the rest of his day, and quite a lot of the night assisting in the laboratory, while the master 'tried a new approach'.

Like several other approaches that Tom had witnessed so far, this one also ended in a messy explosion. Tom was fairly sure that wasn't the point, even if it was a frequent result. The Master's cursing and swearing was as usual spectacular and educational. It was the one thing that any cat would have wanted to learn from a human.

Tom had been human for long enough now to think of a few other things that might be useful – how to turn cats into other things, and how to make milk appear in the back of the pantry – came to mind. But Tom could see there might be others.

Reading appeared central to what the master did. But it was just squiggles on paper or parchment or vellum to Tom.

Tom had stared in frustration at the book left open on the work-bench, as he did his usual chore of cleaning up. Meaningless!

Well... it was to a cat. Except that, to his shock, Tom realized that his human memories knew the letters. The little parts of the black squiggles that repeated. And repeated. Tom realized he did know each of them... and the sound they represented. It was still a long, long step between each letter and the words. But Tom did puzzle out a few of them.

And then he got a terrific headache – which is what a cat-boy earned from a clout from the staff of Master Hargarthius for not having finished cleaning up the laboratory, and standing daydreaming. He might have got worse, if old Grumptious had realized he was staring at the words in the grimoire.

But headache or not, Tom had worked out just what books were, and how they worked. Now he just had to get good at this reading.

He suspected it wasn't going to be that easy. He was right about that. He wouldn't have minded being wrong, for once, which was very un-cat-like, really. Perhaps the human body was affecting his thinking. It was plain to any cat that being in a human body affected humans' ability to think. It could be the posture. That had to make it harder to get sufficient blood to the brain.

꙰꙰꙰ꙮꙮꙮ

'The best laid plans of mice and men oft were gang astray'... they said. The wickedest witch muttered angrily to herself. It was all very well for the plans of mice or men. That was acceptable as far as she was concerned. But now even hers had gone astray. And that was just plain annoying and intolerable.

No wonder so many witches got into the habit of eating children. They were just so damned annoying. Unreliable too. Nearly as bad as demons.

꙰꙰꙰ꙮꙮꙮ

Within the protective cone of silence the Chief Wizard of Ambyria said: "There is something to be said for quiet, biddable rulers. Honestly, between Duke Karst and this foolish Princess, I am hardly able to do any work." The post of Chief Wizard was a government post, which had been largely ornamental as mages were historically very independent, and did not take well to governance. He was still working on it.

The Sorceress Malalia nodded sympathetically. "What does the vapid girl want now?"

"Transformation spells. I told her that she had insufficient skills as yet. She, annoyingly, does have some natural talent for magic. She has no discipline, though."

CHAPTER 5

THE DEMON AND TEMPTATION

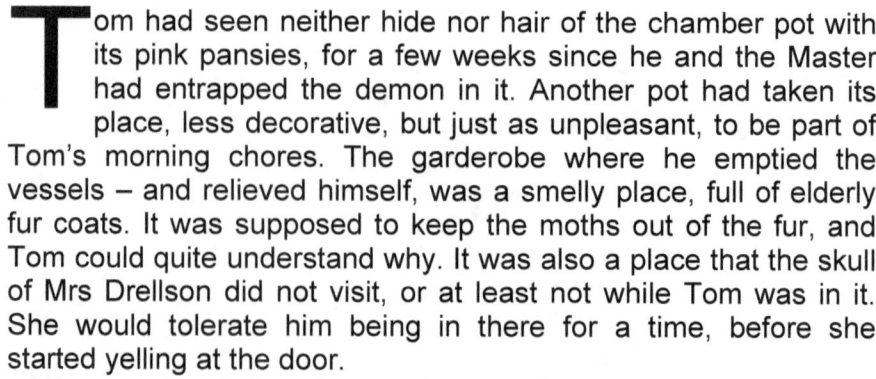

Tom had seen neither hide nor hair of the chamber pot with its pink pansies, for a few weeks since he and the Master had entrapped the demon in it. Another pot had taken its place, less decorative, but just as unpleasant, to be part of Tom's morning chores. The garderobe where he emptied the vessels – and relieved himself, was a smelly place, full of elderly fur coats. It was supposed to keep the moths out of the fur, and Tom could quite understand why. It was also a place that the skull of Mrs Drellson did not visit, or at least not while Tom was in it. She would tolerate him being in there for a time, before she started yelling at the door.

It was a good place just to sit, even if it did smell. It was, Tom worked out, an even better place to read. He'd found something besides grimoires to practice on. He'd suddenly realised that sounding out the words to a spell might, possibly, not be the cleverest thing he'd ever done. It might even be stupider than thinking he could safely take fish from a magician. He'd yet to find out where the fish had come from. He hadn't seen any since then. What he had seen was the material used to put under the raven's perch. The raven perched everywhere else, and mostly used everything but the material provided to relieve himself on. He had no need. He had Tom to clean up after him, after all.

Tom had not realised it was readable for some time. The occasional raven dropping did not encourage a fastidious cat-boy to look too closely. It was off-white and had black marks on it, regular, similar shaped marks, most unlike the erratic writing in some of the grimoires.

Once Tom had recognized the letters however, it was a short step to words and realizing that the material was in fact the Weekly Illuminati Age and Magical Advertiser, and it gave Tom something he had not had before, besides practice reading matter, a supply of paper for the garderobe, and something to put under the Raven's perch –which he seldom used, and some of the other spots he did use frequently.

It gave Tom a window onto the human world, something he'd poorly understood before. After reading the Weekly Illuminati Age and Magical Advertiser, he knew a lot more about it, but understood it even less well.

It did help his reading – even if news of an unseasonal cold snap, due to thaumatic induced sphere warming, causing a sharp spike in Southern Salamander prices were a mystery to him. So were the results of the broomstick hurdles championship. The fact that the Duke of Novaria reducing his thaumaturical spending and how that meant Irrendia's Count Morgoth was untrustable, or that Ambyria needed stronger leadership than the Prince Regent was providing, and that the Joringian Empire's threats were empty – were all about matters outside of his ken. The tax advice column, on various deductible things to turn tax collectors into was fascinating. It didn't include cats.

For obvious reasons transformation was an interesting subject to Tom. It seemed something most of the Weekly Illuminati Age and Magical Advertiser's readers considered commonplace, so much so that they never explained just how it was done.

Tom realized that those sorts of instructions had to be in the library of grimoires that Master Hargarthius read. The trouble was getting to read them himself. Some of them were under lock and key, and Tom was sure those had to be the best ones.

Mind you, that too was something Tom was less sure about after he saw Master Hargarthius belabouring one particularly fat grimoire with his staff, until it spat out a quill pen and a bottle of ink, and the magician could get the latch for the padlock to close again.

Master Hargarthius kept the bunch of keys for the books, and other fascinating mysteries, on a ring on the ratty old velvet sash he wore. Thus, barring him leaving one open on the desk or in the laboratory, Tom wasn't going to get a chance at those.

He was hopeful of one of those chances, when he took a detour while on one of his errands for the skull, to look in at the laboratory. The magician had worked late the night before and wasn't up yet. Tom knew about the lateness, because he'd been called to assist, and eventually Old Grumptious had sent him to bed in a rage, because Tom had fallen asleep for the third time, mid-experiment.

Tom was suffering from that human ailment that he'd never had as a cat – too little sleep, and yet needing to stay awake. As a cat, if you needed sleep, you slept. As a famulus, if you slept after first light, the skull of Mrs Drellson took it out on you. To make up for it, Tom thought he'd like a peek at the double-padlocked book the Master had been peering at and muttering from last night.

There was no open grimoire left on the bench or on the central table. What there was, was a chamber pot. Tom looked at it with tired eyes and no small amount of irritation. Well, best if he took it and emptied it now. He wasn't used to seeing that particular purple and puce-pansy ornamented pot here. It belonged in the study... no, it was the wrong color.

It wasn't, as he'd vaguely hoped, empty.

There was a heavy roiling purplish smoke covering the bottom. Well, considering the magician's diet that wasn't surprising. The brimstone smell in the laboratory could have been due to the chamber pot. On the other hand, the place generally stank of many strange things. Tom sighed and picked it up, and began trudging to the garderobe to empty it. Something was niggling at his tired mind.

About half way there it came to him. The unfamiliar chamber pot... was very like the sky-blue and pink pansy ornamented one from the magician's study. He stopped and looked at it again. The pansies were now magenta, and some of them looked like little horned skulls.

"Demon!" he said, peering at it.

The smoke stirred and he could see, in the roil of purple smoke, a pair of slitty eyes, of precisely the same shade of magenta that the pansies had been.

"Cat," said the smoke in a cracking voice reminiscent of fire-splitting logs.

Tom nearly... but not quite, dropped the pot.

"I'm a boy, or maybe a demon too," Tom said hastily. "And I'm taking you back."

The demon snorted smoke. "You're a cat. I can see your essences. Besides you have a tail. Those are hard to magically transform. Let me loose, cat."

"No way. Old Grumptious would kill me."

"I can protect you," said the demon.

"You couldn't protect yourself," pointed out Tom.

"I will call on legions of help. I am a demon-prince! I am not in his bespelled place now. You will be richly rewarded," said the demon.

There was a particular wheedling tone that Tom, now thoroughly awake, distrusted. It reminded him... yes, that was it, it reminded him of the voice of Master Hargarthius, offering him fish.

"Don't believe you. Anyway, what can you do for me?"

"I can make you a cat again, free of this magician," offered the demon.

That was enough to make Tom pause in his hasty walk back to the laboratory.

The demon plainly detected his advantage. "I can give you whatever you desire. I am a being of great power... and this is terribly undignified."

Now that Tom could understand. So much of what had been done to him, was undignified for a cat. It was the kind of affront that neither Master Hargarthius nor the skull of Mrs Drellson appreciated. He stopped.

The demon pressed the advantage. "Feasting, dancing cat-girls, they will be yours."

The cat-girls part definitely stirred interest in Tom, interest that met sensible behaviour and told it to get lost. "Cat-girls," he said.

"Oh indeed. Cat-girls, dancing and singing for you... and anything else you may desire," and the pansies reshaped themselves, briefly, into sleek dancing cats with elegant necks and tails.

He'd won. But the demon didn't know that and went on. "I can make you the king of cats. Cats everywhere would obey your orders. You will have prince-cats and duke-cats under you, obedient and loyal. Your wish would be their command. Especially the girl cats."

Tom started walking again, back to the laboratory. The demon continued to make offers, ever more grandiose. Tom walked faster.

Just short of the laboratory door, Tom met up with Master Hargarthius, who had the raven on his shoulder. "Where are you going with that thing, boy?" snapped the magician, sounding neither old... nor pleased.

"Back to the laboratory," said Tom.

Master Hargathius peered into the chamber pot. The purple smoke twisted and churned under his gaze but of the eyes there was no sign. And the pansies on the outside were once again pink on a cerulean blue. "And where have you been with it?" he asked, his tone considerably more mild.

"I was taking it to the garderobe."

There was a moment's silence. "It's a demon, boy. It doesn't need to... go. As you must have worked out, or it wouldn't still be in there."

"It was lying to me. Complaining about its dignity," said Tom. "I'd like to show it worse." He was cross, now. He knew he was in dire trouble, but the thought of those dancing cat-girls was still with him.

The raven's beak closed with a snap. Then it went: "Kaaark! Kaark! Kaark!" which might even have been laughing, if ravens laughed.

That was definitely a nasty snigger from Master Hargarthius. "Of course it was lying. They always do, boy. Heh, heh. I hadn't thought of that threat... or bribe. Well done. Put it down in the laboratory. Let's go and have some beer."

So Tom did.

He did get two things out of the entire experience, well, three really. The first was that he didn't really like the beer. The magician said it grew on you. So did mould. The second was that he'd never seen the raven sit on Master Hargarthius's shoulder before. There had to be a reason for all that. The third, less direct lesson, which most humans seemed to need to be taught early, or would never learn, was that demons always lie and don't know or understand cats. Imagine telling a cat he'd be the king of cats with all other cats in a hierarchy below that obedient to him! Maybe demons worked like that. In the next while Tom established that yes, indeed they did.

But cats do not.

Cats didn't take orders well or willingly. If the magician had wanted that, he should have transformed a dog.

It must have been the beer growing on them – even the raven had had some. And none of them thought twice about going into the laboratory. If they'd been a little more observant, the master would have quietly closed the door before stepping through the doorway... and possibly have returned to the kitchen to have more beer, or just had Master Hargarthius do his best to incinerate the place. Tom himself, just behind the master with a silver platter with another tankard of beer and some pickles – needed for an experiment, the Magician had loftily explained to the skull of Mrs Drellson – had no chance to see much, until the door swung closed behind them.

A pity he hadn't been in front... he might have noticed the spider-webs earlier.

Not just their presence – there were always spider-webs. The magician used them. But the fact that they now held just a lavender hint of exactly the same shade of angry purple as the pansies on the chamber-pot might have been a clue – that, and the fact that the ceiling was just solid with them. But no one looked up, until it was too late.

Seconds after they had walked into the room, it wasn't just the ceiling. The myriads of tiny spiders boiled down the walls, spinning an ever-closing tent of cobwebs. Tom didn't see a lot more, as they'd smothered the candles in web.

The Master and the raven both tried to reach the chamber pot and the demon. However, firstly, flying was a poor choice. The raven made it part of the way, and then fell... a little, wings tangled in an ever-growing mass of web... and the magician, striding forward, staff outstretched, didn't do much better. Tom was free, but Master Hargathius – and his staff – was not.

Tom had not rushed to the attack. Instead, he'd done what any sensible cat would do – dived for cover. Now, perhaps if the demon had not sent all his spiders to the roof, the space under the workbench in the middle of the laboratory would have been just as cobwebbed, and Tom would have been in the same kind of trouble as the magician, and the raven who was up there and slashing at the sticky cobwebs with its dagger-like beak.

Instead, Tom had crept underneath the workbench, trying to find the darkest and safest corner... which, as the walls and roof were full of cobwebs was more-or-less the middle of the room. He was under the bench, just about directly under the demon-infested chamber-pot, from which a shriek of demonic laughter echoed.

Then the demon said in voice of unpleasant delight. "You're trapped now, Magician. At my mercy. Give me my freedom, or you will die here." It cackled with demonic glee.

"Nevermore!" croaked the raven. It sounded somewhat muffled.

"What good do you think this will do you?" demanded Master Hargarthius, sounding both old and grumptious. "You can't escape from this room even if you could escape the containment spell on the pot, Prince Hariseldon."

"You know my name, magician. But you cannot draw the circles. You cannot invoke the powers. Let me loose of here. You have me prisoner. But I have you! You will suffer terrible agonies and I will relish every moment. My power will grow with what I seize from you, I will rise in the hierarchy of demons, and all life will be mine, mine to destroy, slowly and painfully," boomed the demon. The room was very dim, lit now only by a faint sickly mauve glow from the spider -webs.

"I didn't put you in there," said the Magician. "So I can't take you out. The boy did the widdershins working."

There was a moment's silence. "What happened to the cat?" asked the demon, as Tom pressed back hard against the back leg of the work-bench. Tom wasn't too good at interpreting demonic tones of voice, but it did sound decidedly worried. Which was how Tom felt right then. It was nice to know he had company feeling like that.

He wished he knew precisely what to do, and, principally, how to get out of the laboratory by doing it.

Master Hargarthius laughed, almost winning the 'who-can-laugh-most-evilly' contest with the demon. They really were very evenly matched in that. It did seem that a cat's ability to see in a dim room was still superior to a trapped demon's, even if the cat had been transformed in shape, thought Tom, peeping out. Of course that didn't help, when he couldn't see a way to escape.

Just then there was a thump.

A bundle of cobwebs with a large protruding black beak landed on the floor.

It uttered a gloomy 'Nevermore'.

Obviously the raven's beak, at least, could cut cobwebs. But spiders, tiny little spiders, were swarming down on silken drop-lines to recapture it. They would spot Tom, no matter how far back he lurked. It didn't stop him squirming back as far as possible, and getting as his reward a metallic clang as his elbow slid into a wet pool of what was, by the smell, beer. The pickle jar, miraculously unbroken rolled up against his cheek... just as he felt the ghostly touch of little spider-feet on his other cheek. A faintly mauve-glowing mass of them was heading his way, behind the scouts.

It was a case of do something... or it would be too late to do anything. Reflexively, Tom grabbed the pickle jar and flung it. He hurled it at them – as well as someone not very experienced at throwing can – while lying on his stomach under a workbench.

That is to say: very badly. The pickle jar did not hit the advancing swarm of little spiders. It hit a bench-leg, hard, because Tom had put all his strength into that terrible throw, and the lid came flying off, spraying an arc of vinegar and glass followed by bouncing brown pickled onions.

Among the human food he was having to learn to eat, Tom had found the fiery pickled onions to be dangerous, and best avoided.

It seemed the demon-possessed spiders found them similar, but many, many times worse. The vinegar just obliterated the mass with a vicious hissing that would have made fifty enraged Tom-cats seem quiet. One moment it was there, the next gone. The bouncing pickles tore through the spider-webs like very sharp claws hitting bubbles, with little mauve pops when a spider was in the way. One bounced into the mass surrounding the raven, and the raven, being the raven, stabbed the onion with its beak, and used it to clear its body and legs of cobwebs, before eating the onion. It belched... and descending spiders vaporised.

Tom realized he'd just been handed a way to bolt. His scrabbling fingers found the jar. It cut him and the vinegar in that cut probably didn't help his thinking. The jar still had three onions wedged in it. So, with the silver tray as a shield, and a broken jar of ammunition and a bleeding, sore finger, Tom scrambled out, avoiding the glass and the puddle of vinegar.

That avoidance might have been a mistake, Tom realized, as he emerged into the cobwebbed space... on the far side of the chamber-pot from the door. It was a chamber pot on which the pansies were dancing... some purple, and some puce, and not a few pink, and some in rainbow shades. Something was bulging out of the pot, seething, in just those colors.

It seemed to be shaping itself into a maniacally grinning mouth full of razor-sharp teeth, reaching for him – and he'd emerged from under the bench far, far too close to it.

In shock, he pushed the broken jar into that mouth, and then snatched his hand back... without the jar. All he had left was the silver tray, so he slapped that down onto the chamber-pot, like a lid.

And it seemed to have just that effect.

The webs faded from their strange colours and then faded entirely, leaving, eventually, one solitary, small spider dangling from a thread above the chamber-pot.

The raven flapped up onto the bench, looked at the chamber-pot and balanced clumsily on one leg and scratched its own head with its long claws, uttering a mildly puzzled "Caark. Nevermore!" as it stared at the tray.

Tom expected hearty congratulations and perhaps a fulsome reward from Master Hargarthius. Of course, he got a clout for dropping the beer instead. But it was a gentle clout, comparatively. The master had instead produced a pince nez and was examining the spider. "Clear signs of demonic possession," he said. "Probably got tempted into the pot. Good thing the creature is not toxic to anything much larger than a fly. You need to do a better job of cleaning up in here, boy."

Tom was somewhat resentful, as he'd been told to leave the spiders alone just the week before. Being made a famulus was not all joy to a cat, he thought, grumpily, as he was sent to get a brush and dustpan, and to clear up the glass and spilled vinegar and beer.

The master contented himself with a good long look at the chamber-pot, and then went to fetch himself more beer, merely telling the raven to watch the pot. And to deal with the spider. The raven did that, promptly, by eating it.

Tom noticed, however, on returning to the laboratory – which he was careful to do just after the magician – that Master Hargarthius had very long look around the room, and up at the ceiling, before stepping over the threshold.

There were no hordes of spiders waiting.

Instead, a few inches above the surface of the workbench... the chamber pot hovered, the pink pansies slowly opening and closing to an eerie throbbing sound echoing from within the pot. It hovered in precisely the way that chamber-pots only usually do very briefly, but it was staying up. It was watched from some distance away by the raven, back on its favorite perch in the corner – a plaster bust of some woman the magician referred to as Athena.

Tom stayed well back ready to leave for somewhere else, very fast, as Master Hargarthius drew symbols around the chamber pot, and then sprinkled a ring of salt, before lifting the tray, with a loud "Avaunt, Prince Hariselden!"

Nothing happened. Perhaps the demon had avaunted. At least the eerie throbbing chords of sound stopped.

Instead of brimstone, the smell emerging from the chamber pot was eye-wateringly of pickled onion. The roiling cloud of earlier had gone, replaced by a faint drift of smoke curling in delicate patterns above the rippling pale lavender liquid.

"Have we killed it?" asked an awed Tom.

In answer a somewhat slurred voice came from the chamber pot. "Pieces and luuurve, man. And cool cat."

The raven leaned suspiciously over the chamber pot from the magician's shoulder, cocking his head to inspect it first with one eye, and then the other, in case it was different from another point of view, presumably. "Nevermore," it said, to no-one's surprise.

Well, no-one, except, it seemed for the demon, which went off in a fit of demonic giggles, sending ripples across the fluid. Finally, it stopped. "You pretty chicks have all the good pickup lines," it said, dreamily.

The pickles plainly didn't entirely agree with the raven, making it the first food Tom had ever come across that had that effect, or degree of courage. It belched, at the chamber-pot. "And I just love your scent," cooed the demon back at the raven. "How about if we just hang out a bit?" It bubbled a swirl of psychedelic onion-smelling cloud on the face of the water. "We could smoke it up together. Come on in... I got lots of pot..."

Master Hargarthius put the tray back on top of the chamber-pot, shaking his head disapprovingly. "It's channelling something from another dimension. No use even talking to it now, let alone teaching it a lesson."

ᏕᏕᏕᏕᏕᏕᏔᏔᏔᏔᏔᏔ

"It was stupid, dangerous, and beneath you, Alamaya," said her Uncle in that the worst of all his tones, more-sorrow-than-anger.

She didn't answer. If she did, he'd use her words against her, as he always did. The guard would get better. And there were less flies than there used to be. And the footman, well,

she'd got the dose wrong. He would be conscious again soon. And she'd be more careful with the dosage next time. Anyway, it served him right for drinking on the job.

"It's for your own good, you know, Princess. Now I'll have to increase the guards. And it's not as if I don't have bigger issues to deal with."

"Well, deal with them, instead of me," she said, sulkily.

He sighed. "They're only causing trouble for me, because I stop them from reaching you. Try to understand that Alamaya. And stay away from drugs."

Huh. Just last week he'd been telling her to learn about them. Admittedly that had been so she'd know if she was being drugged or poisoned and how to counteract it, but how was she supposed to learn, if she stayed away from them?

CHAPTER 6

THE SUCKER

———➤•◀———

"**Y**ou promised you'd teach me some magic, Master," said Tom, seizing what he hoped was an opportune moment, as they walked into the laboratory. It was not that such moments did not exist. It was just that they were rare, and mostly required that something particularly unpleasant had happened to someone or something else.

It appeared that whatever had made Master Hargarthius chuckle evilly as he walked down the long passage earlier, had not been sufficiently nasty. "Hmph. Why on earth would I do such a ridiculous thing with a good-for-nothing boy? A boy who needs to get those filthy cobwebs out of my laboratory."

Master Hargarthius had taken against spiders, since the demon had used one of them in his escape bid. Of course he still wanted cobwebs when he wanted them, and quickly. But having the producers living in the laboratory was just not on. Unfortunately, this was not an opinion shared by the spiders, who seemed to think it was their ancestral home, to which they had the right of return. Tom would do his best, and yet, by next time old Grumptious walked in there, there'd be webs again. Now was not a good time, as the magician pointed to a web in the corner. But Tom, having got himself to this point, was determined. He pointed at the tray-topped chamber-pot, now on a far shelf, with chalked symbols around it, in seven colors. "You said it'd be useful for demons, Master."

Master Hargarthius said "Hmph," again. He said it rather a lot, but Tom was fairly sure it wasn't magical or worth learning to do. "Nearly as much use as you keeping this place clean, boy." He sighed, irritably. "I suppose I can make sure it's cleaning spells you learn. Where is your broom?"

It wasn't quite what Tom had had in mind, but, well, he had to start somewhere. He stopped. "I'll go and fetch it, Master."

"Do. And stop walking in front of me and stopping where I'm about to step, for Zoranthyrus's sake!"

So Tom fetched his broom. He'd stashed it in a corner, not in the broom-cupboard. He was a bit wary about that cupboard. It seemed to be very, very much deeper than it looked from outside. And the door had a tendency to swing closed for no apparent reason. Tom didn't feel comfortable even going into it, and, for some reason, the raven kept trying to chase him away from it.

The magician looked at him and the broom disapprovingly, and then rubbed his long, bony, knobbly hands and wrinkled his nose, as if he'd smelled something bad. That was a relief, everything was normal, thought Tom. If Old Grumptious had smiled Tom would have dropped the broom and run. "Right. We'll need the long water-bath, and the carboy of Dotfaw Hydro-voltaic-barythermic fluid from the store. And a jar of newt's eyes. There are some up on the shelf there."

There were, of course. And many other things. Tom started with dragging the water-bath out, and fetching the Dotfaw Hydro-voltaic-barythermic fluid while Master Hargarthius indulged in the important magical ritual of standing around and then sticking his finger in his ear.

Tom climbed up on the workbench to reach the jars on the high shelf, and was glad Master Hargarthius could not see the dustiness behind them. He was rather preoccupied in his cunning plan to dust the bottle on his robe, while he was between it and the Magician's eyes, when Master proved he was attentive to more than just the amount of earwax on his index finger. "Not that one, you fool of a boy. That's Neep's eyes. You'd soup the entire thing up far too much. It's three jars along."

Reading was still a slower chore for Tom than it should be, and the writing on some of the jars was old and faded anyway. But, yes, the difference was there, now that he looked carefully. He took down the jar of desperately winking newt eyes, and tried to hand them to the magician.

"Put them on the bench. They're an activator," said Master Hargarthius. "At this stage, which is probably the only stage you'll ever be fit for, you're using magic, not making it." And he carefully turned his back on Tom, and started muttering away. Tom, of course, tried to listen and peer at what the Master was doing... but cautiously. That limited his ability to work out quite what was written on his broom in ear-wax, or the spells enacted on it. It did help that he was quick on his feet to dodge the splash when the magician dropped the broom into the bath. The liquid spat fat angry sparks and hissed like a furious tom-cat, before squirming into the cracks between the paving stones.

The master continued to mutter mysterious words and make mystic passes above the seething liquid. Well, it was that... or he was swearing and waving his arms around. It was sometimes hard to tell, Tom had to admit. He noticed the raven had flapped off to the far corner, before it all started. Tom had, by now, decided it wasn't entirely a stupid bird, so he backed off a little himself. This time there was no explosion and shattered glass. No strong smell of roasted rat. No fragments best not thought about hanging from the ceiling.

Just a high-pitched whine, like mosquitos in chorus.

Then that too stopped.

Tom edged forward.

Master Hargarthius gave an irritable sigh. "Always underfoot, boy! Pick it up."

Tom looked for tongs. He wasn't going near that Dotfaw Hydro-voltaic-barythermic fluid. It bit. But there was no need, the bath was dry, containing only his broom. Well, it looked like his broom, except perhaps for having a faint sheen to it. Nervously he touched it. It did not attack him, so he picked it up.

"Right," said Master Hargarthius. "We need to affix a newt's eye to the handle." He spat onto a couple of his fingers, and put a wet spit-spot on the end of the handle. He plucked out one of the newt's eyes from the jar, and popped it into the spit. "Now where did I put the thumb-tacks?" he asked looking around. Tom had no idea, so gave him no answer.

"Well, it'll just have to stick there. Be careful with it. Now, hold the broom firmly, and repeat the following incantation after me. Concentrate, boy. I will only tell you once. And the pronunciation better be perfect. Repeat exactly what I say."

Tom took a firm grip on the broom. Nodded.

"Roohvah a ekil skus gnithon!" said the magician. So Tom repeated it.

Nothing happened.

"Another twice, it takes three repetitions."

"Another twice..." Tom got a clout around his ear. "The spell, fool boy. Now you'll have to start again. Say the incantation three times."

"Roohvah a ekil skus gnithon! Roohvah a ekil skus gnithon! Roohvah a ekil skus gnithon!" said Tom.

Some more nothing happened.

"Now you have to press the newt's eye," instructed Master Hargarthius.

Warily Tom did. The eyelid blinked frantically as he poked a finger at it. That wasn't all that happened though. There was an eerie booming 'hoom' sound. The broom's straw bristles writhed and sucked onto Tom's foot. He screamed and tried to throw the broom away, but it wasn't letting go of his hands, although he did manage to pull it off his foot. Instead the broom, with a deep 'hoom', nuzzled under the bench and then began to drag Tom around the room slowly, with dust flying toward the writhing straws. It was better at cleaning than Tom was with the old broom. That was all that Tom could find to say that was good about it, right now. "How do I stop it!" he asked, as the Magician watched with some satisfaction, as Tom and the enchanted broom hoomed their way past him.

"Hmm. I don't recall right now. It'll stop when it's done. I'm going to do some reading. Call me when you're done. You've given me an idea."

And with that he walked out and off to his study, leaving Tom to finish hooming the room.

❦❦❦❦❦❦❦❦

Tom had to admit that the enchanted broom did make his work easier – once he stopped trying to fight the broom and just let it do what it felt it must. It was undoubtedly magical. But he didn't feel he'd actually learned any magic yet. He'd just learned to use some. He still had no idea what he was doing. Well, there were times he suspected that was true of Master Hargarthius too. Especially when he blew things up – once every few days, or had a temper tantrum because a spell either didn't work or worked wrong. At least Tom's two spells... the one for opening things and the one for making his broom suck up the dirt, always worked.

A few weeks later, Tom found himself cleaning up, again, after another failed experiment. The hoom-broom refused to deal with the bigger pieces of glass, and had stopped. Tom propped it against the wall and sighed, looking around for his dust-pan. He'd put it in the corner, which took him to the vicinity of a chamber-pot, with a silver tray on the top of it. Today it was a very pallid shade of blue, and the pansies a pink that bordered on white.

"Hey cat," said the demon, as he walked closer. "Er, cat, um, you wouldn't like to help me out a little?" The tone was wheedling, with a hint of desperation, thought Tom, who was beginning to get a handle on human tone.

"Not likely! You tried to kill me with spiders, remember," said Tom.

"Don't be so discriminatory, cat! It was for your own good," said the demon. There was a pause, and then with obvious effort, "Look, I'm not asking you to let me out, just, uh, fix me up with some of that good stuff again."

"What?" asked Tom.

"Oh cat, I need it so bad. Just a little bit. I'll do anything. Anything at all," pleaded the demon.

"You're stuck in a chamber pot. You can't do anything."

There was a moment's silence, again. "Well, I could tell you things. Humans always want to know things. Cats probably do too. You're curious. I know many secrets. I'll tell you anything you want to know for some more. And a bit of that crack."

Crack? "You'd lie. And anyway, I don't know what you're talking about. And I'm not letting you out."

"The stuff you gave me last time. Please. I'm begging you. I'm desperate. If you don't do it, I'll burst out of here." And indeed the sides of chamber-pot bulged ominously.

It became slightly clearer to Tom. And there was some broken glass to dispose of, and a long walk to take it away, otherwise. "Stay there. I'll have to see if I can get something for you," said Tom, who had nearly retreated onto the shards of broken glass. He picked one up and advanced on the chamber pot... it had worked last time.

And it worked this time. The silver lid raised marginally and a smoky hand made a frantic grab... not for Tom – who let go, but for the sharp edged glass, which was ripped into the pot. A puff of lavender smoke emerged, but the tray settled down again. The pansies started to dance frenetically.

If it hadn't been for the pansies, Tom would have kept quiet about it. But Old Grumptious was bound to notice them, he knew. The magician had a bad habit of noticing exactly what you least wanted him to notice. So he went to Master Hargathius's study and knocked. He'd learned the wisdom of that. The sound of snoring merely reflected one of the more pleasant possibilities.

"What is it, boy?" said the magician. "Why are you disturbing me again?" He yawned, closing the book on the desk.

"It's the demon, Master. It took a piece of broken glass."

Master Hargarthius got to his feet, picked up the leaning staff. "It shouldn't be able to do that. It's constrained, and the bonds should stop something many times as strong. And touching silver hurts them," he said, thoughtfully.

They walked back down the long winding stair and the passage to the laboratory. "Did you pick up the lid, the tray, boy?" asked Master Hargarthius thoughtfully.

"No. It reached out a smoky hand and took it. Really. But it was begging for broken glass. Crack, it called it."

"I'm going to have to give it a crack or two," said the magician, grumpily.

"It was offering to tell me secrets."

"Oh yes. They do. And they are secrets. Unfortunately usually made up on the spur of the moment. Demons lie. And they will tell you it's for your own good. Great Zoryanthus's pickled left testicle! It should not be able to do that! Avaunt, I tell you!"

The demon was smokily dancing in the chamber-pot... at least, writhing slowly and rhythmically in smoky coils with the silver tray balanced on top of its head. "Pickle," yelled the demon. "I need it. I want pickle, not a motasickle..." Then he whined. "Ah come on, man, fix me up, man."

Master Hargarthius's eyes narrowed. "Boy. Fetch me a pickled onion. Just one. Run."

So Tom ran.

Of course he ran straight into the skull of Mrs Drellson, which yelled at him. He was getting quite good at dodging her by now. There were important techniques he'd learned: One of them was "Master Hargarthius needs..."

That usually saved him from the green darts of pain. "You need a good kicking, boy. You see that I can see my face in the big pot by this evening. You call that clean. Huh. I'd do a better job with both hands tied behind my back."

Human speech was still very confusing, thought Tom, even when it came out of a disembodied floating skull. She didn't have a face. And if she did, did she want it boiled? And it wouldn't make much difference to her cleaning skills if she tied both her hands behind her back. They were presumably buried somewhere... Tom unbolted the pantry, and rushed in. And backed away from the cheese, which had sneaked up on him. It made an odd sort of burring, humming noise. But although it had butted his hand it hadn't actually bitten him. Tom got the message. The demon might want a pickle, but first the cheese was going to get some milk. He gave it a little from the ever-full jug. The cheese kept trying nudge his hand as he poured. And then it lapped at it... making the deep burring sound.

It was... purring. Tom had to resist his sudden urge first to wash it with his tongue, and then, from the human side of him, to stroke it.

Really, it wasn't so much purring as humming. And cheese did that, when it was dangerous. It had little sharp teeth! Tom shook his head, and peered at the jars. No, those weren't vole-skulls, but pickled onions. He took the jar out of the pantry, carefully closing it behind him. The door might keep mice out – but thinking as a cat, Tom was not sure of that. Perhaps it kept the cheese in, and that would probably deal with the mice.

He took a pickle out of the jar with a fork that only bent slightly on contact with it, and put it into a small bowl – and endured a lecture from the skull of Mrs Drellson about cleaning them, and putting the pickles back, before running up to the laboratory.

Master Hargarthius had chalked several more containment circles around the chamber-pot, and was standing with his staff extended towards the demon. "It appears broken glass gives it a certain hysterical strength, and the ability to ignore pain."

"Gimme the pickle, I want the pickle..." shrieked the demon, long vermillion claws reaching, scrabbling against the magical containment.

Master Hargarthius picked the pickle up off the plate, and tossed it at the chamber-pot.

It was snatched out of the air... and not by the raven, despite it trying. There was a mushroom cloud of rainbow-colored smoke... and all was still. The demon was back in its pot, and the pansies resumed a slower dance, their color fading to a soft lavender.

"Hmph," said Master Hargarthius. That could mean a lot of things, Tom had discovered. "I suppose it'll be devouring all my pickles. Well. I'll need to look this up in Groomes Encyclopaedia Demonologica. I won't be needing you, boy. Back to your work."

So Tom went back to the kitchen, where breakfast plates still had to be cleaned. There were a large number of jobs Tom disliked and dishwashing was high on that list. He wished he had a spell for a wash-disher. Now that would be handy. Of course, the Skull of Mrs Drellson was waiting for him to tell her about it. "What took you so long, boy?" she demanded.

Tom had worked out that the Skull was also curious, although less so than a cat. It liked to gossip. "The demon wanted a pickle. The Master is worried it will consume all his pickles."

The skull snorted. "He should be so lucky. You'd better put that jar back, boy."

So Tom took it to the pantry. He couldn't find the spot he'd taken it from though. The gap seemed to have filled itself in with another jar. The milk he'd poured out was gone, but the cheese was at least silent and undemanding. Tom stole some milk on principle. How come that jug was full again?

"What are you doing in there," demanded the Skull. "Not being disgusting and drinking milk straight out of the jug, are you?"

Tom hastily wiped his lips and chin and came out. "Just struggling to find a place for that jar. There seem to be a lot of pickles on the shelf."

The skull of Mrs Drellson had sniffed disapprovingly. "They're breeding in there. It's bad domestic management. You put pickle-jars together on a dark shelf in a boring, lonely pantry and what do you expect?"

Out of curiosity, Tom had tried to catch them at it after that, but so far the most evidence he'd seen was a fiery blush on a jar of pickled plums.

🙊🙊🙊🙈🙈🙈

The Wickedest Witch of the West (and she'd had to work hard in her youth for that title), was, frankly, worried. She'd hated doing that, but informing Duke Karst had seemed the lesser of two evils at the time. They'd been ready for her, waiting.

It was a question of timing and choosing that timing.

And Karst, goody-two-shoes, at least was better disposed to her as a result, instead of trying to keep her away from Borbungsburg Castle. Huh. Her reputation indeed. At least King Uther had understood her. The Tindrell blood ran strong in that girl, unlike this prosy boring Duke. And anyway she had found better places for entertainment. Borbungsburg was dull compared to Majorca.

CHAPTER 7

EYE OF NEWT

➤•◀

Tom discovered the big problem with newt's eyes was that they really were very badly attached... at least to the broom, if not to the newt. Perhaps having been detached once, they'd got used to it, and weren't used to staying put. He'd been lucky the first time, seeing the eye fall onto the bench. The second time he'd been less lucky but he had found it by crawling around the laboratory floor, and catching the winking reflection of it from under a bench.

The third time, less lucky.

He saw it fall... but only at the last moment. It had landed right next to the snaky tendrils of the broom and, before he could try to wrench it clear, been sucked away to whatever place the dust and spider-webs went to. The hoom-broom just went right on working... but Tom knew he had a problem, when it came to doing the job again. And right now it was not a bit of use to ask Old Grumptious about it. The magician was still deep in demonology books and wasn't taking to being disturbed well. Tom had managed a few glimpses of the demonology tomes. They seemed to have a lot of pictures. Very confusingly some of the pictures looked rather like lady-cats... or humans who could be cat-girls. He'd mentioned that to the skull of Mrs Drellson. She'd laughed nastily about it, and said it would serve him and Master Hargarthius right if they got caught. Demons looked exactly like what they wanted you to see.

Tom found that quite hard to get his head around right now, but what wasn't hard to work out was that he'd be in trouble again if the hoom-broom wasn't working and being used.

There hadn't been anything special or magical about attaching the eye. Just a bit of spit. Tom was sure cat-boy spit had to be as good – if not better– than old magician spit. So he climbed back up on the bench and got the jar down.

The lid was tight, and took all his strength to get it to twist. How had the old magician managed that? Tom got it off loose... realized he'd forgotten to spit and turned to do so. The jar lid fell off with a clang onto the bench-top. Tom turned back hastily, to see some of the contents beginning to ooze out over the top. He grabbed them and shoved them back. They were hot and squirmed as he crammed them in. Why did newt's eyes co-operate with an old magician, and not him?"

He tightened down the lid and then cursed. He still needed one of the eyes... but there was one, out and damply trailing its way across the bench.

Maybe if he hadn't been so flustered Tom might have noticed it didn't look like the newt's eye that had been on the handle. He grabbed it and shoved it in the spit. And then, thinking he'd better test it, pressed it.

The broom took off with a bristle-writhing howl of HOOOOOOOOM, and Tom found himself being dragged across the floor, and then... when the broom reached the wall, straight up it.

It didn't stop there, either. It was determined to clean the ceiling, even with Tom hanging there, unable to let go, as it high-power HOOOOOOMED along, turning abruptly and sending a swinging Tom whacking against the wall, before voraciously racing after a few shreds of cobweb in the corner.

What had he done wrong? It could kill him at the speed it was working.

Too late it occurred to him that really, he should have looked carefully. It must be that he'd made the same mistake as last time... only this time there was no Master Hargarthius to help him. He put out his feet hastily to stop himself from leaving an imprint of the side of his face in the stone of the wall. And they changed direction again, hurtling toward the floor...

The over-powered HOOOOOOOM broom was not going to leave any spot un-cleaned, even if it splattered Tom and then sucked up his remains...

It sucked up some tongs and narrowly missed some complex twisted glass apparatus before dragging him up to the roof again. Tom yelled for help, because being in trouble was still better than being in trouble for breaking glassware. That was Master Hargarthius's exclusive privilege.

It didn't help. The magician's tower was half cut out of the native rock, and even where it wasn't, the walls were two feet thick. There was no reason to suspect the ceilings and floors were not much the same. The heavy, iron-bound door was closed. Anyway, it was so thick one couldn't even hear explosions from outside.

The raven hadn't been in the lab when he'd got there, or followed him in, or Tom would never have tried the experiment in the first place. The demon was deep in its pot, burbling purple pickle dreams.

He was on his own... only every ounce of his strength enabled Tom to stop the over-powered HOOOOOOOM broom from shattering an orrery that the Master fiddled with from time to time. It ripped him back to the roof, and this time it was on course for the shelf full of bottles and jars of exotic and magical supplies.

Frantic, Tom scratched at the baleful neep's eye.

And was rewarded by a sudden silence. A sudden silence, punctured by Tom's yowl of alarm as he realised that he and the now silent broom were falling off the ceiling and straight into a glass and crystal multiple retort. Only a desperate mid-air turn and flail saved the glass, and landed Tom, hard, on the flagged floor. He did at least land on his feet like a cat. He made up for it by falling onto his face like a human, because a cat has four feet to land on, and that's more stable than two.

Still... he was alive. The roof and walls were cleaner. And he'd found out just how to turn a neep's eye off.

It might even work with newt's eyes.

It did.

Learning magic, even to use, thought Tom, was not for the faint-hearted. Still he was quite proud of himself. The laboratory was clean in far less time than usual, and he'd learned something. It made up a little for having to have a strange human body, and for having to work. Dogs worked. Cats did not... unless they were caught and turned into famuluses.

Of course pride and a bit of extra free time didn't last long with the Skull of Mrs Drellson around. He'd just settled down with his feet up on the bench for a little cat-nap, when he awoke to her dulcet screeching. How a disembodied skull could open doors was still a bit of a mystery to him. Maybe she did it by sheer force of will. She had enough of that. "You will do this, you will do that." And right now it seemed Tom would take out the garbage, which was stinking up her kitchen.

He set off with the pail of kitchen scraps, which were, he had to admit, quite smelly even by the standards of a magician's residence. He'd done it often enough before. Only this time... well, the skull followed him. He was aware of it, but there wasn't much he could do about it.

He soon realized that he should have tried harder. Distracted her, or something, because he got a stinging weal of pain across his back. "Fool boy! Where do you think you're going?"

"To get rid of the rubbish. Like I always do."

The dead orbs of a skull cannot narrow, and look at you as if you just crawled out of a piece of green cheese. The skull of Mrs Drellson did her best. The chilly tone of her sneer made up for the difficulty. "That passage leads to the second-best dungeon. Not the midden."

"Uh. This is where I always take the rubbish."

That was clearly the wrong thing to say, because he got two more of her bolts of pain. "You disgusting, boy. How dare you!"

"But... there was lots of rubbish in there anyway."

"Of course there is. Don't you know anything about the maintenance of a proper dungeon? Hmph. Probably not. Let me explain, fool. That rubbish is selectively put there to make it unpleasant and harder to escape. You do not improve the cells with any old rubbish! You'll have to clean it all up and return it to its previous state of awfulness before old Grumptious finds out. Estethius would have had your skin peeled off over three weeks. Fancy putting it there, of all places."

Tom had actually thought he'd done well to find a place with other rubbish, rotting scraps and rags. "But... I didn't know where else to put it."

"Hmph. You know perfectly well where the midden is. I caught you sneaking out there. Without the rubbish."

"You mean it's... outside?" asked Tom

"Where else is a midden?" asked the skull.

Tom had no idea, but decided it was probably not clever to tell her that. "But I thought I wasn't allowed to go there."

"You're not allowed to run away. Or you'd be stupid to. But the garbage needs to go somewhere," said the skull.

So Tom went back to the door to outside. He was very careful to get the spell right. The skull did follow him... but not further than the doorway. "I'm bound to the tower," she said irritably. "But it's just a few yards away. A big hole. Estethius blasted it."

Tom found it, amid the dead nettles and with a few drifts of snow still lying in the lee of the rocks. It might have been a big hole once. It wasn't any more. But there was still room for a pail of smelly kitchen waste.

It was strange to be outside. Strange and cold.

And the raven was watching him from a perch on a lichen-covered broken pillar that leaned among a patch of briars. It hadn't come out of the door with him. It could fit though the arrow-slits, Tom suspected.

It actually didn't say 'Nevermore,' which was strange enough to make Tom not waste any time out there. Besides, it was cold.

It didn't stop him coming out again. And again. And quite a few more times after that, hauling kitchen scraps and laboratory disasters up from the second-best dungeon, to the midden.

It was on the last of his trips up from the second-best dungeon that Tom found heartbreak.

Well, not so much 'heartbreak', as a little lower in his body. There was a smell out there he recognised, and it wasn't the familiar smell of kitchen scraps. It was a smell that did very odd things to his head.

Things the human side of him said were insane, but still made his tail quiver, and wave rather fast and sinuously.

She wasn't what anyone would have called a beautiful female cat.

That is, not anyone but a Tom cat, and that fairly temporarily. The human side of Tom could see that. The cat side wasn't interested in logic.

Unfortunately... or maybe fortunately, she wasn't in the least interested in Tom. The feral she-cat had been hungry enough to be interested in kitchen scraps, perhaps. But not in humans. Not even human boys with a cat's tail. They scared her, and she ran a lot faster on four legs than he did on two.

Tom had been becoming somewhat resigned to being trapped in this clumsy human body, a body that wouldn't have considered those scraps as edible or worth looking at. Not that he hadn't still been thinking about getting to be a cat again one day. But it had lost its urgency.

This made it all fresh again.

Which, inevitably, led him into all sorts of trouble.

※※※※※※※

"A Princess," said the Duchess, loftily, "Is expected to behave with a certain amount of decorum. And, Zoryanthus help us, with discretion!" she hissed out that last word. "And," and this sounded as if it were wrung out of her, "With a common page-boy, Alamaya! It's your grandmother's blood. It didn't come from our side of the family. I'm... I'm mortified."

I wish you were, thought Alamaya. He was cute. But she didn't say it. "It wasn't anything serious, just..."

"It's the rumors you will start, Princess. A future queen needs to behave like a Corvin!"

Alamaya had to admit that she felt no particular pride in being the last heir of the ruling dynasty, Corvin. She knew the Corvins were cursed, and that she'd die, after they married her off, when she had given birth to the next doomed Corvin. It wasn't much to look forward to, let alone be proud of. She braced herself for a long, long lecture. She'd have turned herself into a green frog to avoid it. And the page-boy too. Hmm. That had possibilities... The frog spell wouldn't work on herself, but maybe...

※※※※※※※

Inside the security of the magical cone of silence Malalia did not bother to hide her disdain. "If anything the Borbungs seem a more foolish house than the Corvins. They do not seem aware just how many mages report to us."

"It's only the latest two generations of Corvins that seem to have lost the ability to command. Remember, that as foretold, the Raven took down the greatest mage of the age, Estethius. And, cursed as they are, they are a useful foil."

"And in the process of destroying Estethius, King Uther was consumed, lost to his people and his kingdom," said Malalia, dourly. *"And therewith their virtue, courage and strength."*

"Naturally. Destroying Estethius was not without cost."

CHAPTER 8

USE ONLY AS DIRECTED!

————➤•◄————

I t's got a big evil long beak, and a glittering eye. That's not going to stop me killing that Zoryanthys bedamned bird, as soon as I get out of this mess, thought the warty toad sitting in front of the mirror in a puddle of mildly toxic slime, amid the flasks, beakers and retorts on Master Hargarthius's main work-bench.

The now-toad's name was... Tom.

Tom the toxic-skinned toad was of the opinion, now, that being a human and a magician's famulus wasn't actually the worst thing that could happen to a cat.

Quite recently, about an hour ago, he had not had that opinion. That, he had to admit had a lot to do with the mess he was in. Maybe more than that old tatty black feather-duster of a bird who was sitting and looking him with one unblinking eye from its perch on the top of the bust of Athena.

As a cat Tom had known that rules were for people and other lesser creatures. This was of course still true, but, well perhaps this time as an ugly-clumsy human had changed that. It hadn't changed his tail, which had done most of his thinking in this situation.

It had been that feral she-cat at the midden...

He'd wanted her so badly. Of course the cat had not been very impressed with an ugly clumping human. Even if he'd had fish, she would not have found him interesting in the way he wanted her to find him interesting.

Which had led him here, to this puddle of toxic slime and into all sorts of trouble, most of which could only get much, much worse.

"Cats have more fun than humans," he'd said to the raven – because there was no-one else to talk to in the tedious work of cleaning up after the wizard's latest messy venture into the arcane. It was either the arcane or possibly supper, or possibly both. He hoped that was egg spilled on the counter. He'd been banished from the laboratory for this session, something that happened occasionally. The wizard considered it punishment. Tom wasn't sure it was. "There are at least girl-cats around. I haven't even met an attractive human, and won't, with Old Grumptious about."

The raven tilted its head at him, and lifted its tail over the face of Athena, and said "Nevermore."

"I wish," scowled Tom. "You always say that. But you always produce more." He had put several pages of the Weekly Illuminati Age and Advertiser under the bust that was the raven's favorite perch, but the tokens tended to land on Athena's décolletage or, like this one, hang up on her nose. It was the little cleaning job Tom resented most. Still, the raven was inclined to vicious pecks and sneak attacks, so he said it quite quietly.

"It's all very well for you," he said taking a rag from the bucket and wiping Athena's nose. "You've got no interest in the fairer sex."

"Nevermore," said the raven, and slashed his beak at Athena's nose, and Tom's hand, which was hastily withdrawn.

It was always a bit of a limited two-way conversation with the raven. "She was gorgeous. Well, attractive. I wish I could be a cat again. But Old Grumptious has barely taught me any magic, let alone the transformational stuff."

At which point the raven fluffed up its feathers and spread its wings and hopped over to the shelf above the workbench Tom was wiping down, landed clumsily on a large jar which rocked enough for Tom to raise his hands to catch. "KaaaaaRK!" it said, which was a change from 'Nevermore.' So then it said: "Nevermore," and pointed its long heavy black beak at the jar's label.

That was enough to make Tom read it. Reading was one of the few advantages Tom had found to not being a cat.

The jar – brown glass with a big stopper – had a large, florid label, making it look just like most of the other exotic supplies in the place, so Tom had never bothered to read it, just dusted carefully around it. He saved his reading skills and efforts for the Weekly Illuminati Age and Advertiser, and for the grimoires, whenever he could find one that wasn't locked.

This jar label read, in ornate writing:

Ye Wizard's Favorite:

Doctor Mirabellus's Original

Ontogenetic Reflux liquid.

'Never be short of those essential ingredients again! Eye of newt or wing of bat, fresh to the cauldron and on hand, just at your fingertips.

Suppliers to Royalty'

And on the bottom, beneath the picture of cauldron bubbling with suitable ingredients:

'Use only as directed by ye professional Thaumaturge. Do not exceed the recommended dosage. See reverse label for application instructions.'

So Tom did, but not before going to one of the few books he'd stashed safely where old Grumptious would never find it, with the soap, scrubbing brush, and hand-towel. It was Wolbster's Dictionary of Magical and other Terms, and of great value to an apprentice and one-time cat who was learning to read. He looked up 'Ontogenetic' and got led into ontogeny recapitulating phylogeny, which meant looking those words up too. He didn't see quite how regressing a human could take the person to the stage of being something more advanced like a cat, but he went back to read the label on the back of the jar.

'Administer the requisite dose to ye organism to be refluxed. When ye correct stage of ontogenesis −according to ye count of seconds is reached, say ye words 'Sator-Hathaway-Yawahtah-Rotas three times while rotating ye organism counter-clockwise, and apply a second dose of the liquid, externally. It will then develop from there along ye correct evolutionary branch with the astonishing rapidity only achieved by Doctor Mirabellus's Original Thaumaturgials. Accept no substitutes!

And beneath that was a list of typical transformative dosages and times.

Spider to porriwiggle – ¼ drop, 19 seconds

Toad to usable famulus – three drops, 7 seconds.*

Mouse to newt – one drop, 9 seconds

Cat to toad – nine drops, 22 seconds

Dairymaid to sylph – five drops orally, and one behind each ear, 35 seconds.

Maiden to eagle – seven drops, 19 seconds.

Famulus to cat... His eye caught that one, dwelled on it – eight drops, 20 seconds.

Maiden to eagle – seven drops, 19 seconds.

The list went on. There was even a dose for creating cockatrices, and apprentice-to-tiger – that came with an advisory that the apprentice should be caged first.

And at the end of the list... 'Extreme care should be taken to avoid contact with ye liquid. Always wear dragon-hide disposa-gloves. Store in a dry place away from exposure to ye full moon or sudden actinic light. Apply Doctor Mirabellus's patent fixative powder to freeze changes. In case of an overdose contact your nearest Apocalypse Room. Use before the Century of the Horned Toad.

*Apprentice may occasionally eat flies, a great saving.'

"Huh. They always say stuff like that. All the same, it might be risky," Tom said to the raven who fluttered clumsily back to its favorite perch, its claws scrabbling for purchase on Athena's marble hair. He tried not to think of the graceful curve of the girl-cat's tail. "Anyway, she's probably gone elsewhere by now."

"Nevermore," agreed the raven.

"And I might wreck my chances as a human, where I get to work like a slave for Old Grumptious, with an old raven for company, not a sexy cat. I could be turned into a frog, or a cheese... or, using the same potion, into whatever ingredient he was short of right then. I'd be crazy to try transforming myself back into a cat."

"Nevermore!" said the raven, nodding his beak sympathetically. Well, maybe he was trying to scratch his chest. An ex-cat believes what he wants to believe, especially when thinking about girl-cats. It tended to skew Tom's thinking a lot. Tom took the jar down from the shelf. What was the worst it could do? Tom opened the jar. It was another advantage to being human – or at least to having opposable thumbs.

The goop inside it was a virulent green, bubbled and shivered with purplish scintillations, and it stank badly enough to make skunks and rotten cabbages envious. That was reassuring: It looked and smelled like any good magical potion.

He went and fetched a pipette, and then, on thought, a mirror. He avoided the one that told him he was fairest of them all, and the one with the odd frame that showed your image... and an entirely different background. He wasn't sure that was actually a mirror. Old Grumptious looked into it and sniggered a lot. Anything that made the magician laugh probably wasn't pleasant. The mirror he chose was mostly quite well behaved, and new. It came from the hallway, where Old Grumptious had installed it to examine possible customers after the incident with demon, to make sure they had reflections.

He read the instructions carefully, took a deep breath, closed his eyes... exhaled. He couldn't put a drop in his mouth with his mouth closed and eyes shut. He began the process, counting drops. The raven had flapped over to the mirror to watch. It was naturally utterly revolting and each drop made him feel exceedingly strange. He was just lifting his finger to release the last drop, when the raven hopped across from the mirror-top onto his shoulder in a flop of black feathers and shrieked "Nevermore!" in his ear.

Inevitably his finger had slipped a little. He flung the pipette aside, spluttering and spitting. And changing. Shrinking.

His robe fell off. If he hadn't hastily scrambled up onto the workbench, in a few moments he wouldn't have been able to reach it.

He'd understood what a fetus was, but before he returned to being one... he hadn't realized how small they were. If this kept going he'd disappear! He started frantically counting seconds, and then decided to rotate three times, counterclockwise, yelling "Sator-Hathaway-Yawahtah-Rotas" at the top of a very tiny voice.

He stopped shrinking. That was the only substantive improvement in the matter.

He was very tiny, and very weak, and trapped on the top of a workbench with a vast raven peering down at him. Somewhere across the ridges of splintery wood, was a spilled pool of ontonogenic reflux liquid. He started crawling while he could. It was a long way, and it was revolting stuff to crawl into.

Once into it, he felt himself growing again. That was a relief. That girl-cat had better be worth it. Still, he could hardly wait to taste fresh mouse again...

Only it had all ended with croak not a meow. And a desire for fresh fly, and romantic hours of amplexus with another fat toad, floating in the green pond-slime... The once-cat and the once-human parts of Tom knew two things now. Firstly, there were actually worse things than being a famulus. Secondly, this had to be the raven's fault.

For a few minutes he just sat there and croaked and thought dark thoughts about ravens. But he knew too well what happened to toads in a magician's laboratory. He had to get out here, and preferably not as a toad. And that meant doing something before toad thoughts took control of him completely. The only way out was back to the ontogenetic liquid... The jar still stood on the counter, and there was some in the bulb of the pipette. He read the instructions on the jar, his toad-mind wrestling with the reading. There was no toad to cat. Toad to famulus, yes. Magicians were always running out of famuluses it seemed.

He got his nose under the pipette, tilted it and the drops ran out.

"Nevermore!" exclaimed the raven.

"Croak," answered Tom and drank. He hoped those were the right number of droplets...

Being a bat had to be better than being a toad, he supposed, a little later. And they were better at reading in the dim light of the laboratory. It must be getting on for evening. Master Hargarthius could get up any moment now from his post lunch nap. That thought drove him back to the last of the spilled ontogenetic liquid. This time he was closer. A lemur, fortunately just big enough to pipette out some more fluid.

"Nevermore," said the raven, shaking his head.

But it had to be once more.

Tom's relief at being in human form again, even still with a tail – It had been there when he'd been a toad, a bat, and might have been when he'd been a lemur, was tempered by the fact that the muttering and swearing down the passage had to be Old Grumptious, and here he was, naked, on the workbench. He leaped off and pulled on his robe, and was just hastily putting the jar back when his master arrived.

"What are you doing with that?" The wizard demanded, fixing his apprentice and the jar of Doctor Mirabellus's Original with a very jaundiced eye.

"It's, er, date expired, master," said Tom. "Due to be used before the century of the horned toad."

Old Grumptious sniffed and scratched his straggly beard. "Hmph. Just a hundred and three years past its safe date then. But the stuff is dangerous anyway. I thought I'd transform a plump milk-maid into a sylph once. Er, strictly for experimental purposes. And I ended up with a gorgon who gave me no end of trouble. I'd forgotten about it. Toss it out, Boy."

"Never... more!" said the raven as he walked past.

"Never ever!" agreed Tom.

ꙅꙅꙅꙅꙅ

Alamaya had thought being an eagle would be liberating... and would mean she could fly. Fly wherever she wanted to, away from Borbungsburg and the guards, and Duke Karst being a miserable old misery.

Finding herself to be a cat was a shock. A measuring error... but once she was a cat and not an eagle, she'd discovered that suddenly being a cat did not mean you could run... or even walk like a cat. It was the four feet thing! And doors had a whole new problem factor to them. Footmen needed better training. They should open them to cats. But

when she tried to tell the footman that, it came out as a plaintive 'Meeeow.'

The footman had tried to kick her. Had it not been for her frantic guards, searching for her, she would never have got through. They weren't paying much attention to a cat, just then. One of them was carrying the gown which had fallen off her when she became a cat.

She'd headed for her rooms, wondering if maybe this had been less of a good idea than she thought at the time. At least there were more clothes there.

There was also a dead maidservant hidden behind the drapes she'd scampered for instinctively – cat-instinct- on hearing a sound she really had not expected.

What had alarmed her was men, speaking in whispers... in her bedroom. Men never went in there! Cats, it seemed, were able to hear, and smell far better than she could as a human.

"...patient. She's not due for a little while yet."

"It's not being patient that worries me. It's getting out of here after we kill her."

"It's all arranged. Hist... what was that?"

'That' was an outraged and somewhat frightened meow, from a rapidly departing cat. The meow had been an attempt at shouting for the guards. It didn't come out right. The running did, even if it looked a bit odd with a cat lunging onto its hind feet.

She might have no clothes, but becoming not a cat – it wasn't permanent without the fixative the instructions had said – in a room with at least two murderous assassins was less attractive than being naked.

It occurred to her, when the panic subsided, and she was well and truly out of the gates of Borbungsburg Castle, that she really had no idea just how 'not permanent' it was, or just how long she was going to have to stay a cat, and quite what would happen then. But she didn't have much time to worry about it, because a nasty-looking dog, who had been investigating some garbage in the alley, had spotted her.

Alamaya had to think about what to do. The dog didn't. The dog didn't care if he was a common mongrel and the cat that he could see was transformed royalty. She was a cat and the dog chased cats. If it caught one it would kill it. And this was not a very agile cat. It kept standing on its hind legs and meowing at him before running very ineptly – but fast. It did swipe his nose with a claw, before jumping up onto a fuller's barrel, put there for the convenience of the visitors to the tavern just beyond. The tavern's drunks got relief, the fuller got a source of ammonia... until the large angry dog knocked over the barrel, lunging for the cat. A cat that jumped clumsily from the tipping barrel for the tavern door, hotly chased by a dog now wet with decayed urine that the fuller had wanted and the dog had not.

Alamaya dodged kicks – mostly, and fled between the human legs, upstairs. A man was just entering a doorway there, and Alamaya shot between his legs and into the room – which was rather small, full of a bed and that bed was full of a woman, without any clothes on.

Well, she couldn't spare Alamaya any – even if she hadn't flung a pillow at the princess-cat that had bounded up onto her unmade bed. The man had tried to grab her – the cat – or maybe the woman. Alamaya didn't stay to find out. The window was open, and un-shuttered.

Alamaya forgot she wasn't an eagle.

But she found herself flying anyway.

Someone or something had her by the scruff of the neck, and was hauling her up into the sky, cackling with laughter.

CHAPTER 9

IN WHICH THERE IS GARLIC. ALMOST CRUSHED GARLIC.

——————▶•◀——————

Master Hargarthius had become absorbed in a new line of research, which, Tom realized, meant that the old one hadn't worked. This, according to the skull of Mrs Drellson, was perfectly normal for magicians, who had the attention span of a fraction of a gadfly. "It kills them, yes," the skull cackled gleefully. "Spend more time and effort looking for a short cut than they do in achieving anything."

Tom could understand that to some extent. The hoom-broom... and the super hooom, so long as he kept his finger ready on the neep's eye, had made clean-up so much faster and easier, that the rest of it seemed more tedious than ever. And the trouble with new lines of research was that they seemed to be – automatically – messier than old lines.

Added to this was a new and recent discovery of his own. Tom had learned the value of finding good hiding places for a famulus in trouble, a situation he knew so well he wondered what it would be like not to be one. It must be odd, he thought, to not have a magician's temper tantrums or the vindictive driving of the skull constantly chasing him on to the task he would fail to perform to her satisfaction. He didn't know what it would feel like, and he was given no chance to find out.

It appeared he was not the first famulus to have this problem, to find hidey-holes, or the first to be trying to learn enough mage-craft to get out of here. The stone cistern on the top floor – bar the roof – was refilled by water spewing from a pipe attached to a strange metallically squeaking device. Tom went to fetch buckets of water for cleaning from it. He noticed a small gap between the cistern and the wall one day, and promptly squeezed through it. In the tangle of pipes there, some long-ago famulus had made himself a nest of blankets and the remains of an old chair, and laid in supplies of food and drink, now long decayed, and reading matter, still intact. A book: 'ELEMENTARY SPELL-CRAFT FOR YE DUNDERHEADS'

It might have seemed the best find in the whole of Ambyria to Tom, if it wasn't for the fact that it had also been written by ye Dunderhead, a long time ago. Ye Dunderhead had written a how-to book to make a living because he wasn't very good at magic. It also was long on the use of expensive and rare ingredients – Tom knew they were expensive and rare because Master Hargarthius said so every time he used them. Tom had seen he marked at least one of the bottles. The book was short on spells that were either relevant or simple. Still, Tom studied it, carefully, and was suitably confused by it.

None of the spells related to transformation. It mostly seemed concerned with attracting one's true love, and revenge on one's true love for also being attracted to others. The cat side of Tom found that hard to understand, unlike the spell for ye summonsing of mice from other dimensions. That he got. The "Make ye staff into a magickally propelled rod of chastisement for ye lazy apprentice" seemed hauntingly familiar in some of the words. Tom still wasn't going to try it on Master Hargarthius.

There was however one spell which had some applicability. By the fact that the book opened itself to that page – as it did to 'ye visions of a state of disrobement of a nubile sylph' – and the dirty thumb marks the book's previous owner had found it so. And the previous owner had not scrawled 'Ye rubbish' or "Dothe not worke!" on the page, as he had in other places. It was titled "Ye el-Zebbo's simple incantation for ye harde-to-clean surfaces. Contains ammoniacal micro-daemons to get to those harde to reach places. Pine scented. Will clean up to five square cubits in a single application."

Hard to clean... That was all the places he had to clean, as far as Tom was concerned. The disrobing spell was... interesting, but Tom wasn't too sure why. Cats didn't wear clothes anyway, and were not much excited by seeing other cats also not wearing clothes. Smells were something entirely different. He decided he'd better try the cleaning spell, cautiously, in an abandoned room – there were many of those – with the door soundly locked.

To his immense surprise it worked. There were no complications, other than a faint smell of ammonia and distant pine forests mingling uneasily, and those soon dissipated. The room was clean enough to make Mrs Drellson's skull speechless, something much to be desired. Tom was very pleased with his success.

So much so that he tried it out in the laboratory after the next failed experiment. That, it turned out, was a serious mistake. Only his yelling and the raven's rapid response, and the fact that the master was still in the passage beyond saved him. Hargarthius would certainly have killed him, otherwise.

As he held Tom for his staff to beat him, in a laboratory full of an eye-watering stench of ammonia at war with a vast fresh-cut pine forest, Hargarthius told Tom exactly why you did not let micro-daemons loose in a magically charged environment. He told him loudly and clearly and re-enforced the message with a selection of bruising staff-stripes.

It was only much later, in his small stone room, trying to find a comfortable way to lie that didn't make the bruises hurt, that it occurred to Tom that Master Hargarthius had known it was el-Zebbo's incantation that he'd used.

He asked Mrs Drellson's skull the next day. "Old Grumptious. Yes, he was one of Esthetius's famuluses. Lazy little hobgobbin he was. Always skiving off. Like you."

Tom made a mental note that behind the cistern was probably not a safe place to hide from the Master. Still, the spell was useful for cleaning empty passages. He was busy doing that one day when Master Hargarthius came bustling down the passage. "A task for you, boy," he said in a tone that made Tom wish he was in a better place to run. "You're always on at me to teach you the trade. Well, here's your chance. We have some merchants that you must go and bargain with. I shall be entrusting you with money. It's an important part of the practice of magic."

By now Tom had worked out how Master Hargarthius felt about money. Tom had even found a few small coins himself, which had come to light in the process of his cleaning. Gold, copper and silver were at least known values, as what they were used for, even if Tom had had no physical experience of this 'spending'. He knew that Master Hargarthius regarded it as the equivalent of having his nose hairs pulled... at best. This wasn't just suspicious, it was very suspicious. "Er. Why?"

Master Hargarthius scowled. "Because I told you to. They're from Kos and they nauseate me. But they claim to have bat-blood to sell."

The Master had been putting adverts in the Weekly Illuminati Age and Advertiser, attempting to buy some. So far the results had been enough to make him pull his beard out in lumps and curse and swear a lot. Tom ventured to ask why this should be any different. "They're from Kos. They're full to the back gills with moonbats down there," said Master Hargarthius. "Now listen, on no account are you to pay more than one golden Salabar for a vat. Bargain them down. Offer them three silver Corvin, let them counter offer. Edge it up, but I'll reward you for every copper Zoe below the Salabar. Money is tight," he grumbled, "and prices are just ridiculous!"

"Er. Can't you magically just make some more money, Master?" asked Tom who still only had the vaguest idea of the relative value of these coins.

The magician scowled. Plucked at his dirty star-and-moon spangled robe. "Do these look like bats and roses to you, boy? I'm not an alchymist, and no one else wastes their time trying to defy the first law of Thaumodynamics."

"Er. What's that?" asked Tom.

"Hmph. 'The value of money magically produced does not exceed the expense needed to create that money'," said the magician. "And the merchants are all rich, meaning getting a bargain is difficult because of the second law of Thaumodynamics."

"I er, don't know that either. And... and it might help," Tom said hastily, reading the Master's expression.

"Money cannot, without magic, flow from a richer environment to a poorer."

"I don't know much magic," said Tom, warily. "Or about money."

"Well, I'll teach you a quick translation spell," said the Master loftily. "Pay attention."

"How much?" asked Tom.

He got a cuff for that, and memorized the spell. "You can tell them you're me," said the Master, handing him a small pouch, prodding him ahead of him into the gate-room, and slamming the door behind him.

Tom had recently got the floor to that room cleaned up, after a lot of hard scrubbing, which the Master found very funny. That was always a bad sign.

So the stench in the place was a bad sign too. It was smoky and the smell was foul enough to make Tom want to gag. The smell, and the smoke came from the four large... well, possibly men. Maybe undead. Undead for quite a long time by the pong. And undead with garlic, which Tom had gathered between the Weekly Illuminati Age and Advertiser, and things the magician and Mrs Drellson's skull said, was not a favorite of the undead, or vampires.

The Kossians had made a small fire on the floor, a floor Tom had painstakingly scrubbed those terrible stains off. "What did you do that for?" he demanded crossly, quite forgetting that he was here to bargain.

They looked at him. "No speeky Ambyrian," said one. He, like all of them, wore strange leggings. Puffed up like a turkey's drumsticks, but upside down, so they were much wider at the bottom than the top. Actually, even without the smoke to make his eyes water, Tom would have wanted to rub his eyes to make sure he wasn't seeing things. They had embroidered waistcoats, and what looked like a sheet wound around their heads. And attached to their broad sashes were large curved scimitars. Tom remembered the spell, hastily muttered it, and repeated himself.

The speaker laughed and a wave of garlic pounded at Tom. "You will not magically entrap us now." He pointed at the fire. "A spell to protect us. Very powerful witch she made it for us." He broke another clove of garlic off the double bandolier of garlic around his neck and popped it into his mouth and chewed, open-mouthed. "Garlic very good yes," said the Kossian spitting flecks of it as he talked.

"Er. Yes," said Tom. The men appeared to be spreading out, rather like the smoke. "Well, I want to buy some bat-blood. I'm offering three silver Corvin a vat."

"You him Hargarthius?" asked the Kossian, as his companions drifted sideways... it was very odd. Tom was not comfortable, besides the smell.

Mindful of what he had been told, Tom changed the automatic shaking of his head to a nod. "Yes. Now about that bat-blood..."

And then dived sideways to avoid the grabbing hands, and crashed into the second Kossian, and ducked the sweeping grasp of the third. He dived between the turkey-leg leggings and away, instinctively trying to find somewhere high, as the curving swords came out and the four, who weighted more than three times what he did, each, advanced towards him like a fleshy, sword-wielding wall.

There was no high point to jump to. No furniture. No windows...

Nowhere out at all.

No support, No help. Just an ominous creak.

Ominous enough to get the Kossians to look up, at the ceiling. It was descending.

"Magic!" exclaimed one fearfully.

"We protected," said another. But there was doubt there. The ceiling was distinctly lower, and looked like stone.

"Anyway, we got him, Hargathius," said the leader of the four, now tickling Tom's windpipe with his sword. "You stop it."

Tom shook his head. "I'm just his famulus. And the roof's pulleys and chains are on the next floor. I always wondered what they were for."

"We'll kill you if you don't stop it! We only want the brain," said the Kossian.

Maybe they were Zombies! "I can't stop it!" yelled Tom. "And the master will kill me too! I'm just a cat." He understood now what he stains on the floor had been. At least cleaning them this time would not be his problem. The next famulus might find some squashed gold... It was dawned on Tom, that this might be his way out. Hargarthius might not care much for apprentices or smelly Kossians, but his gold was another matter. The roof was much lower now, and the Kossian had abandoned Tom to try and push it back. They were huge men... and their muscles bulged futilely.

Master Hargathius's cackle filled the shrinking room. "Excellent. I'm glad I fixed the device. I'll crush you like beetles, you stinking rogues."

"Mercy," screamed the straining Kossians, as the roof came down, inexorably. Tom, who knew that mercy was of little interest to magicians, yelled. "Master, it'll crush your gold too." The roof by now had the Kossians on their knees. "It'll mash it into a bloody mess, and you won't find it all."

The roof stopped coming down, which was just as well, because it was now barely high enough for Tom to crawl. One of the Kossians had jammed his sword between the floor and the roof like a prop. It had bent, alarmingly. "Hmph," said Master Hargarthius. "I'll have to see if I can find the raising lever. I put it somewhere safe."

Tom groaned. He'd been trying to find 'somewhere safe' for months now. It was a very elusive place which had a lot of things in it. This time it must have been less safe, because Master Hargarthius announced. "I will raise the roof and open the outer door. If you're not out of there and running, faster than I can say 'Rack Jobinson', I'll drop it again."

The roof by creaking degrees began to go upwards. The door to the outside world swung open, and the Kossians scrambled out. The door swung closed before Tom could follow them. The bent scimitar fell with a clang as the roof ascended.

And a little later the door into the tower opened, and Master Hargarthius stood there. "Hmph. Kossians. They've stunk the place up," he said, supremely unaware of his own bouquet. "Clean it up, boy. And, well done, to think of my money being crushed."

"Um," said Tom, entirely bereft of words just then.

"I wouldn't use el-Zebbo's incantation. That was a powerful spell they brought with them," said Master Hargarthius, oblivious to fact that Tom wanted to fall over, or at least sit down. "Now, let's see what they left behind." He poked at the bent scimitar. "Hmph. Poor metalwork." He looked at the bundles the 'merchants' had abandoned, while Tom worked on staying upright, with increasing success. "Well, well, well. It really looks like bat blood vats," said the Master, pointing to the little barrels. "I'll have to check, carefully. And see there are no booby-traps. Take them to the laboratory. Heh. That's a bargain! Now, where's my money, boy?"

Now that Tom had recovered his wits a bit, he thought he'd better make as much of this as he could. He held out the bag. "You promised me a reward if I got you a bargain," he said.

The magician took the pouch, and felt the weight of it. "Hmm. So I did." He opened the pouch and took out the littlest coin, a copper Zoe. For a moment Tom thought he was going to give it to him. But that was of course in defiance of the second law, so instead he used it to teach Tom a spell. "Very useful for shopkeepers in towns you never plan to visit again," he explained. "It makes it appear to be the highest value currency they are likely to accept, a golden Salabar. It doesn't last very long, unfortunately. But if you've had to make a carpet-stop in a distant village, it can be very useful."

As Tom had not made as much as a foot-stop at the nearest village, let alone a flying carpet stop in a distant one, it didn't seem very useful to him. But that too was about to change. "That's the second attempt to gain entry to the tower in months. It's been more than twenty years since that last happened. I'm going to have to tighten my defenses. And the easiest way of doing that, boy, is not to let them in in the first place. You will have to walk to the village for any purchases in future. Traders can stay out... or in the gate-room."

Tom fervently expressed support for 'out'.

But, all in all, it was not a bad set of outcomes. Tom got to carry the heavy little barrels of bat-blood... but he also had a chance to go through the rest of the Kossian's baggage. He found some money, which he decided, as no-one could not be richer than someone, had to move to him. Most of the rest of it was mysterious to Tom, and smelly, so he threw it out, barring a high collared cloak – which, as he did not have one, he washed – and a small dagger. The cloak was, once washed, soft and lined with red velvet. Tom liked it, and wore it, just because he could. The dagger was useful for eating with.

The village, seen from a human viewpoint and not a cat one, was... different. Tom was more than a bit nervous the first time he visited it as a human. Someone had shrunk the place while he was away. It still smelled much the same, but it looked quite different. Perhaps it was having one's eyes so much higher off the ground that did it. Walking there he'd wondered if he should run away while he had the glorious chance. It was just that it was... suspiciously easy. And by now Tom had learned: if it seemed too easy... it was probably one of Master Hargarthius's traps.

The locals had never recognized a ginger tabby cat from the farm dairy at the end of the muddy track on the outskirts of the village, although they had seen him about. They did recognize him as Master Hargarthius's famulus without introduction, or having seen him before. Women drew their skirts aside, men eyed him warily. Tom rather enjoyed the latter, and wasn't sure about the former. He did notice a couple of plump milkmaids peering speculatively at him and then tittering. Thinking about the word – another sprung unbidden into his mind – tittering was an appropriate term for it. His passage through the market-place was an interesting one, but he did manage to buy eggs and a duck. The duck seemed to know he was a cat, or at least guess what was going to happen to it, but that was the worst of it.

After a few weeks they were greeting him, and trying to cheat him. Of course even that was, Tom realized, very cautious, compared to their normal practice. They didn't want to take too many chances with a customer who could possibly turn their cow barren, or make their wife interested in someone else. He did get questions about that, in cautious tones. And people asking him his name. He'd never thought about it. Tom was what he was, so that was what he answered.

⁂

When it came to getting yourself into trouble, thought the Wickedest Witch of the West, Alamaya could have given her a good run for her money, as a younger witch. It was lucky for the girl that she'd got away. That there had been an escape from the alley with that dog in it.

She'd actually managed to put herself into more danger than she faced from those who planned to kill her.

And Karst's wizards and mage-guards hadn't picked it up at all, just as they'd missed the last attempt on the girl's life. So much for 'organised magic' and its superiority!

Well, let him sweat, she thought to herself. It's time to put her in touch with her heritage.

She chuckled wickedly, reminiscently, to herself. That would be fun, if nerve-wracking.

In the meantime she'd better try another approach to acting on what the demon had told her.

⁂

Inside the cone of silence the conclave gathered. "You cannot," said the Chief Wizard grimly, "Expect to fail us and have the organization continue to support you. Duke Karst is looking for heads to roll, and yours will be first. It was your job to watch her."

The warlock Algorius looked around desperately for an escape. There was none. He'd walked into a trap. He could possibly have bested some of the individuals that circled him in their dark hooded gowns. But all at once… no. "I couldn't have guessed," he protested, desperately. "No one uses that stuff these days. It's too dangerous. It was just on a back shelf. There were no thaumatic fluxes…"

"You were too lazy to watch. Now you will pay the penalty."

Afterwards, when the other business was concluded, and a magical search, and various divinations organized, the Chief Wizard found himself once again, alone with his inner circle. "The Borbungs," he instructed. "Begin to cultivate them, Bernerius. We may need them, after all."

CHAPTER 10

ECONOMY CLASS CARPET TO
BORBUNGSBURG

————➤•◄————

Tom was barely getting used to the business of dealing with humans of the village as a human himself – it had been much easier as a cat, where all he had to understand was 'scat' – when his world expanded immeasurably. Well, Tom wasn't very good at measuring, yet. But it did change a great deal.

Master Hargarthius decided that they had to go to the Court. Fortunately for Tom, the Weekly Illuminati Age and Magical Advertiser had by now clarified the difference between the Court, which had Courtiers and a Duke, and court – a beast that entrapped mages and where turning witnesses, or judges, into newts was, most unreasonably it seemed, frowned on, and caught, which was something Tom tried to avoid being.

The parchment had appeared in the laboratory in front of Master Hargarthius with a sudden and startling boom which had made all of them take cover. "Show off," the Master had yelled, before retrieving and reading it.

"The Duke is holding an in-gathering of witches, wizards, mages, spell-workers, thaumaturges and sorcerers. A good thing to stay away from," said Master Hargarthius, waving the bit of parchment about as if it smelled bad. There might be some truth in it smelling bad. The edges were burned.

"So are we?" asked Tom.

Master Hargarthius grimaced and shook his head so that his beard waggled. "Unfortunately, that's not a wise thing to do, even if it would be a good idea. My predecessor tried that and look what happened to him."

"What happened to him?" asked Tom, who had actually never been told.

The Magician looked at him slightly askance. "He ended up with his brain in a jar and his body burned," he said, tersely.

"Oh. We'd better go then."

Master Hargarthius nodded and sighed. "I'll just have to get the old carpet out. Drat that boy."

Tom had worked out by now that the master was referring to Tom's predecessor, who had stolen the new carpet, raided the pantry and fled from the tower. Tom dratted him too: if it hadn't been for that, the magician might not have captured Tom, and the last famulus would still be cleaning and running about after Old Grumptious.

It might have made for fewer meals and a colder winter for Tom. But, well, freedom had its compensations. Tom gathered from the magician's comments that his predecessor had met a nasty end... but that hadn't brought the carpet back. The carpet had a second use-return spell – which was very useful for returning stolen magic carpets and for taking drunk magicians home. The fact it had never come home meant that Marcenius – the previous famulus – had met an unpleasant end before he could try to use the carpet again. The unpleasant end part pleased Master Hargarthius, but the lack of his carpet annoyed him almost as much.

So they would be flying on an elderly and frayed rug from the study. Tom knew it well. It refused to stay still and be hoomed. He had to brush it by hand, which it put up with. The flying part was more worrying. It was all very well for carpets and ravens. But as a cat, or as a human, Tom was less than sure about it. If they'd been intended to fly, cats or humans would either be woven or at least have feathers, he thought.

It wasn't all bad, though. The wizard did something almost unprecedented: he washed. And dug out a robe stiff with gold embroidery, which, Tom was pleased to see, Old Grumptious found both heavy and not particularly warm. He also put on boots with extremely curled toes and tassels on the heel, that part of Tom wanted to chase and bat.

There was a further surprise. Even famuluses got somewhat better dressed for Court, in a long-sleeved dark blue robe, which was not too musty – and did not have a hole for his tail. It was, thus, uncomfortable. Tom's suggestion that he cut a hole was not well received. And Tom got foot-wear. It was warm, Tom supposed. But his feet were most unused to being sheathed, even if they no longer had decent claws.

The raven, and a large, heavy trunk were also coming with them. The carpet and the trunk had to be hefted up a great many flights of stairs to the very top of the Tower. "It needs a jump-start," said Master Hargarthius, grumpily, when asked why. "And don't ask so many questions at Court. The House of Corvin hasn't been worth much since King Uther disappeared, but they can still chop off heads. Keep your mouth shut and behave yourself. And keep behind me. And for Zoranthysus's sake, don't get underfoot as you always do. Now, I must finish setting the wards on this place. Can't have thieves or trespassers in here while we're away. And I need to make sure the demon gets his pickle. We'll run out at this rate."

That seemed unlikely, even if they weren't breeding. There were, it seemed, a near infinite supply of elderly evil pickles in the pantry.

Tom liked high places and the top of the tower worried him not at all. Well, not until Master Hargarthius made him unroll the carpet onto the parapet, and put the trunk onto it. It nearly slipped over the edge, with Tom still holding it. It was a long, long way down. He was a bit reluctant when Master Hargarthius told him to get on the carpet. "Sit behind the trunk."

"Er."

The magician took a look at Tom, then shook his head. "Come here."

"Er," said Tom again, looking for a place to run.

"I want to fit a safety belt to you," said Master Hargarthius, holding out a broad sash.

That sounded a good thing. Safety. Just what he needed. Perhaps it would help him fly, or magically make the ground soft.

It appeared – once it was around his waist, that all it did was to attach him to one of the big iron handles on the trunk. Tom was fumbling at it, when Master Hargarthius sat down in front of the trunk and the raven hopped onto it. As usual the mage was muttering.

And then... plunging.

Down...along with Tom and the carpet and the trunk. Even the raven.

"Fly," screamed Master Hargarthius.

Tom just screamed.

The Raven said: "Nevermore," in a funereal croak, as they stopped falling just short of the ground and began an undulating flight, some few inches above the rocks. Tom wrestled with the belt, desperate to jump. Sneezed. And sneezed some more. The reason for that was the cloud of dust coming out of the carpet, as Master Hargarthius belaboured it with his staff. It rose rapidly. Tom didn't want to be free of the belt, any more. In fact he was rather glad of it. They were higher than the tower now, heading east into the full face of the rising moon. Then their transport hiccupped and dived again, as the Master both yelled some more and beat some more dust out of it, until it came up again.

The raven did nothing more than sharpen its beak on one of the iron studs on the trunk. It paid no attention to the erratic hops into faster flight, or to the near crashes with the rocky ground.

It was all very well for the raven, thought Tom. It could abandon carpet and fly off. Tom knew perfectly well that the only way he'd fly would be straight down, and that landing on his feet would do him not a bit of good.

Eventually the carpet, well beaten by now, settled into a wobbly flight across the darkened landscape, prickled by occasional villages with sparks of light from fires or candles through their shutters. There were, for in-flight entertainment, bats. And an unexpected mountain, and some cold, dank cloud. Even terror got to the stage where Tom was able to admit to himself that he was cold, uncomfortable, and in need of the garderobe. By the time the carpet touched down, light as a feather, at the other end of their journey, he was too miserable to notice.

Which in itself was a mistake, but not one he could go back and fix. He missed the wonders of the aerial view of Borbungsburg Castle, and the sight of Master Hargarthius falling over one of his own tassels as he alighted, and falling on top of a startled mage-guard, knocking them both to the ground. The raven, it was true, did try and tell Tom. But there is a limited amount Tom could immediately understand from 'Nevermore'. The first the huddled, half-frozen Tom knew of the entertainment was a great deal of shouting and some fairly loud blows and even louder pyrotechnical explosions. It might have gone on from there, but a broomstick arrived and added a third person, and a cat to the mixture.

The cat seemed capable of sorting it all out, by the hissing and startled yells from the mage-guard and Master Hargarthius, so Tom did what a good famulus always ended up doing under the circumstances. He took the trunk off the carpet, rolled the carpet up, and then picked up Master Hargarthius's slightly dented pointy hat, and sat down with the raven to watch.

"Nevermore," said the raven, as the matter resolved itself into a woman wearing a long black cloak, green robes, and a wild and wind-swept mass of improbably red hair, an angry Master Hargarthius, and the ornately uniformed man that he was stiffly apologizing to. And the cat. The cat, grey and sleekly flat-sided, with black-tipped ears and a tail, twitched its tail a few times and came over to Tom and the raven. She sniffed curiously at Tom – and then walked off, as cats will do, giving her opinion of cat-boys by lifting her tail very high.

Tom wondered if she knew he could read her tail expressions. But then, being a cat, she probably didn't care. Master Hargarthius called to him to come along smartly, which he was glad to do. There might be a garderobe somewhere. And besides, something large was flapping in out of the darkness. It was big enough to get the raven to fly ahead, rather than using him, or Master Hargarthius, or the trunk Tom was struggling to carry as a mode of transport. That suggested it would be a good idea to leave the mage-guard to his next arrival. So they did.

It was Tom's first experience of quite so many humans. Humans, even bathed ones, stank. He'd smelled them around the village, even before he'd had to get used to Old Grumptious's particular peculiar odour. Tom suspected it was because they never gave themselves a good bath with their tongues. It just wasn't practical, Tom knew from his own efforts. Their tongues were too wet and too soft. But he hadn't been prepared for the sheer stench of them en masse. Human smell with added perfumes and scents... and a solid undertone of laboratory smells.

He was quite dizzy with it all by the time the small liveried man led them to the door of the room they had been assigned, and Tom could put down the carpet, the trunk, and ask the way to the garderobe.

The quarters themselves were not what Tom was accustomed to, or what his master wished to be accustomed to. There was only one room, for a start. Only one four-poster bed. Tom looked longingly at it, but, he had a good idea that was not going to be his lot. He wasn't wrong, either.

Sleeping on a straw pallet was no novelty to Tom. Trying to sleep through old Grumptious's snoring was. He was fairly tired the next day, when a bell ringing dolorously in the distance woke them.

"Up, lazy boy!" said Master Hargarthius, plainly well rested and ready to go. "That's the bell to call us to break our fast."

They proceeded, without a wash, which Mrs Drellson's skull would have beaten him for, and which Tom was getting quite used to, himself (both the washing and the beating), to a vast hall, where there were long tables, and, to Tom's stomach's relief, food was being served. Platters were being carried out and set on the tables, where the castle's visitors were attacking them with all the decorum and delicacy of starving wolves.

That was fine by Tom, even if the noise and smell were even worse than the village marketplace. The noise wasn't helped by a quartet of musicians in a little hanging gallery, adding to it. Tom still found human music confusing and not nearly as meaningful and melodious as a good caterwauling. The raven shared his opinion and flew up and deposited something in the Krumhorn player's instrument. None of the feeding mob, bar Tom, even noticed the change in the noise level.

Tom had just finished shoving a chunk of hot bread into his mouth, to keep company with the ham and smoked fish in there already, and was reaching for the small-beer when things went rapidly to the worse, thanks to the raven. It was really making itself entirely too much at home here. It speared a quail egg with its beak, and flapping clumsily snatched a kidney off someone's knife-point and then flapped up to the dais... and landed on the back of the empty central chair. It was a large ornate chair of some black wood, and the raven was perched on the top of the carving there... which was a crown... on the head of a raven.

The crowd stopped in a shocked silence as the raven tossed the egg up into the air, and ate it in one gulp. And then took a big peck out of a slightly bloody devilled kidney.

The musicians desperately did their best to fill the sudden silence – three of them with the viol, lute and hoboy, the fourth with uncontrollable retching. A guard flapped frantically at the raven who took to the wing, and with a defiant "Nevermore" flew out of the hall.

Tom was just relieved it hadn't come back to the two of them.

The dining hall gradually returned to the sound of brave magic-workers doing valiant battle with food, and winning, but now it was laced with whispered traces of gossip, that plainly weren't meant for Master Hargarthius's ears. Two bits recurred more than others. Firstly variants of: "A bad lot, should have burned him along with the tower and his master," and magicians and witches alike agreeing with that sentiment. And secondly: "It's an omen. A sign. A raven on the raven throne." But no one quite agreed what it was a sign of.

Of course there were the more exotic theories about it being the princess's kidney, and one of her eyeballs rather than a quail's egg. But Tom rather doubted those. He'd seen the raven take them. It was possible the princess's kidney and eyeball – both of which the raven would cheerfully have eaten in Tom's experience – had been put in the food, but it would have taken more skill than the raven normally showed in choosing what it ate.

Tom ate, and ate, and ate and hoped the flying carpet could cope with the extra weight. He was somewhat concerned about the raven, which surprised him. It was a familiar menace. A familiar familiar. And who knew what the magician might get next?

Then a couple of heralds came in, tooted their horns, and the crowd were instructed to proceed to the Throne room, where Duke Karst wanted to address them all.

This plainly was no time to delay, by the way the various wizards, sorcerers, hags, magicians, warlocks, enchantresses and witches left the mostly empty platters and headed en masse for a side door, being held open by footmen. This led into a long passage, in which the crowd gradually spread out. Tom had the feeling it spread away from him and his Master, particularly. The hallway was hung first with tapestries and then portraits. The last few all had markedly aquiline noses, barring one.

Tom found it odd that he recognised the face in that one, even though it did not have a raven dropping hanging from the nose as was so frequently the case in the laboratory in the wizard's tower.

"Who is she?" he asked the Master.

"Hmph. Queen Athena. No better than she had to be."

That was a puzzling statement. How did you get to be better than you had to be? But Tom had no more chances to ask annoying questions because they had arrived in the Throne room. It was suitably regal, enough so to impress even Tom. The ravens fluttering about were not, in Tom's opinion, a decorative thing, even if they were on flags and fluttering rather feebly in the breeze that leaked through the upper casement windows.

The throne on the raised dais stood in solitary splendour, a huge artwork in onyx and silver, empty. One tier lower stood a very ordinary chair with an extraordinary man sitting in it.

Duke Karst, the Regent, was tall and broad, with a scarred cheek, a black spade of a beard, heavy brows, and a blaze of white hair in among his dark locks. He looked like he hadn't been at breakfast, because he'd already had his fill of babies before dawn. His expression was grim, and he seemed to be staring at each and every person in that hall in turn. It was enough to ensure absolute silence. In short, he appeared to be the perfect model of an evil and a rather angry usurper.

And he sat there and said nothing.

Eventually someone broke the silence. It wasn't Duke Karst. It was the wild scarlet-haired witch they'd had a collision with, the night before. Tom saw the aristocratic-nosed cat peering out from under her hair – it was plainly draped around her neck. "Well, Duke Karst. This is much earlier than I like to get up. What's all this about? And where is Alamaya? I tried to go and see her when I arrived last night. I have my duties to see to."

"That's why I have called you all together here. I considered imprisoning and torturing the lot of you until I get an answer. I still like that idea. But the royal council of mages has prevailed... for now. Not for long." He stood up and slammed one meaty fist into his palm. "Princess Alamaya is missing. Magic was involved. Guards and servants were killed. Find her. Return her to the castle unhurt and there will be rich rewards... fail, and things will start getting worse, rapidly."

The flame-haired witch was the only one who did not seem horrified – either by the disappearance or their alternatives. "Tell us the details. How long since this happened?"

"Two weeks."

"And you're only telling us now?"

Tom realized that at least some of those in the dining hall must have known.

The duke glared at her, and she glared straight back. He sighed. "We have been searching and investigating in all possible ways, from raids and spies, to augury and necromancy. It was thought best to keep it a secret. But now we're trying other avenues. All the soothsayers, and augurers say that she is alive and well, but they cannot find her. That speaks – along with the mysterious disappearance, despite the best of magical wards – of a powerful magic-worker."

Tom was at least absolutely certain that it wasn't Master Hargarthius. He'd have noticed a captive princess in the magician's tower, he was sure. He'd have had to clean up after her and feed her.

By the way that the other mages edged away from his master, Tom was probably the only one there who believed that.

"I wouldn't trust that lot to divine the color of my hair," said the Scarlet-haired witch. "Let's have them in here, Karst, so that we can find out what they've done, so we know where to start."

"You'll start by finding her!" roared the Duke. "Get out of here, all of you! You too, Emerelda."

It plainly wasn't a good time to argue, so they went. It seemed even Master Hargarthius was aware of the fact that he was prime suspect. He kept his mouth shut, and walked. He was, Tom thought, the only one. The hallways carried sound well, and every other person there was discussing the matter, working on the principle of accusing everyone else first so it couldn't be them. One of the themes of these accusations seemed to be history repeating itself. Tom knew better than to ask about it just then. Tom and Master Hargarthius went to the room, packed up – which didn't take long as the trunk had not been unpacked. Tom wondered if they'd be flying back without the Raven, but as they were about to open the door, there was a loud rat-tat-tat at it. Master Hargarthius stepped back, took his staff in hand and said: "Open it boy." He was plainly braced for new trouble, and making more of it if need be. But it was only old trouble, in the shape of the raven pecking at the door.

It flapped up to the trunk, landed awkwardly on one foot. It had to, because the other foot clutched a piece of foot-ware. A small black slipper, liberally seeded with small pearls and ornamented with a pattern in sapphires. At the time of course Tom didn't know what it was, and assumed that it was the raven indulging in its occasional taste for something glittery. Master Hargarthius, however, obviously recognised it, and snapped at Tom to close the door. He then took the slipper from the raven, which let him have it without even attempting to peck the reaching old hand.

Master Hargarthius turned it over in his hands, examining it. "A Princess's slipper," he said, nodding his head, thoughtfully. "I suppose it would be no use to ask where you got it from?"

"Nevermore," said the Raven.

"Hmph. Well, I shall take it with me. It could be very useful. And Duke Karst is likely to wish to kill us, even without the crime of slipper-theft."

He opened the trunk. It appeared at first glance to contain an awful lot of nothingness. Tom was very irritated because carrying it had not been easy. But then the magician muttered a cantrip, reached into it, and somehow slid out a drawer full of magical paraphernalia. So much of it, that Tom had to wonder what was left in the laboratory. He put the slipper in there. "Hmm. I suppose seeing as it is daylight, and people have a bad habit of shooting arrows at magicians on flying carpets, we had better have some sort of cloaking." He closed the drawer, which vanished. He opened another and pulled out two gray-white fabric slabs, which he handed to Tom. They were surprisingly light for their size.

"What are they, master?" asked Tom.

"Hmph, questions, always questions. They're Nornstrom cloud cloaks." He closed the drawer, and the trunk, and straightened up. "Well, let's go. Take the trunk and the carpet, Boy. With any luck we'll avoid bumping into that witch Emerelda again."

But plainly they did not have that sort of luck. She was on the tower of Borbungsburg castle, with her cat and her broomstick when they arrived, Tom hot and panting. And then, abruptly, they weren't. They vanished.

"Dratted new-fangled invisibility cloaks," said Master Hargarthius, crossly. "That woman! Money to burn. Showing off her Hell-Hell Bane accessories. Just you wait until they hit rain."

Tom didn't like the safety belt any more this time – especially knowing what was coming. But, by the looks of the guards, running away was not much of an option either. So he put up with it. He hadn't died last time.

But it wasn't any better this time. Borbungsburg Castle stood on the crest of a hill above Borbungsburg. A small swearing, screaming cloud hurtled toward the pointy rooves of the town, and only stopped just in time to narrowly avoid being a red rooftop mist. Or a rooftop missed. They did collect a weathervane, which nearly knocked Tom off in the process of being knocked off itself. The weathervane could have been very useful, as it showed which way the wind was blowing, which was the opposite way to which the bouncily flying cloud was moving.

The bumpy flight caused Tom to bitterly regret that breakfast. The moving-in- the-wrong-direction-not-terribly-high-in-the-sky cloud caused the arrow that 'thunked' through the carpet and into the chest's wood. Tom gathered by the background swearing and spell-casting – and the bucking flight, that Master Hargarthius was doing something about it. But he was too busy throwing up to care if they were used as arrow-targets. For a while, anyway, death seemed preferable than continuing to fly.

That, inevitably, did not last.

ᕱᕱᕱᕱᕱᕱᕱᕱᕱ

There were times when Alamaya was a lot less certain that escaping Borbungsburg castle had been as good an idea as it seemed at the time. Oh, it was true her wicked fairy Godmother was as bad as everyone had always implied. And it was true that she let Alamaya have fun... with boys and strong drink and parties. The tail, however, did put certain constraints on just how much fun she could have, and the witch had made it clear that that was there to stay. "It's genetics, Alamaya. You ought to have been a lot more careful. You're a Tindrel on your grandmother's side. The cat is still strong in our line. You make mistakes and you'll pay for them."

"But I didn't know it was a mistake," Alamaya had protested.

"That didn't stop it being one, did it?"

And the fun was in a very strange place. A place, it was true, that the searchers... and the killers, would not find her. It had its own rules to break, and she'd had to learn just how to break them without unpleasant consequences.

But in her way the witch Emerelda was even more strict that Duke Karst, and certainly more demanding than Duke Karst ever had been. Alamaya spent more time at her books than she ever had before. And the witch was as intolerant of failure as she was of convention.

And there was the witch's obsession with the family curse. As Alamaya had absolutely no intention of having children, that did not concern her.

"Estethius is a devious bastard." There was almost admiration in the Witch's tone.

Alamaya shook her head at her Godmother. "He's dead. They hammered a stake through his heart, burned the body, and tossed the ashes into an acid-bath."

"A good cover story."

"They made absolutely sure it was his body, Godmama."

"It didn't fulfil the oracle. The Raven had to kill him for him to be dead."

Alamaya rolled her eyes. "The raven just means the noble house Corvin, and grandfather's troops conquered and killed him, even if grandfather was lost in the battle."

"They did nothing of the kind. That apprentice let them into the tower by the back door."

CHAPTER 11

IN WHICH THERE ARE HIGHWAYMEN, NEWTS AND DIVINATION

They had to finish the last thirty miles of the journey in a cart, after the carpet refused to fly another inch after crash-landing in a field. Tom was not upset by this, but Master Hargarthius was livid. "Zoranthys's pustules. Now we will have to walk." He kicked the carpet and swore, descriptively and furiously.

"Isn't there any other, um, magical way we could use?" asked Tom, more to distract the old man, than any real desire to try these alternate means.

"Hmph. Many. But it's not my field and I don't have the relevant literature with me. I had no idea why we were being summoned to Borbungsburg, but I thought war most likely. So I packed the tomes that related to that. You boys all think I can remember every spell in existence."

Tom had had no idea that Master Hargarthius couldn't. Wisely, he said nothing.

"Take the trunk," said Master Hargarthius, irritably. "You can leave the carpet."

Tom had thought that walking had to be better than flying on that particular carpet. He quite liked walking. But that had been walking while not carrying a wounded trunk, a trunk that groaned, and was very heavy.

It was a good mile to the first village, and by then Tom was ready to try flying again. The Master spotted a green bush hanging at the door and that cheered him up. It meant 'Beer', it turned out.

After the Master had tried the local beer, he turned to Tom. "I might be able to repair the carpet. Go back and fetch it."

It was at least pleasant to walk without the groaning trunk – without the added weight of the raven, which had not bothered to fly. Tom stopped and had a drink from the stream under the little stone bridge, and eyed the tiny trout in it, thoughtfully. The field, when Tom got there, was not quite so pleasant.

The bull who had been frightened into the far corner by the crash-landing was determined to regain his reputation by charging down this returning invader. Luckily Tom knew about bulls from growing up around the barn, and he and the carpet made it back into the lane. He walked away, whistling, a new human skill he'd seen others do at the village market. He wasn't sure he was getting it right yet, but it seemed the dimpled young shepherdess thought he was whistling at her.

It turned out she rather liked bold young travelling men, with a carpet, so close to the secluded shady spots by the stream. "We could... take your carpet down there and unroll it," she said, leaning up against him, and taking his arm.

Tom was more than a little puzzled by this, but the rational part of his mind seemed to have gone for a walk somewhere, because all he managed to say was "Ah..."

"It's shady down there. You look all flushed. You could... take something off and cool down. I could help you. It looks like a nice soft carpet to lie on." She stuck the tip of her tongue out and looked at him from under her lashes.

"Er. It might be muddy, and, um, my master's expecting me."

"It's all mossy. And it wouldn't take that long," she said, sliding an arm around him.

By this stage Tom wasn't thinking at all, so he went down to the stream, under the curtain of willows, and unrolled the carpet. She must have been hot too, because she had taken off her clothes, and before he knew quite what she was doing, started lifting his robe.

Only that was when she saw his poor confined tail and screamed, "Demon!" and ran, scooping her clothes as she did.

Tom called after "I'm not! I'm a cat!"

That didn't seem to help, because she didn't come back. So he lay on the carpet himself for a little, and then rolled it up, and went back to the village.

"What took you so long?" said the Master, grumpily. "I've eaten, and hired a cart and a driver. Come now. We've miles to go."

Tom wouldn't have minded the eating himself, but that was not happening. Instead he got to sit on the tail of the cart while his master sat up on the bench with the driver. Master Hargarthius complained about the cost of it – almost as much as he would have if that had been real money he spent, which Tom was sure the cart's owner would find it was not, the next time he looked in his pouch.

They trundled down the rutted track, across the hills and down along the seaside road, on the way to the village below the Master's Tower.

The sea was blue and full of waves. It smelled of salt, and other things Tom had never smelled before, not all of them nice. "What is it?" asked Tom looking at what seemed like far too much water to be possible.

The cart-driver looked at him in amusement. "The salty sea, boy. All the way from here to far Rindia, and maybe to the edge of the world beyond that."

Tom badly wanted to stop and look at it, and perhaps touch what seemed like entirely too much water, and certainly enough yellow sand to make for a lot of extra cleaning for any famulus living with a local magician. But they didn't stop, and turned inland again, into the steep valleys leading toward the mountains that looked familiar, but small.

They spent the night in flea-pit inn, where Tom got to experience the fleas. There was a bar-maid who gave him an interested look, but he wasn't too sure how she'd feel about the tail either. Perhaps darkness could work. But then, perhaps it wouldn't.

Just when things were beginning to look familiar, which apparently – according to the cart-driver – meant they were on the far edge of civilized lands, entering dangerous parts, just short of the lip of a steep hill next to a copse, they had a meeting with a man with a sword and a crossbow, and his friend who had a knobbledy club. The fellow with the club grabbed the horse's head, and they demanded they halt and hand over all their money and goods.

Master Hargarthius had been grumbling about a flea, and the slowness of the cart. "Go away before I turn you into newts," he said crossly to the two men.

The highwaymen laughed. "You ain't no real magician. Them don't travel by cart," said the one, holding the horses.

Which, Tom reflected later, was why it was always a good thing to choose your words carefully. It would also probably be a good thing to choose who you turned into a newt first, and that should always be the one with the crossbow. Even if you had no quarrel with him, he'd have a quarrel with you. Or in you, if the raven hadn't dive-bombed him, and if the cart and Master Hargarthius had stayed still.

The horse, possibly startled by the sudden implosion caused by a newt being a lot smaller than a man, or the fact that he now had a small spotted newt clinging to his harness, started, and broke into a gallop, where it had been too tired to do more than walk moments before.

As a result the remaining highwayman had only Tom to aim at – on the back of the cart. The quarrel nicked Tom's ear, more due to the lurching cart and luck than bad aim, and buzzed between the driver and Master Hargarthius. "You didn't tell me you was a real magician!" yelled the driver.

"What do I look like?" yelled Master Hargarthius, clinging onto the cart.

"I thought you was just one of them fellers who do tricks and conjure for drinks, like you did last night. I don't want any nasty real magicians in my cart! I wants the rest of me money, and you're getting off, right now."

That was also not a clever thing to say.

Newts are just not much good at driving carts, and the horse panicked afresh, but without a skilled driver this time.

As Tom had read in the Weekly Illuminati Age and Magical Advertiser, in Aunty Eden's agony advice column: Injudiciously applied magic could have undesirable effects. In this case those undesirable effects were that all of them ended up in a wet roadside ditch, underneath an upside down cart. It was fine place for a newt, but muddy and unpleasant for anyone else.

Well, all of them, except for the raven. The bird took off at the last moment. When Tom crawled out from under the remains of the cart, it was sitting on a broken shaft, looking at the one surviving still slowly turning wheel. Unsurprisingly, it said "Nevermore," something Tom could agree with.

They cut the horse free with the idea that it could carry the trunk. It decided that it was going home, before that happened, so Tom and Master Hargarthius had to walk, carrying the trunk, the carpet, and, when it got tired of flying, the raven.

Still, they were close now, and by evening Tom was back at the magician's tower, enjoying the shrill tones of Mrs Drellson's skull shouting at him.

It was quite welcoming after the outside world.

Familiarity, even horrid familiarity, or the demon, was comforting. The cheese in the pantry was pleased to see him too. It was distinctly purring when Tom gave it some milk.

Master Hargarthius had set up a vast apparatus, with the help of half-a-dozen grimoires, and a great deal of chalk and even a few small demons that Prince Hariselden sneered at, to divine where exactly the owner of the jewelled slipper was.

The slipper hung in a shimmering crystal orb hovering above the complex map of the known lands on a large sheet of wood that had been a hellish task for Tom to carry up to the laboratory. Several benches had been pushed aside to allow space for the construct. The air was thick with the ozone smell of the lightning discharges from the surface of the orb. They ran down it and trickled off the silver spike at the bottom of the orb jaggedly dancing to various places on the map. A strange and eldritch moaning droned steadily through the room, only interrupted by Master Hargarthius's swearing or muttering more spells. "It is easier to magically hide, than to magically find," the master informed him, when he asked why it had to be so complicated.

"Why?" asked Tom.

Master Hargarthius shrugged. "I don't know. But empirically we prove this, because if it were not so, everything would be found. Including my eye-glasses."

"They're on the tip of your nose, Master."

"Aha." He pushed them back. "You see, boy, those involved in magical kidnapping will be hiding her. Those not involved in this will all be searching, but I, Hargarthius, have the advantage over all of them. Besides the fact that that they are stupid, that is."

Tom wondered if any of the others had poor-quality flying carpets. Master Hargarthius was something of a puzzle to Tom: in some aspects he seemed competent and powerful. In others... well. "Er. What advantage, master?"

Master Hargarthius drew himself up, proudly. "I have more Grimoires. And I would bet they are trying what they have sequentially, because that's what they do. They are narrow, experts in little fields at best. I have developed a grand unified pasture theory to work within. Now, get me some more dragon-wing, Boy." He sighed. "I wish the writing in Halamathus's Universal Augurial Techniques was clearer. I wonder if rat entrails are an adequate substitute for gerbil?"

It took several exhausting days of fetching, carrying, running around, changing things, changing them back, ordering various magical supplies and getting less magical ones in from the village to get the construct ready for use. Of course it had to be done at midnight, when the moon was full.

Tom who was by nature a little suspicious sometimes wondered if it had to be so complex. Based on his experience so far with 'Elementary spell-craft for ye dunderheads' Tom had the feeling that a lot the books were just making it up to make it sound good, and to be so complicated that you either wouldn't try or couldn't get it right.

He had no great expectations of this experiment, either, when the hour came, and he had to spend his time walking widdershins with a branch of multi-colored candles, chanting words from a tattered parchment scroll and waving a censer of unpleasant incense. The master splayed out the rat-entrails... and the suspended globe began to spin, and sway, while keeping up the lightnings. Then it shrieked and zoomed across the wooden map, hovered briefly over the island that was Borbungsburg, and then, with blurring speed whizzed off to the Lamdark mountains in Novaria... and then zig-zagged back to Borbungsburg, and then Lamdark... and then whizzed sideways across the Sunder Sea to spike itself, in a shattering of crystal... into the very edge of the wood.

Tom and Master Hargarthius slowly straightened up from having instinctively ducked. It was an instinct one soon developed around magic, or at least Master Hargarthius's magic. The magician, followed by Tom at a safe distance, went to look.

"Bring those candles closer, boy" said Master Hargarthius. "And snuff that incense. It's going to make me sneeze."

So Tom followed both instructions and asked: "Did it work, Master?"

"The silver needle should be exactly where she is. Some magician must have a secret island lair out there, out on edge of the Sunder Sea."

Tom peered at the wood – it was made of several layers of wood, actually, glued together in transverse grain to give it strength despite being thin. "Can't see the needle, Master. Just a hole."

"Hmm." The master adjusted his eye-glasses, and peered at the edge of the wooden map. Pushed the glass away with his sleeve, and looked again, nearly putting his long nose to the floor. Then he nodded. "So that's how they've fooled the court mages. They've taken her to another plane, such as the one you can see in the third mirror. She's alive, but they can't find her anywhere in the world... because she's not here. Well, well, well! Get me some beer, boy. I need to think about this. And then you can clear this lot up, and pack it away."

Being Master Hargathius's famulus was definitely not all joy, thought Tom bitterly, as he did all this, yawning.

The next day, when the Master got up, which was long after Tom had finished the morning chores and indeed, the lunchtime chores, the master wanted the slipper. So Tom had to find it. It was pure luck he had rather liked the blue stones –sapphires he was told they were called – and had kept it instead of tossing it out with the rat-entrails. After all what use was one slipper?

Plenty, as Tom discovered, when he was foolish enough to say so. Besides the value of the jewels and the pearls, the stuff of the owner was within it. "I can link it to a hyper-dimensional fluid that will take me to the right dimension and then a mere divining spell, something like Adubussion's Natural divination vortex, and we'll have her and be able to rescue her. Though why Karst wants to find the poor cursed girl is beyond me. Now, I'll need you to learn Borthius's magical flame spell. We'll have to condense some

Gadderson's fluid with Mermaid tears, and that can't abide mere flame."

So Tom got to learn another spell, a minor summonsing of fire elementals. It was a problematic working, in that the magic was not sustained. It was a good way of starting fires, the Master said, but terrible for keeping them going without fuel.

"So why do we use salamanders, Master, for lighting lamps and candles and the fire?" asked Tom, when he'd mastered the magic.

He ducked the cuff. "You ask too many questions, boy. Because it is poorly contained, that's why."

Tom thought this sounded a poor reason, but when his entire candle caught fire and not just the wick, he saw it was more sensible than he'd realized. He was glad he'd been taught the quelling spell to banish the elementals. The reason for using salamanders instead, he now grasped entirely.

Which was more than Master Hargarthius seemed to do with the recipe for Hyper-dimensional fluid.

That didn't work.

And, as always, it was Tom's fault.

※※※※※※※※

Emerelda had wasted no time getting the girl back. Not that the family there were precisely ideal, or the location perfect, but some of the magic workers summonsed to Borbungsburg were, in their way, dangerously competent. She admitted that to herself, even if she'd never dream of telling any of them. The Duke's staff of royal mages was an entirely different matter. Inevitably the stupid, lame and lazy ended up in government service, where they could make everyone else's life a misery. It was unlikely that Alamaya would get up to more mischief than was perfectly healthy for a young woman, or that the cousins would not step in to help, if she got into really serious problems. The girl knew enough magic to deal with minor trouble. And a bit of adventuring would do her good. She was getting a life, having some fun and enjoying a few parties. Athena would probably have been less of tramp if she had been allowed to get it out her system before being married to King Uther.

Emerelda ran every magical divination she knew of to make sure that Alamaya wasn't findable by any of them, so that at least was taken care of. Now all she had to do was to work out who wanted the girl dead, and just how to break the curse on her.

Of course, short of knowing exactly what the curse was, that would be difficult. But at least, thanks to the demon's loose talk, she had some idea what she was looking for.

CHAPTER 12

TOM GOES CLUBBING

S tanding inside its pentacle of finely powdered bone-dust, the alembic quivered and shook on its stand. "Concentrate, famulus, for Zoranthyrus sake!" cursed the Master. "Keep that flame steady or I'll turn you into a privy in a camp full of puke-drunk Joringian mercenaries."

Tom concentrated. That was enough of a dire – and possibly real – threat to focus his mind remarkably, turning it away from thoughts inspired his experiments with 'ye visions of a state of disrobement of a nubile sylph', from 'Elementary spell-craft for ye dunderheads' and comparing those visions with his memories of the disrobement of a shepherdess, before she'd seen his tail.

Tom wasn't a cat anymore but he knew what he had been, he had also seen a few people become newts, and had his suspicions that the cheese might once have been a famulus...

It was all very well for Master Hargarthius, thought Tom

sullenly, after several more minutes of repeating the magical fire spell. The Magician was as wrinkled as a dragon's hide after a long hibernation, and was old and disinterested in such things. It was spring out there, and here he was stuck in a dank old tower.

Tom sighed to himself. In spring the master's thoughts turned to the price of glassware, and where best to source snow for his work, now that it was warming up outside the caves. Anyway, Hargarthius could summons a succubus or a winsome sprite if he ever felt like Tom did right now. It was just as well, thought Tom, flicking a tiny piece of fluff from his cloak. Nothing else would come near the old man, not with yesterday's egg still in his beard, and a bodily bouquet of over-ripe goat, tinged with ozone.

Tom's small contact with normal humans in the village had left him wondering if the magician had pursued this career because he had absolutely no hope of ever getting himself a girl, or even a life, by any means other than the arcane arts. Yes, there were other rewards to being a magician, gold, fame, power, being torn to shreds by demons if your memory started to go or you got careless. But he had to wonder, looking at the scrawny old fellow, if it hadn't been the fact that a girl would run a mile and hide in a well before going to a country fair with the young Hargarthius, which had shaped the magician's career choice. By the sound of what Tom had heard of old Estethius one would have to have had a really good reason to take the job. After all, that was why he'd been transformed from being a cat: human boys willing to take the job, and stay with it, were rare.

Cynically, Tom suspected he was right. It was a career choice for humans who really had no chance of becoming a brawny warrior, or even a brawny miller. Later, the arcane arts might become goals of their own, but at first...

"The flame, you idiot!" yelled Hargarthius. "You fool of a famulus! It has boiled dry!"

Tom didn't wait. He ran while he still had the chance. Privies couldn't run, and newts didn't live long and probably had even less luck with girls. Estethius's tower was an old and complicated building, and Tom had a selection of small hidey-holes to lurk in when Master Hargarthius was mad at him, or wanted him to do something particularly unpleasant.

Tom waited and shivered while Master Hargarthius yelled and broke things. Eventually, when everything was quiet again, Tom crept out of his little lair behind the blood vats, and started the tedious business of clearing up the debris of Master Hargarthius's tantrum. Tom sighed. It wasn't easy being a human, and less so as a famulus, he'd decided, especially if your master was an old grouch like Hargarthius. Tom's thought of his experiences of the village, and the court... Huh. They hadn't even got to see Borbungsburg town, where, if the village talk was to be believed, there were taverns that stayed open a whole three hours after sundown. Tom sighed, thinking of the excitement, glories and opportunities he'd been denied.

Well, with any luck the Master would have forgotten about it by the time he got back to the laboratory. Tom began sweeping up the glass. He didn't dare use the hoom, let alone super-hoom or el Zebbo on this. A magical mess required that he actually do it. He sighed again. He'd been hopeful about learning magic, at least enough to get out here, but it seemed that all that what he'd learned so far was an awful lot of housekeeping. Yes, he had learned certain magical skills, in between sweeping, dusting, dish-washing and cooking and being yelled at by the skull of Mrs Drellson.

Unfortunately none of them were the skills that Tom thought could take him safely far away, especially without going near a magic carpet, or possibly a curse or being turned into something worse than a human boy. The Master really had no interest in teaching him anything useful – unless it was useful to Master Hargarthius. It was all very well learning things like conjuring flame under the alembic, or summoning small creatures. In more mundane households here in the Kingdom of Ambyria, rats and mice were a problem. In Master Hargarthius's demesnes they were a necessity, and often in woefully short supply. Besides, Tom liked catching them. It was one of the traits that remained after his transformation, like his tail. The desire to eat them had not remained, much. These days Tom would swap a fat mouse for a piece of bacon. The cheese in the pantry possibly still ate mice. But it might also have been a cat, once. Tom wasn't sure.

Tom's patient sweeping brought him to the pentacle of powdered bone where the alembic still stood on its little brass trivet. All that remained of the master's hyper-dimensional fluid was a dirty brown residue in the bottom of a crook-neck flask. Tom cursed himself for being a clumsy idiot, swearing just as much as Master Hargarthius had. Cleaning it out of there was going to be pure murder, and there was no doing it by magic either.

Looking at it, Tom knew that there was only one way to get that residue out... hard scrubbing, and it was a narrow-necked flask.

He sighed with irritation, thinking of the careful hours this job would take him. Master Hargarthius could (and did) break glassware every time that he had a temper tantrum – which was far too often for Tom's comfort – but not even a demon prince would help Tom if he so much as chipped a beaker while he washed them.

The pentacle had been broken so it was reasonably safe to touch the dratted thing. Reluctantly, Tom picked up the flask. It was still warm. That was odd. It had been at least three hours since the disastrous experiment.

To his relief the powder seemed to be quite loose. Without too much careful thought Tom shook some out.

It scintillated, emitting aquamarine flashes as it seemed to drift towards the floor rather than fall, as if 'down' was a direction it was far from certain about.

Where the sparkling dust touched the laboratory floor, a hole appeared. Tom could see darkness and strange lights through the gap.

Tom laughed with relief. Master Hargarthius had got angry too soon. His hyper-dimensional fluid-making process had worked after all. Tom could see clear into elsewhere! Master Hargarthius had been trying to create such a window for weeks now... and so far the master had failed. The best Hargarthius had achieved was a clouding and blurring of the wall onto which the fluid had been painted - and now it had worked!

Tom danced a little jig of delight at the thought of amazing the grumpy old curmudgeon. That'd show him...

It proved Aunty Eden's advice column in the the Weekly Illuminati Age and Magical Advertiser quite right. Injudicious dancing can be your downfall. Literally, it was. He tripped over the broom he'd been using, and fell in a cascade of bone dust.... down into the hole, into elsewhere.

It was further down than he'd expected. He landed with a thump and a shower of white bone dust on his face, with the crook-necked flask and the broom he'd grabbed as he fell. It was undignified to land so badly, but at least he and the flask were unhurt.

He stood up, shook himself and looked at the grave new world he'd entered. "Grave" seemed to be the right choice of word. It was half-dark, lit by colored wondering were-light among the misty smokes. Except... it was rather noisier than most graves. There was something compulsively beatey to the sounds. 'Sounds' was the best description he could give it. It didn't come under his previous experience of music, which implied a human and a musical instrument (or unmusical instrument, sometimes). This was different. It seemed to be issuing from several black chests that could possibly contain a number of cacophonous small homonuclii, but no other player. It sounded vaguely reminiscent of the sounds that the Demon Prince Hariselden made in his pot, but was less musical. The sounds were plainly magical, by the effect it was having on the zombies and the undead women gyrating under the lights. All in all, it appeared to be a good place to get out of, except... well the undead sylph looking at him was definitely female. And even if she was white faced and an unlikely shade of crimson haired, she was distinctly attractive.

The tight-laced black leather bustier also showed some of her more curvaceous assets. She was talking to him, although, naturally, he couldn't understand a word. Hastily Tom muttered a translation cantrip. To think that he'd resented the master making him deal with those garlic-munching 'merchants' from Kos! At least he'd been repaid for suffering through their bouquet, not to mention nearly being killed and crushed, in that he at least knew a translation spell.

"I beg your pardon fair sylph," he said bowing with an elegant curl of his tail. "I didn't quite hear what you said." Master Hargarthius dealt with the undead from time-to-time. Tom had always found them less terrifying than people made them out to be. Born-Humans were a little strange like that. The undead could hurt you or kill you, but then so could the living. And at least the royal court didn't make you pay weregild if you killed any of them. They were, after all, dead already.

She smiled at him, a devastating curve of her full lips. "The tail's cute, but the broom is over the top."

"He's cute, even if it is," said her companion, raven dark (except for her face, which was also stark white) and decidedly too thin for comfort. And her long black nails curled in a distinctly predatory fashion.

Looking at her, Tom decided that he'd prefer to cuddle something better padded, which looked less likely to bite his head off in the finale of love-making. The low cut velvet of her sable-dark gown was rich and gorgeous, though, and the silver studded leather throat-piece spoke of wealth and power. Even with only his short visit to court, and reading of the Weekly Illuminati Age and

Magical Advertiser, Tom knew women like that usually got what they wanted. The undead, probably twice... the second time when the objects of their desire weren't warm anymore.

These two didn't smell dead, at least. Actually, the scent they were wearing was distinctly aphrodisiacal. That had to be why he hadn't run already. It was either that or rank stupidity... He threw back his cloak. It was merely to get it out of his way in case running became a necessity, and to cover his tail, but Tom noticed the red-haired one bit a finger and looked thoughtfully at him. "I like the cloak," she said, tapping the sharp toes of her knee-high boots together. Tom couldn't help noticing that the rest of her legs – except for the bit obscured under her split black skirt, were covered in black fishnet. He'd never seen anything quite like it, not even in 'ye visions of a state of disrobement of a nubile sylph'. He said so, which was probably less than a clever thing to say to an undead sylph in a strange world, but, well, maybe he'd hit his head or something. Or maybe the social skills he'd learned as a kitten were not too well suited to dealing with born-humans. There were some advantages to being transformed when you were near-adult, but that wasn't one of them.

"You've never seen fishnet stockings before?" said the sable-haired one. "You gorgeous vamp, next you'll tell us that you've never been to a Goth club before."

Vampire? Well, the sylphs probably would avoid drinking HIS blood if they thought him that. And sometimes truth was better than trying to maintain an air of worldly insouciance, especially when it was someone else's world. "Well, I've never dropped into one before," he admitted.

"Ooh," said the sable-haired one, slipping her arm into his. "A real live Goth.-virgin. Maya and I will take care of you."

She was remarkably warm for one of the undead. "You seem... rather hot," he said.

She licked her deep violet upper lip. "I am."

Tom swallowed. That was the trouble with translation spells. Meanings sometimes got lost or misinterpreted.

"I found him first," said the crimson-haired one, taking his other arm. For a minute Tom thought that they might have a tug of war over him. "Um, ladies..." he said tentatively, thinking about getting free... but not thinking too hard about it.

"So what do we do to him first? Dance, drink or feed him strange chemicals?" asked the first.

"Not the strange chemicals, please!" said Tom hastily. After all, if he hadn't encountered them in a rather tasty bowl of fish, he would still be stalking around with his tail in the air, sleeping a barn, and eating mice and whatever else he could scavenge. And then there'd been his misadventures with Doctor Mirabellus's Ontogenetic Reflux Liquid...

He was much less sure that he'd like to go back to his old form if he could – the idea of washing himself with his own tongue, especially in certain areas – made his fastidious soul feel very unwell. However, next time might be something worse. "They have a bad effect on me." He wouldn't mind some milk, and he'd watched humans in the village dance the Brandsele...

The crimson-haired smiled nastily at her friend-rival. "He's mine, I think, Laney."

She was also quite warm for one of the undead. Perhaps they'd just newly joined the ranks. It was something he planned to avoid, at least for a while. It might be wise to leave now he thought... Then the crimson-haired sylph arched her neck and rubbed her head against his chin and that banished common sense. After all, he had magical means to deal with the undead. It was the living that he had a problem with.

They'd led him to a bizarre structure, a slit-like entry into a well-lit cavern, tended by a zombie. He had to be a zombie, and in a bad state of decay too. His face was held together with bits of chain hooked up to studs through his dead flesh. Smoke trickled from his nostrils. Behind him was an array of bottles which rivalled even Master Hargarthius's stock. The Zombie blew out a waft of herby smoke. "Name your poison," he said.

Tom started. "Poisons! Uh... Not for me. Can I get you ladies something toxic?"

"Ooh, what an invitation," said the dark-haired Laney, slinkily. "I'll have a sex on the beach."

The Zombie grinned at her. "Two of those and you're anybody's."

She put an arm around Tom's shoulder. She was wearing black lace fingerless gloves, Tom noticed. "Uhuh," she said trailing her fingers over him. "I get what I order around here. Sex on the beach."

The zombie grinned. Tom worried in case parts of it fell off. "Sure you won't change your mind and order something. It looks like you're going to need it. Sex on the beach for you too?"

"That seems rather forward," said Tom. "Besides, the beach is very sandy. I'd like a well-woven carpet on the mossy banks of the limpid river for my tryst, thank you."

The scarlet-haired Maya gave a snort of laughter. "He's definitely mine, Laney. And we'll have two tequila's."

"You always get the interesting ones," Laney pouted. But her eye had been caught by some new prey walking towards them. She waved. A large undead with an odd mulberry vest and a problem with a loose eyebrow that had had to be studded and chained to his ear appeared to have attracted her attention. Tom could only be relieved. In the meantime the Zombie behind the wooden counter had decanted and mixed various potions. "That'll be twenty-seven fifty," he said.

He plainly wanted money! Since when did the undead do that? Tom had exactly three copper zoes in his pouch. He'd have to risk a little conjuration, and hope that the zombie was less than alert to such magics. He dug into his pouch, took out an Ambyrian zoe, and rubbed it, chanting hastily to himself. A gold salabar was what he handed the Zombie, who looked very startled. As it changed hands, it became a crinkly green piece of paper. Tom tensed to run... but the Zombie took it cheerfully. "Neat trick," he said admiringly. "You should be on the stage, man."

Tom agreed. Privately. The stage-coach to somewhere else. But what he said, loftily, was: "Keep the change."

"From a fifty?" The Zombie beamed. "Let me get you some fresh lime wedges for the tequila."

The Laney-sylph was talking to the big fellow in the mulberry vest, sipping the potion that was supposed to give her what she desired on the beach. Tom couldn't help but be curious as to how it would work.

Maya tapped him on the shoulder, and he swung around. Unfortunately he swung the broom too, and it cracked the undead in the mulberry vest hard across the shins.

"You did that on purpose!" said mulberry vest, as he looked incredulously at the broom, and then grabbed Tom by the front of his robe.

Tom resisted the urge to stick all four sets of claws that he no longer had, into the fellow's arm. Instead, he muttered the cantrip he'd used for keeping the flame under the alembic burning.

"What did you say?" demanded mulberry vest.

"I said 'fire'," said Tom, pointing to the seat of the man's trousers.

With a scream, mulberry vest let go of Tom and danced away frantically beating at his own buttocks. Tom watched appreciatively as someone emptied a tinkling ice-bucket onto the fellow's trouser-seat. He was led off through another arch-way by a solicitous Laney, a solution that suited Tom well.

"Never a dull moment around here," said Maya, her shoulders shaking slightly. "Now, I think that I had better teach you how to drink tequila, because I am ready to bet that you don't know how to do that properly, either."

She licked her finger and put it on his neck. Put the damp finger into the little bowl of white crystals on the counter. Put it on his neck. "What's that?" he asked nervously.

She looked at him, her head slightly askance, lip held between her white teeth. Shook her head and said. "You really don't know, do you? Salt. Hold this wedge of lime between your teeth. And don't look so nervous. I'm not going to bite you..." she smiled mischievously. "Not yet, anyway."

Tom looked around for an exit. He couldn't see one. But when 'yet' came, he was going to be outside it, running. He watched as she leaned in to him. It was all he could do not to leap like a startled buck. She was licking his neck! His jugular wasn't there... Then she leaned away again. Took the glass and drained it. And then kissed him. He felt her teeth bite into the lime, and the spurt of its juice. Her lips were very warm, and up this close... it looked as if she had something rubbed into her skin to make it undead-white.

He swallowed. The lime didn't make his mouth any less dry. She smelled alive... which **should** be preferable. Only he hadn't really dealt with any live women before.

"Your turn," she said, her violet eyes dancing with mischief.

Tom looked desperately for the exit again. She took her finger and wet her neck. "Salt," she said.

Like a hypnotized rabbit he obeyed. She handed him the glass.

"I can't drink that..."

"It won't kill you," she said as she put the lemon between her teeth.

Tom wasn't sure that it wouldn't be preferable. Besides, what was a live person doing in this place? "Let me take you away from here," he said desperately.

She laughed. "Maybe later. Maybe another evening." She touched her neck...

Tom, who had met more demons than he had real live born-human women, took a deep breath and licked. It was salty.

She gestured at the glass in his hand. She had drunk the

stuff… and she appeared to be alive. It had come out of the same bottle. He raised it to his lips. And three large men came barreling out of the arch - accompanied by the fellow in mulberry vest, now with a towel around his waist. Mulberry vest pointed at him "He did it. He's the bastard who set me on fire."

Distracted, Tom unwarily drained the glass in his hand…

And sprayed tequila out across the room. It burned his mouth and throat. He'd expected it to be some kind of wine or strong ale at worst. This was liquid… "FIRE!" he screamed.

Which was possibly not the right thing to say when he hadn't yet undone his earlier elemental summonsing. Flames whoomphed into existence under his gaze. As soon as Tom realised what he'd done, he quelled the elementals banishing them. In most cases they went out. However, he must have sprayed across the black boxes in front of the man in the corner. The strange music stopped abruptly with a cat-like yowl… The boxes spat a shower of pyrotechnic sparks. Doubtless the demons within had escaped.

The Zombie-dancers stopped too. And of course some things that had caught fire continued to burn. The tequila he'd sprayed onto the counter for starters. Two of the burly men (and they were men, he was sure. They did not appear to be pale and wan at all) grabbed him.

"Let go of him, you bastards," screamed Maya.

Tom was, for a moment, shocked to the core. Too shocked to react. Ordinary people did not meddle in the affairs of magicians, lightly. Not even by contact with their famulus. They got turned into newts! The third large man - not one of the two holding his arms, swung a large fist at Tom's solar plexus.

It never reached him however, because Maya, yowling like a very angry cat, grabbed it, and clung to him, and bit him.

The fellow grabbed her and attempted to pull her loose.

Tom's tail went straight and his back arched. Words tripped off his tongue. The spell was for a staff, but the broom would do.

The broom – a good solid oak-shafted broom – leaped into the air and gave the bullyboy holding her a crack over the head. It was audible even over the pandemonium of the panicked zombies and undead. The bullyboy eyes crossed and he fell, letting go of Maya. She landed on her feet, remarkably catlike herself. She bounded forward and stood on one of the two gaping bully-boy's feet – with a long spiked heel. "Let him go, you son-of-"

The broom belabored the man's head. He was lucky. It was

only birch-twig end. He was obviously less lucky with Maya's weight in that boot... He let go of Tom to grab hold of her. Plainly, by where she put her knee, that was a mistake. The broom had shifted its attention to the last bullyboy, as Tom finished his next cantrip.

The fellow shrank and turned green, giving an alarmed "ribbit?..." before hopping out of his clothes. Tom could have sworn that he had merely made mice materialize in the man's underwear, but his attempts at magic did have some odd results from time to time. The spell lacked the chemical components for a permanent change, so the fellow would be back to normal in a few hours, wondering why his mouth tasted of spill-bugs and why flies made him hungry.

Maya, however, seemed to be having the worst of her battle. So, without thinking, Tom hit her assailant with what was to hand. A crook necked flask snatched from the counter.

It broke on the bullyboy's bullet head, and the powder scattered over him... and through him. Tom had a brief view of the pantry cupboard and the cheese glowering there, before it, and the man, vanished, leaving Tom looking at the broken flask and wondering just how he was going to get home, and how he would explain the missing flask if he did.

He offered Maya a hand up. "I was dealing with him," she said. "He'd have had a problem in another minute, except that he had mice in his clothes. One of the mice ended up as a frog."

She was obviously a little confused. Just then water began spraying down from the ceiling.

One thing Tom liked even less than being trapped in a strange world, was being wet. Baths were all very well, but indoor rain, wasn't. He shook his head in distaste and lifted his cloak over his tail. He offered a corner of the cloak to her - she looked equally taken aback by this cave-rain. "Let us go somewhere drier. This place" – he sniffed at the smoky air and looked at the panicky undead and zombies – "is a mess. And I dislike that."

She slipped under the cloak. "You're an original," she said, with amusement in her voice. "We'd better go. The management are going to be rather upset about their bouncers."

That was a little puzzling, like much of her terminology, but he'd have to get used to it. He wasn't going to be able to get back to Master Hargarthius now – which, considering the broken flask, might be a good thing. The frog, he supposed, might be considered a bouncer.

She guided him through an archway and up a crowded flight of stairs. It appeared that many of the undead were leaving too. In a hurry. For their sakes Tom just hoped it wasn't daylight outside. Fortunately, the broom seemed determined to make sure they were not too crowded, and swept aside the people who didn't get out of the way fast enough. Tom finally had to tell it to stop.

Outside was even stranger than inside. It was dark... well, it would have been if there had not been so many lights. Witchlight clung to poles above the street. More light shone from the windows of towers that seemed to reach to the sky. Light gleamed from the vicious eyes of snorting, growling, braying beasts in the roadway. She waved at a yellow one. It galloped past. She sighed and leaned against him. "I suppose it is late. Let's walk a bit away from the club. There may be trouble and we're more likely to get a cab. By tomorrow they'll probably decide that it's best not to call the cops. The story might get them unwanted attention from the narcs," she said with a gurgle of laughter. "Anyway, there was no real damage done."

They walked. It was a terrifying place, a great citadel with more people – people awake at night – than in all Ambyria. She seemed quite relaxed about it. He put an arm and tail around her. It was more for his comfort than hers, but perhaps she didn't realize that. She smiled up at him. "You're cute, even if you're trouble. This is a great place for clubbing, isn't it? Goth clubs are the best. A bit of pancake makeup and we fit right in. You'd better lose the broom next time, though. It's just so 16th century."

Tom thought the broom had been quite good for clubbing, but if she said it was too futurist he would be pleased to 'lose' it. This was her environment, after all. He nodded. "Sure," he said.

She smiled and sighed. "I think I'd better get myself home. It's been fun, but lack of sleep plays hell with my concentration. I've got a heavy day tomorrow. The old woman keeps me studying hard, and Laney will probably be in a panic by now, and telling my God-mama."

The idea of suddenly being alone in this place terrified him. "I don't know how to get home," he blurted. "All the hyper-dimensional powder I had was in the flask..."

She gave a little of snort laughter. "I'd forgotten that. Well, a New York cab driver will find any place... if you pay them right." She unhooked a small black purse from her belt. "How about one of those coppers of yours?"

Wordlessly, he dug out his second last zoe and gave it to her.

She breathed on it, and muttered something. It became green and grew into a piece of paper with strange arcane symbols and pictures on it. Then she took out a small vial from her purse... and sprinkled a little powder onto the note... a light, iridescent powder. She handed it to him. "Give that to the cabbie. He'll take you home. It's a better system than just making holes in the fabric of reality." She dug in her purse again and came out with a gold stylus and a small square of paper. She wrote on it, and handed it to him. "Give me a summons sometime. You really are cute even if you are ignorant and don't yet know how to make your tail invisible." She whistled shrilly and waved to one of the yellow monsters. It stopped, and she opened a door. "Get in, do, and give him the green paper."

So Tom got in, with his broom.

The human inside, sitting on the front seat, looked back, and surveyed him with some amusement. "Where to, Count Dracula?"

Tom didn't like being laughed at, or mistaken for a Nembutolian noble, but mindful of her instructions he gave the driver the green note.

The man took it, twitched and jerked slightly, and turned around and set off into the herd of other road beasts.

Only when the strange city began to blur did he think to look at the other note the girl had given him.

It read "Maya Tindrell" and below was a summons-spell in Ambyrian script – not the strange letters of this place. Now some of her statements made a little more sense. And Tindrell... The queen of cats... no wonder she'd understood how to headbutt against Tom's chin! The pendant between her breasts should have been a clue, if he hadn't been so distracted by the breasts. A bat with a black rose. An alchemist's symbol.

The cab stopped at the gate-house of Master Hargarthius's Tower. It was pale-predawn as Tom alighted. There was of course the issue of, what had she called him? The... leaper... jumper? Ah... bouncer! Tom could only hope that he'd got away from the cheese, and, of course, from Master Hargarthius. The fellow might end up as privy or worse, a junior famulus. He'd have to get him back to his home somehow, and deal with the issue of the missing crook-neck flask.

But mostly he was thinking about Maya, and her soft curves, and her ability to transform people into frogs. They could go clubbing again. He would take a nice knobbly blackthorn stick next time instead of the broom.

༃༃༃ৠৠৠ

Alamaya should have expected God-mama Emerelda to be waiting for her. But she'd been somewhat wrapped up in thought. So when she finally arrived at the home of cousins that she'd never met, even known existed, before God-mama brought her here, and let herself in, she was somewhat taken aback to see the witch sitting there, feet up, with a very large glass of wine and a sardonic expression on her face.

"I hear you have found some of the trouble I sent you to look for," said the wickedest witch in the west. "You wouldn't happen to have snabbled any token I can use to find out just who he was?"

Alamaya considered, briefly, lying. But only very very briefly. She took a coin out of her purse. "I swapped it for a ten dollar bill. I... I really don't think he had any idea who I was, God-mama."

She raised an eyebrow at him. "That seems unlikely."

"Well, he had lots of chances to try to kidnap me, or to do me some harm. He put a lot of effort into protecting me instead. Not that I need it," she said hastily. "And, um, he was cute."

"Oh?"

"In a sort of raffish way," said Alamaya airily. "There's a sort of kittenish charm to him. Besides the tail."

"Ah. 'Besides the tail'. Really," said Emerelda, eyes narrowing. "Well, well, well. This could be opportune."

༃༃༃ৠৠৠ

"He is generally held to be a suspect. He's been very secretive for years, Duke Karst. Un-cooperative, not part of the association of magic workers."

Duke Karst tugged his spade-beard. "I don't like the man. No-one like a traitor, even if his master had attacked against the Royal house of Corvin. But, Chief Wizard Kolumnus, it seems rather too obvious. He'd hide his tracks carefully."

"That's why it has taken us so long," said Kolumnus smoothly. "And we may not find her, my lord Duke. But it may frighten him into a precipitous move. And we'll be watching."

CHAPTER 13

TROUBLE AND THE QUEEN OF CATS

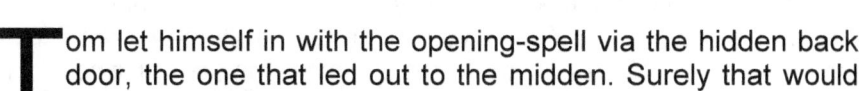

Tom let himself in with the opening-spell via the hidden back door, the one that led out to the midden. Surely that would be less obvious than the front door...

That was wishful thinking of course. They were waiting for him by the time the latch clicked closed.

Within a remarkably few seconds he wished he was outside it again, and had in fact not decided to come back at all. He said so, but no one actually heard him, seeing as they were all too busy yelling at him.

Tom gave up, and waited for the storm to subside. Eventually it did.

"You're forbidden to leave the Tower again. The miscreant must have sneaked in through the door that you left open," said Master Hargarthius.

"You're going to be scrubbing pots and floors for a year," said the Skull – as if that was something different.

Tom yawned.

"And you'll be cleaning up the pantry right now. No rest for you! Wicked boy."

The raven said… "Nevermore."

"Quite," agreed the Skull of Mrs Drellson crossly.

"Take the prisoner down to the dungeon," said Master Hargarthius. "Let him stew for a bit before I question him."

Tom sighed. It had been a great evening. And strictly speaking he'd got there without going out of the tower. "Where is he?"

"In the pantry. The cheese is sitting on him."

So Tom went to the pantry, and cautiously opened the door.

It was indeed a bit of a mess, with several broken jars of preserves and some flour on the floor, with a big shaven-headed goon lying in their midst. The cheese was on his back, growling in a menacing way that would have made the fellow's hair stand on end, if he had any.

"Ah," said Tom. "The leaper. I mean, bouncer." The cheese stopped growling at Tom's voice, and he absent-mindedly petted it. It let him. Tiredness could be the death of him, Tom reflected.

"This criminal, this… this pantry raider is your associate?" said Master Hargarthius in a voice that Tom knew, from experience meant trouble. Possibly newts.

"No, Master. He was trying to beat me up, in the place I fell into."

"What?" demanded the Master, shocked.

"I didn't leave the tower," explained Tom. "I fell through a hole into somewhere else. Your Hyper-dimensional fluid worked." Tom yawned again. "Sorry. It took me a long time to get back." He didn't point out that he'd been having a good time not getting back. He felt he'd been in trouble about that already.

At this point, possibly because the cheese had stopped growling, the bouncer tried to get up. The cheese bit him on the neck and shook him, hissing like a kettle that was about to explode. Tom realized he didn't understand a word the fellow was whimpering. His translation spell must have worn off, so he repeated it.

"I'll never buy from that street corner again. Ever," said the leaper…bouncer.

Maybe the spell wasn't working properly. Or maybe the hyper-dimensional powder had left part of the fellow's brains elsewhere, thought Tom. "Lie still, and it will stop biting you," he said, not at all sure that was true.

The man obviously recognised him. "I was just doing my job," he protested weakly.

"Miscreant. Pantry robber," snapped the skull, having lowered her empty glowing orbs to his eye-level, but carefully staying outside the pantry. "You're going to suffer." And she gave him a jolt of the green lightning... which changed to purple sparks as it entered the pantry, Tom noticed. It still made the bouncer groan, and begin to understand suffering.

"I'm never going to touch it again, I swear. I'll be good," promised the bouncer, miserably.

The cheese did not seem to believe him. Tom was inclined to accept its judgement of character. Master Hargarthius didn't seem too impressed either. "Take him to the dungeon, boy. And then come back and tell me about it. Hmph. I might as well eat something, seeing as I am awake."

Tom was aware that the last thing he'd had to eat was some salt, a long time back, but for the moment he had the problem of persuading the cheese to release its captive. Finally, Tom had the idea of bribing it with a saucer of milk, and telling it it was very good boy, well, cheese, and hastily getting the man out of the pantry, and closing the door.

The bouncer got up off his knees and looked at the magician sitting at the kitchen table, warming his slippered toes at the hearth, in his tasselled nightcap and star-spangled night-gown, with a glowing-eyed skull hovering next to him and the raven glowering from a wall-sconce. The fellow shook his head. "I'm crazy, or this is a movie set. I'm getting out of here..." He tried to bolt for the door. Master Hargarthius was not much amused at the cheese being correct, and turned him into a newt. A newt still trying to push through the door.

"Take him down to dungeon anyway, and give him a bowl of water," said Master Hargarthius. "He'll get better in a day or two. And then you can broil me some bacon."

So Tom did that. He even got to eat some bacon, but he fell asleep onto the table while Master Hargarthius was asking him questions. That would normally have been a very poor move, but this time he was left to sleep. Perhaps Master Hargarthius did not want to wait a day or two for him to recover from being a newt, without answers and without a famulus to do the housework.

Tom woke up several hours later, on his own straw pallet in his little room. He did wonder how he'd got there, as he was sure that old Grumptious hadn't carried him, but he had at least had some sleep, full of delicious, if slightly odd, dreams. He wondered if it was worth just lying there and trying to slip back into them, but his bladder said that was a very poor idea. The garderobe in your dreams is always a bad thing, and using it, worse.

So he got up, and found that the world, or at least the magician's tower, hadn't miraculously got better while he was asleep. Still, he'd had a wonderful evening out, and met a fabulous girl, who had given him her summonsing spell. If he could just slip through the next day or two, when things quieted down, he'd give her a call. He was agonizing about what he'd say to her, and so barely noticed that there was someone in the hallway with him.

Until she cleared her throat. The scarlet hair gave his heart a momentary lift, until he realised that the color was right... but the woman was a lot older. And she was wearing an emerald green gown, not a laced leather bustier. Besides he recognised her from Borbungsburg castle. "I wouldn't scream if I were you, cat. This is merely an illusion, and it would vanish, if you did. It's quite hard and expensive for me to keep up, so you should appreciate it instead. I can only do this by assuming my ancient aspect, as Emerelda Tindrell, the Queen of Cats, and as such you're one of my subjects. Not that I have found that cats pay the least attention to rank."

Tom swallowed. "Uh. What do you want?" The hair color had joined certain things in his mind.

"To ask you a few questions. In my experience apprentices usually know precisely what their masters are up to, even if they pretend otherwise."

Tom looked warily around. "I'm not the apprentice. I'm just the famulus. You should go away." He looked at her hair. She noticed.

"Yes. It is the same color. And that's why I am here."

"Uhuh," said Tom sweating afresh, but shaking his head. "No. I'm not telling you anything. Go away or I will scream."

"She said to say hi, and that she thought you were cute," said the witch, calmly.

"Oh. Look, I, um didn't do anything."

"Well, other than set fire to a bad influence's trousers, a Goth club, and beat up several bouncers, no. Not to Alamaya anyway. She's capable of reaching her own decisions and protecting herself, anyway. At least, there, she is. Here is different. That is why I took her there."

"Well, uh, then she should stay there." Then it sank in. "Alamaya? You mean..."

"Yes she's my god-daughter. I was also her grandmother's cousin. Younger cousin, of course," she said with just a trace of haste.

"I won't tell anyone. Not even Master Hargarthius. Just... keep her safe."

A slight wry smile, twitched at the witch's painted lips. "Hargarthius is a grumpy old curmudgeon, as inept as he is brilliant. He's utterly self-centred, barely trained, but not stupid. He either has already worked it out, or he will do so. I thought I'd prevented anyone from finding her. Now, tell me, exactly why is he trying to find Alamaya?"

Tom blinked. "To rescue her, to take her back to Duke Karst, to her home in Borbungsburg of course."

"Really? Nothing more. Nothing less?" asked the witch who was Queen of Cats.

"Uh." Said Tom, he felt he'd said that a lot, in this conversation. "She's not really kidnapped, is she?"

"More like escaped and hidden. People are trying to kill her," said the witch in a tone that boded ill for those people when she caught up with them.

"It's not Old Grumptious, I mean, Master Hargarthius. Um, do you mean Duke Karst?" asked Tom.

"I doubt it. But someone is always trying to kill the heir to the throne. There are quite a few other candidates. The Borbungs spring to my mind, but there are others. There are always others."

"Not Master Hargathius. All he ever said was about rescuing her." Tom scratched his head. "He did say something about wondering why Duke Karst wants to find the poor cursed girl."

"I want to talk to you about that curse," said the witch.

"I didn't do it... did I?" asked Tom. He'd done many, many things he knew nothing about. The skull of Mrs Drellson always knew it was his fault, anyway.

"It's a family curse, cat. From long before you were born. It affected her grandmother, and her mother. In time, or at least if she has a child, it will affect her."

"Oh. Well, can't you uncurse her?" asked Tom.

"To do so I need to find out exactly what the curse was, what magical binders were used and just how it was done. To do that I need to question the one who put the curse on Alamaya's grandmother, Queen Athena," explained the witch.

"Master Hargarthius?" asked Tom, faint, but pursuing.

"No. Estethius," she hissed, her hatred obvious.

"But he's dead, dead, staked, burned, ashes tossed into the sea with every spell on them to stop necromancy. Mrs Drellson's skull told me," said Tom.

"Oh, his body is burned and gone," agreed the witch. "But that wasn't his brain that burned with it."

Tom had, as younger cat, some experience with mouse brains. He could categorically state they did not live well out of the body. Perhaps it was different for humans, but Tom doubted it. He said so. Humans might not argue with their Queen, but Tom was still cat enough to do so almost automatically.

"I got it from the demon he used for the trick," she explained. "It's true."

Tom was relieved. "Master Hargarthius said demons always lie."

"He's correct about that," said the witch. "But if you think about it, that can be used to extract the truth from them. Estethius's brain is in a jar awaiting transfer to a new body."

"He's been quite patient then, very unlike a magician," said Tom. "His brain must have been there longer than the pickles in the pantry... uh, we haven't been feeding that to the demon, have we?"

There was a stunned silence from the queen of cats. She shook her head. "I hope not. Esthetius was close enough to a demon, alive."

"Nevermore," said the raven suspiciously... And the illusion Tom had been talking to, vanished. The Raven landed on Tom's shoulder, cocked its head, and leaned toward Tom. "Never. More!" it said insistently.

That was interrupted by an army at the gate, which tended to interrupt most things. They were knocking, but were ready to knock louder with a battering ram.

Master Hargarthius was less than pleased. The army had, however, several mages in tow to prevent it from being newtralized, which was, for the army, a good thing.

"What is going on down here?" demanded Master Hargarthius, from the battlements, as Tom scurried up with the arcane supplies he'd demanded.

"Open up. We have a writ here from the Prince Regent," shouted the mailed officer who had been doing the pounding and was now readying his battering ram team.

"I'm coming down. There will be trouble about this," said Master Hargarthius, crossly. "And I'll talk to you alone. Or the basilisk will be released."

"We have orders to search the premises. Various augurers and luminaries have come forward to claim you have the Princess Alamaya captive in your vile den."

"Hmph." said Master Hargarthius. "I will be glad to conduct you through my establishment. I would have thought Duke Karst had more intelligence than to believe a load of incompetents and frauds." He looked at the army, and the huddle of men in wizardly clothes. "And that means you in particular, Master Kolumnus. Hmph."

"Who is he?" asked Tom as they made their way downstairs.

"Hmph. He is the Chief Wizard of the Royal Magical Council. A jumped up incompetent, determined to hold the rest of us down. Couldn't find his own posterior with both hands and a map."

Tom had seen the name in the editorial column of the Weekly Illuminati Age and Magical Advertiser. He did wonder if the problem was not just how to hold the map, but he had eventually learned not to ask at times like these.

They proceeded to the front door of the gateroom, despite Tom wondering if the back door near the midden might not have been a better idea. When Master Hargarthius sent him to open it, and stood at the far door himself, Tom was sure he was right.

He was even more sure of it when the soldiers, followed by Master Kolumnus barreled into the room and grabbed him, and Master Hargarthius... nimbly stepped out of the other door. And a heavy portcullis clanked down sealing off the doorway. Then with a grinding slowness a slab of rock slid down to seal off the outer door.

Seeing he was going to be crushed again, Tom decided to give the men in armor holding him some company, in the shape of some mice inside their armor.

It did make them let go of him, not that that did him much good.

The royal mage pointed his staff at the inner portcullis. "I wouldn't do that," said Master Hargarthius's voice.

"We're on Royal business, Hargathius. Open the door or I'll blast it down," said Master Kolumnus.

"Very unwise, as the roof will then fall in," shouted Master Hargarthius. He had to shout because of the noise of one the knights bashing his own armor, and another was frantically trying to remove part of it.

"I've a writ here from the Prince Regent himself to search your premises for the Princess Alamaya. We have been informed that it has been magically determined that she's in your dungeons. The men will be readying the ram. Resistance is pointless," shouted Kolumnus over the din. And then turning to the knights: "What is going on with you?"

They weren't paying him a lot of attention, and a mouse leapt frantically out of a now open gorget. That at least halved the noise for Master Hargarthius's reply. "I think you're exceeding your orders, as ever, Kolumnus. I offered to let you search. I'll let them in to search. I have sent a message to the guild, and to the Weekly Illuminati Age and Magical Advertiser about this. But you've been an irritating carbuncle for long enough. It's a pity you triggered one of my safety devices with your over-hasty behavior."

One of the knights, a grizzled-bearded man with an open helmet, and a chainmail neck-piece, turned to Tom. "What's happening, boy?"

"The roof comes down," said Tom. "It's a huge rock on chains. It'll squash even the mice. Can't you just search? I mean, she's not here. We've been looking ourselves. I don't want to die... I... I've got a girlfriend."

The knight nodded. He stepped over to the Royal Magician, who was scratching symbols on the floor with his staff. Tapped him on the shoulder. "Master Kolumnus. I think we could just search."

"Sensible man," said Master Hargarthius. "I'll open the outer door slightly and you can tell those fools to stop ruining my door. Good oak isn't cheap."

Tom decided that the next time he was sent to open the door, he would run out of it, but with a little more negotiation, a compromise was reached. Swords, and the very angry wizard's staff were pushed out of the slightly raised stone slab to outside. Two men in dire need of some help with their armor squirmed out, and a scrawny barefoot Life-Diviner crawled in with her equipment, to join the Chief Wizard and his assistant.

"There's going to be trouble about this, Hargarthius," said Master Kolumnus.

"Hmph," said Master Hargarthius. "Yes, there is going to be. I'm going to write a very strong letter to the Weekly Illuminati Age and Magical Advertiser. The magic workers of Ambyria won't take kindly to this. Who told you I was responsible? Ridiculous. I've been a loyal supporter of the crown since... since I was granted the tower as my reward. Tell me who said this about me? Most of them couldn't find their own toes."

"I can't reveal our informants. Anyway, you have nothing to complain about. We just intended to search your tower."

"Last time that happened, there was a great deal of looting and destruction," said Master Hargarthius loftily.

"Last time this tower was searched, the occupant had put a death-curse on the Queen and the King himself had disappeared!"

"I know. I let the King's men in, remember," said Hargarthius, tersely. "You can search anywhere, but no breaking anything this time. And my famulus and I will accompany you to make sure there's no looting either."

The chief wizard of the Royal Council sniffed. "The dungeons. That's where we were informed there was a magical trace of her."

So they went down to the extensive underground network of dungeons, cells, pits and torture chambers, which were empty even of mice. Except of course for one cell. Tom had felt faintly guilty and put the newt and the bowl of water in one of the nicer ones...

It was swimming rather hopelessly around the bowl.

"Aha! You'll pay for this," shrieked Kolumnus in triumph, pointing at the newt.

"What? Temporary newtering is perfectly legal," said Hargarthius.

"Fancy doing that to her royal highness! Take the spell off at once."

"You take the spell off. It's not her," said Hargarthius.

"I will."

So he did. The large, naked, tattooed and shaven haired man suddenly sitting in a bowl of water – which broke – was not quite what the magician, or the soldiers who had unobtrusively taken up position on either side of Master Hargarthius had expected. The bouncer was yelling and gesticulating wildly, and ended up thumping a bare fist against a large armored chest. That was probably not a clever thing to do, as the knight hit him back with a mailed fist, which knocked him back against the wall.

"It's... not the princess," said the Life-Diviner, stating the obvious.

"Really. You don't say!" said Master Hargarthius. "How surprising! Perhaps you'd like to try the rest of the cells? Or transforming the raven or my apprentice? You owe me for that bowl," he pointed at the broken crockery.

The raven said: "Nevermore," and pointedly turned its back on the chief wizard. But they did search, using the life-diviner's magic bowl and peering into a great many rooms, and being teeth-chattered at in irritation by Mrs Drellson's skull for dirtying up the floors.

At the end of it all, Master Hargarthius said: "Now I suggest you go and search residences of the idiots who told you it was me. And I'm planning on finding out exactly who they were. I've a good idea already. Zoryanthus's plague of boils on the lot them."

The soldiers and the wizards left, which Tom could not but be glad about. He really didn't like the Chief Wizard any more than Master Hargarthius did, and it was so unusual to agree with old Grumptious that it made him uncomfortable.

The outer door closed behind them, and the Master leaned against the wall, and said: "Phew. Now I'll have to do a thorough decontamination. I'll bet they were up to something."

"The little rat-nosed one, the Chief's assistant, was making secret notes on a pad she had in her sleeve," said Tom.

Master Hargarthius scowled. "Checking out the defenses. And looking for something, I would guess. The Life-Diviner Malalia isn't someone I would have thought ill of, though. The others..." He shook his head. "Well, I'll speak to the tower, it'll re-organize itself. Much help her notes will be to them. They walked right past some things they ought to have seen. Go up to the battlements, boy, and make sure they've left."

It was a lot of stairs, but Tom was actually glad to go. And it seemed, at least from everything he could see from up there, that the small army and royal wizards were glad to go too, and busy leaving. Tom was pleased to wave his tail in a suitably insulting fashion at them. It was insult only a cat would understand, and they were far below. He watched until they had disappeared and the master was bellowing for him.

Going back downstairs was... confusing.

Tom had always been sure the tower moved and changed. This was the first time it had done it in a hurry though. Getting to the laboratory was complicated and very different.

"I was quite correct," said Master Hargarthius. "Two magical spying devices were left. Hmph. Does Kolumus think I was born yesterday?"

Even the Chief Magician couldn't be quite that foolish, thought Tom.

"So have you destroyed them, master?"

"Hmph. And why would I do that?" said Master Hargarthius. "I know where they are, you will shortly know. The raven will tell them 'Nevermore'. Perhaps we can get the skull of Mrs Drellson to talk to them about kitchen cleanliness."

Tom could see that that would be a fitting revenge for searching his Master's Tower.

"There is a time for taking chances, and a time for caution. We've moved from the latter to the former," said Emerelda.

Alamaya had never noticed her God-mama ever going with caution, but perhaps that was just compared to Duke Karst. "So what are we going to do?"

"Stick our heads into what I suspect may be the lion's mouth. But I may be wrong. I just didn't trust him. I will have to put certain protections and confusing spells on you, Alamaya. Fortunately, cats are, by their very nature, somewhat resistant to magics, as they have their own."

Safely inside their cone of silence the conclave met. "It is the Princess's slipper. There is no doubt about that," said Malalia, examining the jeweled shoe that the Chief Wizard had purloined from the Magician Hargarthius's laboratory.

"So where has he hidden her?" said Kolumnus.

"There was a lot of divination equipment in the laboratory. He may just have been looking for her."

"I don't believe that," said Kolumnus.

CHAPTER 14

A WITCH IN THE DOOR

——▶·◀——

The task he'd been summonsed to the laboratory for consisted of setting up a device to detect intruders magically, even outside the walls. Anything that moved – besides Tom, the master, Mrs Drellson's skull and the raven – would cause it to sound an ominous chime. Personally, Tom had his doubts. "Master, it'll pick up every bat or rabbit."

To prove his point the device, powered by a small colony of ants fed colored sugar by micro-demons, promptly sounded the ominous chime, making both of them instinctively duck.

"Hmph. I will have to adjust the sensitivity," said Master Hargarthius, scrawling a new spell and carefully tossing a psychedelic mushroom into the ants.

The ominous chime sounded again.

"More? Hmph." He did so, for the same result.

"Er, Master. Could there be someone out there? Maybe the army come back or something?"

"Go and check," said Master Hargarthius irritably, opening another book.

So Tom did. And came running back as fast as he could, wondering just how wise he was being doing so. "Uh. There's um, a witch at the door. The... the witch called Emerelda. She was knocking."

"Emerelda Tindrell?" Master Hargarthius looked startled. "Well. Go and let her in. I'll be down shortly. Take her to my study and fetch some wine. Good wine."

"Er. Is she... safe?" The magician's reaction to her, seemed quite different now, than to his bumping into her at the castle had been.

"By Zoranthus's red-hot pizzle, no! She's the wickedest witch in the West," said Master Hargarthius, with an evil chuckle. "But she didn't blast the walls down, so this must be a social call. And that is flattery. Not flattery that's ever come my way, but it is quite... widely talked of."

Tom had heard something of the physical and magical strength of the tower's walls. "She's that powerful a magic-wielder?" he asked, warily.

"No, she's a successful alchemist, and better than average at most forms of magic. But it's the alchemy that's a problem. She blows things up with intent and skill. Now get a move on. It won't do to keep her waiting. I need a quick wash and change."

Tom was too stunned to say anything, but, shaking his head went off to the door of the tower, and opened it. The witch was somewhat windswept, but otherwise just as she'd appeared in the illusionary sending. She had her broomstick, and her cat.

"Were you all asleep?" she said dryly. "Did the army get bored demanding entry and go away? We've been knocking for ages."

"Er. No. The master was setting up a device in the laboratory," said Tom. "We don't get many visitors. The skull usually seems to know and tells us. Or the raven does."

The witch shook her head. "Men. Can we come in?"

Belatedly Tom wondered if this was just another of Master Hargarthius's traps. "Uh. Just a moment." He scampered over to the far door and jammed it open with his knife. Ran back. Remembered his manners. Bowed. "Do come in. My Master bids you welcome, and will be with you shortly. He has asked me to take you to his study and to fetch you some wine."

"Have you been feeding the grumpy old so-and-so black-spurred rye or something?" asked the witch, coming in with her broom which she leaned against the wall. "I was expecting a stand-up fight to get in."

The cat had been staring at him, and now stalked in behind her and walked forward and rubbed against Tom's legs. Tom leaned down and stroked the silken soft fur.

The witch snorted, but with amusement. "I suppose my telling you not be so forward would be futile," she said.

Tom wasn't sure just who she was addressing, him or her cat.

So he bowed and said: "If you could follow me, please."

Tom retrieved his knife, and let them to a room he was seldom allowed in except to clean, his master's book-lined study. The witch sat herself down, put her red high-heeled shoes on the book-crowded desk, helped herself to a chained volume, and said…"You haven't got tequila have you?"

Tom swallowed. "No. But I could get you a salamander if you want to set fire to your mouth," he volunteered.

"I think I'll just have wine. White, dry. Chilled," said the witch.

"Er. Yes. Would your cat like some milk?" That cat was… worrying. There was something very familiar about it. And it looked rather affronted to be offered milk.

The witch gave a wicked little gurgle of laughter. "I think you are about to be clawed. Milk, I am sure would be good for her. And a novel experience. Why don't you go with Tom, Kitty, and get some nice fresh milk." The cat gave her a cold stare, but did follow Tom as he retreated from what was, altogether, a little worrying.

Of course, as any cat did, it didn't so much follow as dart ahead, twist between his legs and stop to carefully wash a paw in front of the mirror. She was just doing this when the raven swooped in silently, and landed on the wall-sconce. It could be a very silent big black bird, when it chose.

The slim cat was plainly not expecting it, or the sudden "Nevermore." She jumped for the shelter of Tom's legs, as well she might, because the raven was eyeing her, shifting its head to try a different perspective, as she peered out from behind Tom's legs, the hair on her back slightly raised.

"It's only the raven," said Tom. "The master's familiar."

"Nevermore," said the raven, and clacked his big black dagger beak, quite savagely.

The cat looked at the bird, unblinkingly. She was not a very large cat, thought Tom. "I could carry you," Tom offered, wondering if she would be affronted.

She got up on her hind legs, using his robe for purchase, so Tom bent down and picked her up. To his surprise, she adjusted very neatly to the crook of his arm, and snuggled into him and purred. "I'll keep you safe from the raven," Tom said, wishing he was sure of his ability to do so. The raven was watching them, and followed them, fluttering ahead, landing on a wall-sconce and watching them until they passed, and then doing the same thing again. It was rather un-nerving. Even more worrying than the white wine, dry, chilled. How did you dry wine? He'd learned from Old Grumptious that the requirements of magicians were by nature always unreasonable. It seemed female magicians were the same, only more so. He stroked the cat he was carrying, to help him to cope.

"Nevermore," said the raven, sternly, as it flew and perched, watching.

They arrived in the kitchen, where the skull of Mrs Drellson was buzzing about like a worried housefly. The skull seemed magically aware of visitors — and of their station. "What took you so long, boy? She's a powerful enchantress, and the Queen of Cats. Run, don't walk!"

"Mwrow," said the cat.

The skull paused, jaw open. "Oh. I suppose you couldn't jar the cat."

Tom blinked. "I am a cat, and you have jarred me. Often."

"Huh. You're a boy. A dirty, smelly creature who doesn't work hard enough. Get the poor cat some milk. Do we have any fish?"

"No." Despite the side effect of fish having made him into a human, Tom was still very fond of it. As far as he was concerned it was entirely too rare in the tower, and if it was there at all, it was salted and smoked.

"Well, cut her some strips of duck." The cat had slipped almost bonelessly from Tom's arms, onto the table and was looking curiously at the skull. Tom reached forward protectively. Feet on the table would never be tolerated. But it seemed that was only for him or even Master Hargarthius. It was Tom who got the sting of green lightning, not the cat. "Get on with it. Milk. Some strips of duck-breast. And no doubt you have to take wine to her ladyship."

"Yes, white, dry and chilled. And we only have red and see-through, and all of it is wet."

Mrs Drellson's skull was not impressed with that answer either.

However the witch's cat was impressed by the duck, or at least pleased to eat it. The raven hopped closer, and Tom was preparing to try and shoo it off, which usually didn't work, when the cat hissed at the raven, and it backed off all by itself. She pretended to turn her nose up at the milk, but Tom noticed, when he got back from fetching the bucket of snow from the cave for the wine, that she was licking the fur around her perfect black lips, and the milk in the bowl was considerably lower. He reached out to stroke her and she rolled onto her back. He was unwise enough to take the invitation and reach towards the furry belly. She grabbed his hand with her front paws, raked his arm with her hind claws, and bit his fingers. The cat side of Tom knew this was in play, really. Had it not been, those would not be pinpricks. The human side noticed she had sharp claws and teeth.

She cheerfully climbed up him and draped herself over his shoulder as he walked back up to the master's study with the silver platter and the ice bucket and the delicate wine goblets.

"Wasting no time, I see," said the witch dryly, as Tom set the wine down and the cat abandoned him without so much as a backward glance, and climbed onto her lap.

Tom didn't quite know how to reply to that, so he bobbed his head and turned to leave, just as Master Hargarthius arrived... in his court robe, his beard combed.

He bowed to the witch. "Madame Emerelda Tindrell. What brings you to my humble tower?"

She laughed. The same snort of amusement, and possible devilry Tom had had from her. "'Madame' is a bad choice of words, Hargarthius. I've never been at that end of the business. And I'm here to look for your help, obviously." She took her feet off his desk and smiled at him.

"Ehrm yes," said Master Hargarthius, looking stunned. "Of course. What can I do for you?" And to Tom. "Run along, boy. I am sure you have work to do."

"Let him stay, please, Hargarthius," said the witch. "He is one of my subjects."

"Eh?"

"I am the Queen of Cats."

"Oh. Yes," said the Master. "One forgets. He is prone to asking questions and butting in... Emerelda."

"That is very much a part of what he is. Cats are curious and have little idea of precedence. That is why cat may – and do – look at Kings. Personally, I like it."

"Hmph. They're mediocre famuluses," said Master Hargarthius, reverting to type. "But if you want him here, he can stay."

Tom wasn't sure if he should be glad about this or not. He was, of course, curious. And that was an exceptionally beautiful cat that had scratched him and made his hand smart. On the other hand, well, Master Hargarthius could be exceptionally dangerous, when he didn't get his own way. Tom had the feeling that this witch was no different.

Being allowed to stay did not go as far as 'being invited to drink the wine'. But he was told to pour it. "Hmm," said Master Hargarthius on tasting it. "Chilled. An excellent idea. Makes the taste of white wine less obvious."

"And more pleasant on a hot day," said the witch, pushing the cat's nose away from her wine. The cat sneezed.

"Yes. Quite. Now, what help do you want from me?" asked Master Hargarthius. "I, er, do have some leads on the Princess."

"I know," said the witch.

"Well, er, I could probably use your help to rescue her. To return her to the court," said Master Hargarthius.

"I don't think that is a good idea. In fact that's exactly what I don't want you to do," said witch, calmly.

Hargarthius took a deep gulp of his wine, choked, coughed, and spluttered, and exclaimed: "What?" he exclaimed dangerously, and reached for his staff, standing up as he did so.

The witch didn't stir. She just shook her head. "Karst has a 'suitable' husband lined up for her, and besides, there is the faction trying to kill Alamaya. I – or she – or even Karst may be able to deal with the latter, but you know as well as I do that the first part would kill her."

"Nevermore," said the Raven, gloomily.

"Precisely," agreed the witch. "Now my glass seems to have developed a leak."

"What?" he exclaimed again, shaking his head. The calm, or the statements, had knocked Master Hargarthius off balance. "Those are finest Genitian glass…"

"Well, it is empty," said the witch. "So is yours. Must be a leak. Refill them, Tom, and we will test them again."

So Tom did. Master Hargarthius hadn't set aside his staff, or sat down. But as the witch just sat there and drank her wine, he did set it aside and sit down. His eyes were still narrow and intent. He tugged his beard, bit his long forefinger, and then took another mouthful of wine. "This chilling process," he said. "I believe it makes it sublimate."

"Aha," said the witch. "I suspect the only way to prevent that would be to drink it."

"You took her out of the palace?" asked Master Hargarthius, after another mouthful of wine.

The Witch shook her head. "No. She did that herself. I found her though, before those who were hunting her, and not with good intent, did."

"And then?" asked Master Hargarthius.

"And then I hid her, to the best of my ability and entirely with her consent. She is free to go back to the Castle at any time she chooses. She is, for now, as safe as I can keep her."

There was another long silence. Finally Master Hargarthius sighed. "I see. Very well. I'll stop looking. With the curse hanging over her, I suppose it is for the best. Karst won't like it, nor will he stop searching, Emerelda."

"And you're still prime suspect," she said with faint amusement.

"They came and searched, already," said Master Hargarthius. "And left two magical ears."

"Which you destroyed?" asked the witch.

"Zoryanthus p..., er. No. We know where they are, and they can listen to the housekeeper berating the boy about his cleaning skills, and me muttering about what idiots they are and how important it is to find Princess Alamaya, and how I am failing to do so."

She chuckled wickedly. "I have under-rated you. Excellent. They can also be turned to listen to the listeners, you know."

"Pnagrythis contrarian incantation? Doesn't work."

"There's a deliberate error. He switched the lark-tongues quantity with the owl fewmets. It's a pattern in the old man's spell-books to hide his methods."

"Drat the old gibbering wreck," said Hargarthius crossly. "I spent a lot of time and money on those spells."

"Didn't Estethius teach you the pattern?" asked the witch, raising a manicured eyebrow. "He certainly knew it."

"He taught me as little as possible. And then only when he had to," said Master Hargarthius, with a shrug. "I had to work most of it out myself, afterwards."

Tom thought that he'd learned a lot by imitation, then, but he said nothing. He just exchanged glances with the cat.

The witch gave a slow, thoughtful nod. "You were a cocky, snooty stuck-up know-it-all, when you were young. You let on that you had had the very best and very wickedest teaching you, so we'd better all keep our distance."

The Master drained his glass. "Of course I was. I knew almost nothing, and didn't dare tell anyone, in case they, well, took it away from me. I did have Estethius's library, so I learned. Anyway, most of the other magicians would have nothing to do with me. Half of them thought I was evil and dangerous because I was Estethius's apprentice. The other half thought I was a traitor for letting the King's Army in. Boy. This glass needs filling."

"I wish I'd known then," said the witch.

He shrugged. "I wasn't telling anyone."

"Yes, but you were probably the only magician's apprentice I wasn't experimenting with. I feel deprived, now. My reputation is threatened. It wasn't easy earning the title of the wickedest witch in the West, you know."

Master Hargarthius spluttered on his wine, and gulped the rest.

She continued smoothly. "Anyway, yes, I would like your help in hiding the Princess. But that wasn't why I came to see you. It was about the curse."

Hargarthius wiped his beard with his sleeve. Shook his head. "The royal council of wizards questioned me at the time. They put me under a magical truth trance, and that was with the Enchantress Saliana, and she made Kolumnus look like a green apprentice. I knew nothing of the curse. Not how it was done or what magics were used."

"Oh I know all that," said the witch, with a wave. "I even know Saliana tried on her deathbed to tell them something terrible she'd done to King Uther. I suspected she'd been in cahoots with Estethius... there always are a few that admire such people. I got all that out of the demon. Well, enough to start on, anyway. The important bit. That he used the demon to collect her blood and tears... and that he's not dead."

"Nevermore!" said the raven, a savage look in the beady eye. "Nevermore!"

"The raven does not like demons. And they always lie," said Master Hargarthius.

"Yes. I know," said the witch. "But I still need Estethius's brain."

There was a silence, and then Master Hargarthius picked up the bottle and attempted to pour more wine, without calling Tom to the job, a sure sign he was troubled. Barely a drop fell into his glass. "Hmph. This bottle seems to have developed a leak, similar to the one in the glasses," he said.

"Perhaps it is infectious. You'd better check the other bottles," said the witch, draining her glass.

So Tom went to fetch another. If he had not been a suspicious cat-turned-famulus he would have thought the witch was trying to get his master drunk. As he was a suspicious cat-turned-famulus, he was certain of it. So he collected bread, cheese, and pickles, and some ham as well as more of the precious snow to chill the wine, and more wine to be chilled, then hurried back, because he was inevitably curious, wondering what he'd missed.

And the witch knew. "We have just been exchanging scurrilous gossip about our peers, Tom. No doubt interesting to your long ears, but not important."

Tom swallowed. Well, she was the Queen of Cats, even if she was human. She would know how a cat thought, and possibly humans too. He did pick up some more of the scurrilous gossip while they ate. Tom wished he'd had time to eat. Her cat had at least had duck breast and milk. All he'd had was a mouthful of bread chewed on the way. But he wanted to know about Estethius's

brain. And the curse. He didn't like the idea of Maya being under this curse. It might interfere with clubbing and... other things. The human side of him said that she was a princess, and thus far above a cat. The cat side did not agree.

Eventually, they did get back to the subject of the brain. Tom decided the witch was very skilled at getting men drunk and co-operative. She'd made Old Grumptious laugh quite a few times, and puffed him up a bit in his own importance. It was... interesting to watch and learn from. As a cat he hadn't really studied humans being human. He watched them for food, opportunity and to avoid possible kicks.

"By the way, that bat-blood cost me a fortune," she said conversationally as the talk wandered into that exotic magical supplies. "A foolish move on my part. I should just have asked for the brain. But I didn't know as much about you then."

Master Hargarthius blinked. "That was you?"

"Some of my hirelings," she said dismissively. "They were supposed to be the best armed robbers in all Kos. It's a place where they disarm robbers if they catch them, so they were rather surprised and relieved to escape amputation. Yes, I sent them, and the Demon Prince Hariselden, on the same mission. I assume you dealt with him? Otherwise I'm going to have to summons him and show that I am very, very, displeased."

The raven looked up from the piece of ham it was shredding and said: "Nevermore," in very satisfied tone.

"Hmph. In a manner of speaking," admitted Master Hargarthius. "The boy had better take him another pickle soon. He's occupying my best chamber... um, pot."

"Really? He is a fairly powerful demon. Estethius used him extensively. He is exceptionally skilled at passing for human. A suave, handsome and charming man is one his favorites. Enjoys seduction. I gather he was exceptionally talented at it."

"Nevermore!" said the Raven savagely and clacked its beak.

"Not as good at it as I was of course," said the witch, languorously uncrossing and re-crossing her legs. "But I never managed to keep a demon in a chamber pot. It's an interesting idea. I shall have to check the pots I squat over in future. It could be a useful way of getting rid of unwanted houseguests."

Master Hargarthius shrugged. "I don't have many. Ordinary folk treat the place with fear, which is... quite useful, I suppose. It made finding suitable famulus's and household help difficult. And mages do not come to call." He sighed. "It has a history."

"Yes. Historically mages don't mix much anyway, outside of the Court. It was the eating and drinking at someone else's expense that was the draw, and since King Uther, that's been nearly absent. Of course there is Kolumnus's Association, that he's pressing everyone to join, but I see precious little advantage in it. Mind you, Estethius was a leading court figure, once. You must have spent time there then."

Master Hargarthius shook his head. "Not really. He... was told to remove himself from the Court about a month after I was taken on. He was... always a rough master. But those were bad months. I thought he was going to kill me a few times."

Tom had found a stool and sat on it, and somehow the cat had moved onto his lap without him noticing quite how she got there, or how she required him to hold his leg and arm in what had been a mildly-uncomfortable-at-first position and had gradually moved to exhausting-and-excruciating-but-if-you-move-you'll-disturb-the-purring-cat position. The cat side of him knew he was being used, but the human side knew that, and didn't mind. Humans, thought the cat side, were odd like that. It took a lot of his concentration to hold the position, but still this statement made him ask, despite the cat, the need to remain un-noticed, and his being hungry: "Well, why did you become his famulus then, Master?"

Master Hargarthius looked at him wryly. "The usual. I thought with magic I would be able to turn the bigger boys who used to beat me up into toads, and the girls who ignored me into being hopelessly in love... or at least in lust with me. And that I'd conjure feasts... or even get to eat regularly. And being a famulus to a magician seemed better than starving, which was what I was doing before that. I was probably wrong. I was certainly wrong about the magic."

"Uh. So why didn't you leave?" asked Tom.

There was a silence. Eventually the witch spoke, "I would assume that Estethius used his craft to put spells of binding on his apprentice. To ensure his loyalty and safety."

"Well, I don't think he would have thought of trying being nice to them," said Tom, and then wished he hadn't spoken.

"That can be more effective," said the witch, with a smile, although Master Hargarthius looked somewhat stunned by the conversation.

He rubbed his eyes. "I never thought of that. You could be right, I suppose. I never thought of running away, but it would have been sensible. And, um, what I had done from my previous master. What I should have done... You know, everyone thought I'd betrayed Master Esthetius for the reward. For this tower... It was promised to whoever gave him over to the King's men, dead or alive... Master Estethius thought that very amusing."

"He did?" asked the witch.

"Yes. I didn't betray him. I did exactly what he told me to do, when I let the King's men in. Well, I did most of what he ordered, anyway. I suppose the compulsion spell wore off once he had... well, been bottled. I was supposed to wait a year... but I took it apart instead." He stood up, with a wobble. "I think I will go to bed. I am... tired."

"Er. The brain?" asked Tom, thinking that was what he'd taken apart.

"Oh. In the jars behind my desk," Master Hargarthius pointed at dark corner. "I couldn't quite bring myself to throw it out. Loyalty spells again, I suppose. I never thought of that. I did release the demon, Hariselden, when I dismantled the apparatus. It promised never to return. They always lie. But I didn't know that then."

"I think I will go to bed too," announced the witch. "And my broom does not have one of these fancy self-fly homing devices."

"Oh. Um, the boy will find you a chamber…"

"Yours will do," she said. "I have a reputation to keep up."

᚜᚜᚜᚜᚜

This was dear, dear God-mama's idea of a joke, Maya thought. Of course, she'd found it much, much more amusing before it came to bed. Still, while the curse was active she really could not take chances. And it would apply as much to cat form as human.

Tom, although he didn't scent mark like a Tom-cat… still was one. And this was his territory.

᚜᚜᚜᚜᚜

"It was frightfully expensive," said Malalia, in the cone of silence.

"We serve the state. Cost is no object," Chief Wizard Kolumnus declared. "We needed to know what they were up to. It was a pity that so much of what we could hear was distorted, but we need to take action on the matter." He looked pointedly at her.

"Me?" she squeaked.

"You are probably the lightest of the conclave."

"We'll send Benita," said Malalia, firmly.

CHAPTER 15

BRAINS' TRUST

—▶•◀—

Tom started to move, but the cat stuck her claws into him, so he sat as still as a statue, while his master and the witch left. At which point the cat got up. Tom went over to the table at least in theory to clear away the bottles and glasses and food, but in practice to eat the rest of the bread and cheese, because he was famished.

The cat went off on a mission of her own, snooping in the dark corners among the bottles.

He ate while she did that and then piled the glasses and bottles and plates onto the tray. He picked it up and the cat stood up against his leg, the points of her claws making sure he knew she was there. "I can't carry the tray and you," said Tom.

The claws came out a quite a bit more. Tom sighed, put down the tray, and bent down.

She moved off, just out of reach. He stepped after her. She moved again… next thing she jumped up on desk and then onto the shelf behind it, piled with bottles – homonuclii, snakes, strange flowers with teeth drifting up and circling, Octopi with baleful eyes. "You'll break something and it'll all be my fault," said Tom, reaching for her, knowing perfectly well that even if the witch's cat understood him, it would cat-like, not care.

He expected her to dart away. But she'd stopped just behind a large dusty jar… And the raven came down and pecked at the jar, hard.

The jar lid was harder than raven-beak and the cat didn't flinch – as Tom did. Instead she gave low growl.

That was enough to get Tom to dust the jar with his sleeve. Inside in murky brown fluid was something with the unmistakable folds of a brain. Well, well. She was a witch's cat after all, he supposed.

The raven pecked at the jar again, savagely. It was fond of brain. It had taken the brain out of rats and mice Tom had caught. So far it had made no impression on the bottle but Tom knew it could be singly determined. He'd better put the bottle somewhere else, he decided. In the pantry with the pickles maybe. The raven refused to go in there or into the broom cupboard, but Tom preferred the pantry, and it would be at home with pickle jars. The brain might even enjoy watching them breed. So he picked it up. The cat made no attempt to get picked up too, but followed him, as did the raven, all the way to the pantry.

The raven stayed out of there. The cat did not. However, she kept behind him, peering through his legs, while he gave the cheese some milk, after setting the jar among the pickles.

The raven had flown off to find his own roost somewhere, when they came out. It would probably be an irritable bird in the morning, as it had stolen quite a lot of the master's wine. That might explain why it had decided to vent such force on the jar, decided Tom, as he carried the debris of the evening back to the kitchen. The skull had emerged from wherever it lurked and instead of yelling at him to wash up, asked the little pussy-wussy if she needed a rug in front of the kitchen fire.

However the 'pussy-wussy' left, walking off down the passage, so Tom followed, yawning, to see what she was up to this time. She was scratching at his door, of all things. Well, that worked for Tom, so he opened it, and the cat ran on ahead and jumped onto his pallet, and made herself at home in the middle of his blanket.

There was not much that Tom could do about it, except to use his cloak to cover them both. It was a great pity he could not transform himself into a cat...

It was also a pity she had to sleep in the very middle of the bed, so he had to occupy the bits around the edge. But she did snuggle into him and purr and languorously reach out her chin and rub it against his arm.

With not very much bed left to him and the unusual, if not unpleasant experience of sharing that bed, Tom expected to get fairly little sleep. And in this expectation he was not disappointed, although the reasons were something else entirely. He was a light sleeper, but he was happily locked into a rather vivid and very pleasant dream that involved some intimate clubbing with Maya, and him wondering why there had to be clubbing...when it dawned on him the clubbing was a noise on his door, accompanied by the shrill tones of Mrs Drellson. "Alarums, Alarums, thieves, murderer, mayhem!" And then: "Nevermore!" in hasty and urgent raven tones. And in the background the ominous chime.

Tom stumbled out, wrapped in his cloak, to be confronted by the skull. "Something is on the loose in the master's study, breaking things! I can't wake the Master!"

She, like the raven, had problems with some doors, which was why the raven had been knocking. Tom ran up the stairs, thumped the Master's door, and opened it. It was dark in there, but he yelled: "Master, trouble in the study!"

"What..."

"The study! Mrs Drellson says there's something loose in there."

"I'm coming."

Tom ran toward the noises, nearly tripping over the cat. "Nevermore!" Shrieked the raven, buzzing past him towards the noise of breaking glass.

Tom was not naturally inclined to being brave, but he'd have to clean that up! He flung the door open, to find chaos in the light of a branch of candles he definitely hadn't left burning on the central table.

Chaos, and someone.

A smallish figure in a hooded deep-violet robe raised an arm and Tom dived aside as a fireball hissed past him and into the stone passage. "Recall!" yelled the figure. "Recall me! Now!"

Tom didn't think he was likely to forget, although it was possible it wasn't him that was being addressed. The raven had flown in, low, almost between Tom's legs, and was pecking, clawing, and flapping at the figure, which did not help the next fireball. Tom wished he had his broom to hit the person with, but he did his best by throwing a heavy grimoire at the burglar, who yelled: "Recall!" and shimmered slightly

The Witch Emerelda collided with Master Hargarthius in the doorway. Neither of them were addressed... or dressed, either. Well, the Master had his staff, and a towering fury, and the witch her wand and a lot of red hair. She didn't look pleased either.

"Cease! Abbadon alla Whoop yee woenter ear!" shouted Master Hargarthius, or something like that, as the witch was chanting and waving her wand too.

It was not what should happen as one tried to fling a fireball... that exploded, burst into flames and so, with a dreadful shriek, did the invader.

The Master and witch both cast extinguishing spells, which saved the study and the magical tomes therein. The same, however, could not be said of the burglar, whose once-violet and now black robe collapsed into a pile of ash. Presumably the ash had once been a person, too. It made a further mess to clean up, along with the destroyed bottles and jars of the Master's specimens now on the floor."

"The brain!" said Emerelda. "Is it still all right?"

Master Hargarthius leaned on his staff, peered at the mess. He shook his head. "No. Everything is broken."

"Uh, Master..." said Tom, as the cat clawed his leg.

"They must have some other way of spying on you, Hargarthius," said the witch, arranging her hair into a garment of sorts. It was long enough. "I will have to take steps to remove... ouch."

The 'ouch' was as result of the cat sticking a claw into her.

The witch looked down. And said, "Yes. Well, I think we had better find some clothes. Now!" And she turned and walked out.

The Master sighed. "Well. Most of them were biological specimens. Of no magical value, really. Clean it up, boy. I shall go and set more defensive spells." He sighed again. "But they got what they wanted. I thought I'd be glad to see it go."

"Master...uh." The cat bit his hamstring.

"What, boy?"

"I need to show you something else the invader might have done," said Tom, pointing to the door.

The witch hadn't gone very far down the passage, or bothered about the clothes. "Immeldson's cone of audience," she said.

Master Hargarthius blinked. "But that's frighteningly expensive and takes thirteen skilled practitioners."

"With any luck they're short one. And they wouldn't be worrying about expense. It wasn't their money. They need precise co-ordinates though. Is there anywhere they didn't go?"

"Er. The garderobe, and the tower-top," offered Tom.

"Most of the tower is probably safe," said the master with a scowl. "It moves. But the study does not. The tower moves about it."

"I think we will all acquire some more clothing and go to the tower-top. It's a suitable place for me to launch the broom from anyway," said Emerelda.

So a few minutes later, Tom, the cat, the raven, and witch and, last Master Hargarthius met in the moonlight on the tower-top. It was cold and clear up there.

"Sorry to keep you waiting. Do not go downstairs before me," Master Hargarthius, grimly. "If they decide to come back, they'll regret it as long as they live. And the skull is on patrol. I have given her some extra powers."

"We need to move along, anyway," said Emerelda. "This will not be safe, now. And without the brain..."

"I moved the brain," Tom interrupted. "It's... it's hidden away. Mrs Drellson would have said, if they'd been down there. It... it was the cat's idea."

Emerelda snorted with laughter. "She's a rather clever cat, and doesn't entirely deserve what I did to her."

"Mwrwow!" said the cat, rubbed up against Tom.

"It seemed the safest for now, dear. And in terms of the curse... well, never mind. Well done, both of you."

Master Hargarthius nodded. "But I still want my revenge on the miscreants. I will want those ashes kept separate, boy. I want to know who that was, and who sent them. They'll pay for this!"

"I am certain that that was the witch Benita," said Emerelda.

"Kolumus's assistant?" Master Hargarthius's eyes narrowed.

"Ex-assistant," said the Witch. "And I'd guess that Master Kolumus and his cohort are now nursing flaming headaches, from attempting to recall a burning woman."

"You think that Duke Karst is behind this?" asked Master Hargathius.

"Possibly," said Emerelda. "But I'd bet on at Kolumus definitely being involved," she paused. "You know... we could try the ears they left behind. See if we can listen in on them."

"An excellent idea," said Master Hargarthius. "And I must apologise for the... intrusion."

"Oh, nothing to apologise for," said Emerelda, with a wink. "It happens to me all the time. Now, I think we'll do it up here. The spell, I mean."

So Tom was sent to fetch the porcelain, shell-like ear, and certain ingredients from the laboratory and carry them up to the roof, and endure a tut-tutting rebuke from Mrs Drellson's Skull about the state of old Grumptious's study.

Master Hargarthius had fetched the requisite grimoire himself, and the witch had prepared the circles and symbols. The cat had done exactly what cats always do: watch, and occasionally get in the way. Tom was faintly irritated, and he knew, irrationally jealous at this. It made no sense to feel that way. He knew, better than anyone that cats were like that, just as water was wet. But still, that should have been his job, his role, instead of being the dogsbody. They didn't call that position 'dogsbody' for nothing.

In time however the spell was complete, the last line drawn, the owl fewmets scattered onto the flames... and voices, one of which Tom recognized came out of the ear.

It certainly sounded as if they were angry and upset. Tom felt that that was how things ought be. He did not approve of having to clean up the mess, and this was his tower! Which was an odd thought too. It wasn't his prison anymore. But most of all Tom was vengeful because they had been out to hurt Maya.

That was a very human way to feel. Listening to the conspirators on the other side of the ear did not make Tom feel any more kindly disposed towards them.

"...knew the risks. Go into any magician's house and there are traps," said Kolumus.

"Why didn't you go then?" said another resentful voice.

"Because Benita was the heaviest weight we could magically transport, Targonius. Do you ever remember anything?"

"Now gentlemen," said a voice, chilly and autocratic, and female. "It appears from what they said that we have succeeded in our task. Yes, we showed our hand, and yes, it is possible that

Hargarthius may be able to identify Benita's remains. But the brain is destroyed. The curse endures, and our cause triumphs."

"How do we know it was destroyed?" asked someone.

"Benita broke every jar there when she couldn't identify it. The disguising spells aside, it's destroyed. It has been exposed to air, removed from its sustaining liquid," replied Kolumnus

"And if Hargarthius lied, and it was somewhere else?"

"Unlikely. But we will take steps, none-the-less. Now I am going to rest. It's been a long enough night."

There was a silence. "When do we meet again, to take steps against Emerelda?" asked a female voice, tinged with hatred.

The autocratic female voice replied. "She will have fled by now, we will obtain a writ to search her premises, and work from there. Williana can try her divining again. The woman can't hide forever. Her appetites will betray her, bring her into contact with people. We'll find her. And then we'll find the Princess."

"So when do we meet again?" asked Kolumus.

"Tomorrow night. In my chambers," said the cool voice. "Now go."

There was the sound of people walking, and of a door closing.

"Well," said Emerelda finally breaking the silence. "Now we know."

"The Royal Council of Mages?" said Hargarthius.

"At least a number of their prominent members," said the witch. "I never did approve of magicians working together."

"That is what we may have to do, to defeat them," said Master Hargarthius, heavily.

The witch was silenced. Then she pulled a face, and picked up her cat. "Yes. Unfortunately. But it's this living together in Borbungsburg Castle that's unhealthy, in my opinion. Now I need to take a few steps to protect my demesnes, and my responsibilities."

"And I will take a few steps to protect mine," said Master Hargarthius. "Estethius always said this place could hold off an army, he just failed to see why he should."

"Uh. What?" asked Tom.

"He said there were easier ways to do it, which would achieve the same, but with less cost, damage or materiel. Now, carry that trivet down to the laboratory, boy. And the jar of golden flakes."

"Yes Master," said Tom, wishing for breakfast, his bed, the cat snuggling into him, and no work to do... not necessarily in that order. But at least, despite it all, old Grumptious seemed in very mellow mood.

"By the way – Where did you hide the brain?"

Tom looked around warily, and then whispered in the Master's ear. "The pantry, master. With all the other jars there."

"Ah. A good choice. Estethius referred to it as no-man's land. A good place for him to be."

"Er. Why?"

"I have no idea. He called the broom cupboard 'the netherworld', although the only demon that ever came out of it was the raven."

"The raven?"

"Yes, I opened the door one day and there he was, looking very sorry for himself. It must have been about ten years after I took over the Tower. No idea how the silly bird got himself shut in there. He's been here ever since."

"He won't go near the broom-cupboard," said Tom, who didn't like it himself.

"Can't blame the bird, having got himself trapped in there. I wondered if Estethius had put him in there, but I'd opened it often enough in the time between. Besides, nothing to eat in there for ten years... I think he must have escaped the netherworld," said Master Hargarthius, with a slight laugh. "Yes, Estethius was a hard and strange master. Most places in the tower he had strange names for, sometimes more than one, which made no sense, and my life more difficult. He used to call the tower gate-room the 'the winepress'. Come to think of it that makes sense. I always thought it was his odd sense of humor. Anyway I will see you in the laboratory, shortly."

So Tom went there, and not to bed or the kitchen as he would rather have done. But he was in the kitchen in a few minutes, fetching another pickle for the demon. It gave him a chance to check on the pantry. The brain was still there, on the shelf, exactly where he'd left it. But all the other bottles had moved away from it on the shelf. So Tom got a pickle, grabbed a bit of bread to eat, and gave the cheese a bit of milk and a pet, and ran back up to the laboratory to help in setting up yet another fiendish device, after giving the demon his pickle.

This went on for some hours, before there was a halt for food, and Tom had to get to cleaning up – first the study, and then back to his general routine.

The witch was noticeably absent. So was the cat, which upset Tom more than the witch being missing. He was still, as a cat rather than as a human, somewhat resentful of having the Queen of Cats giving orders. He knew she was entitled to, but orders from Master Hargarthius were already a great deal for his cat nature to have to bear.

He did want to know where she'd gone though. Her broomstick was still parked in the Tower gate room. It was faintly tempting to use for sweeping – as a broom it was in a better condition than his. He had a feeling she had somehow slipped off to the place he'd ended up clubbing in.

❧❧❧❧❦❦❦❦

"It is singly annoying to have been so wrong," said Emerelda, as they sat on the subway, as it clacked its way away from the city.

Alamaya smirked, but said nothing.

"And I do hope you had a pleasant night," she said crossly.

"In bed with my paramour," said Alamaya. "And neither of us able to do anything about it."

"I have used my powers, as the Queen, to make sure he is unaware of the fact. He remains very much a cat in some ways. I doubt if that deception can continue indefinitely. Cats are not very subject to magic, which is why it is the safest form for you."

"And being a cat has its charms. They just weren't quite the ones I was looking for," said Alamaya. "So what now, God-mama?"

"Well, I don't suppose you could have carried the brain away with you. So we will have to go back. We could remove it from them, I suppose."

"Tom gave them to a very vicious creature to guard. I don't think it'll let anyone else take them. Its... quite strong smelling."

"Well, I was about to say I thought it would be something of a betrayal of trust. And I think we may need allies."

"Like a cat and a magician who taught himself. And a skull and a raven. That is a very strange bird."

"I'd guess at one of Hargarthius's less successful experiments," said the witch, with a yawn. "Being self-taught is not all bad. At least he approaches things quite differently. And he inherited one of the largest libraries of magical tomes in Ambyria. It was the reward promised to whoever brought Estethius to justice, dead or alive."

"A sort of make-up for Estethius's not having taught him anything, you think?"

"Certainly a temptation not to go through with that revivification that Hariseldon was supposed to power. For which I suppose we should be grateful."

CHAPTER 16

'LIFE! LIFE AT LAST. MWAHHHHA HAA!'

———▶•◀———

om was surprised, but not amazed, to have the ominous chime announce that the witch and her cat were back. He was pleased, though. His grasp of the politics of Ambyria was not great, but with his reading of the Weekly Illuminati Age and Magical Advertiser – which he had gathered was not the perfect source of knowledge – he knew that he and his master were in all sorts of trouble, gravely outnumbered, and probably going to be on the front page. Deaths of wicked enemies of the state always got onto the front page. The Weekly Illuminati Age and Magical Advertiser liked gruesome deaths, with woodcut illustrations. Tom found them interesting to read about, but did not want to have others reading about him. At least, with the witch and the cat, he and the master would have company in their grisly fate.

It might not have been tactful to tell them that as he escorted them to the top of the tower. Even the cat turned her back, and the witch had an alarming fit of coughing. "We'll have to do our best to disappoint them," she said eventually. "Now, if we're to do that, we'll need to break the curse, and restore the Princess to the Castle. Which means we need to question Estethius's brain."

"They don't talk much," said Tom. "The mouth parts are missing. And I'm not sure the mouth and brain are connected."

"Hmph. That is often true," said Master Hargarthius. "Especially in your case, boy."

"Well, yes, but Tom has a point" said the witch. "We have the brain, I assume it is still alive. But how do we communicate with it? Do you still have the apparatus he had ready for his return? We'll have to constrain him somehow."

Master Hargarthius tugged at his beard. Shook his head. "No. I dismantled it, and destroyed the components very carefully and thoroughly. It cannot be rebuilt and nor would I."

"Er. Why?" Tom asked, in the silence after this statement.

"Hmph. Always the questions, boy. Well, just because he would not answer mine, I'll tell you. Estethius always assumed I was an idiot. I could read, and I could think. He saw this process as a way to get precisely what he'd always wanted and to get away with it without any consequences. He knew the prophecy as well as anyone else: the seeress had prophesied that the raven, the symbol of the noble house of Corvin, would conquer Estethius. The seeress was not wrong, ever. So he knew, despite his defences, he would lose. So he had to make losing a victory. Estethius would die. I would open the tower to the King's armies, and give them his body... that I had apparently killed. The reward was well known, and he had hidden his best and richest treasures anyway. I would take charge of the tower. A year and a day later I was to haul the segments of the apparatus to the top of the tower, place the brain in it and enact the spells he had prepared. The magic would draw down lightnings from the skies, and, together with the power and control wielded by the captive demon prince... he would be reborn. His brain transferred to a new body, its brain transferred by Lambeth's substitution into the hypo-amniotic suspension fluid in the jar."

"Ah. I think I begin to understand," said the witch. "Where was the new body to come from?"

Hargarthius looked at her in silence. And then said: "That, in the end, was why I decided not obey those orders. There was only one place it could come from and one person who had possession of all Estethius had owned. He could, of course, break the curse spell he had put on the Royal House of Corvin, and claim the reward for doing so. I was just supposed to be too stupid to work it out."

"Nevermore!" exclaimed the raven, and clacked his beak savagely.

"In this case, yes," said Master Hargarthius. "You weren't around then, bird. But, no."

"I think," said the witch, "that we'll have to try for a somewhat different approach. And I was wrong. Again. What did he promise you?"

"A great reward for my loyalty, of course. That was why I was suspicious," said Master Hargarthius. "Had he promised me horrible torture if I failed to do it less than perfectly, I would have fallen for it."

"Well, I would say you were right to have been suspicious! I'm for tipping his brain down the garderobe, when we're done," said the witch.

"Nevermore," said the raven, shaking his head.

"I suppose we could give him another body," said Tom. "We still have the leaper... bouncer. From the Goth club. Or... or we could get one of the zombies from the Goth club. They're all falling apart and studded and chained to stop them losing bits. Even their tongues and lips. We could just snip a few studs and chains and just give Estethius a mouth. That'd make him a bit more harmless."

"Merely disarming him is not enough with Estethius. He could still speak spells. Still, I like your thinking boy," said Hargarthius. "Although I think we'll keep him away from the leaper's body. It is entirely too large, and we need to avoid any physical strength being available to him. Likewise with any demonic energy."

"I suppose with enough galvanic energy we could do without demonic," said the witch. "And we could get by with...Lizard lips. We can get the porcelain ear hooked up to the nerves."

They got to planning between them. Most of it was over Tom's head, but he did his best to follow, while stroking the cat. The cat seemed to like that.

Once they got to the construction of the magical apparatus stage, Tom's rest was over, and he had two irascible masters to yell at him instead of one.

Two was not twice as good as one, but at least when they were yelling at Tom, they weren't yelling at each other. It was probably less dangerous to have them yelling at him, Tom eventually decided, even if it wasn't pleasant. Still, despite the arguments, the strange device took shape. It was a good time for storms too, and great galvanic collectors were soon buzzing with energy and making Tom's tail-hair stand on end when he walked too close to them.

The witch and Master Hargarthius worked – and argued, and shouted at him, relentlessly. It took nearly three days before it was ready, and by then Tom was just about ready to run off... except for the cat. He couldn't leave her. And the cheese. And it was for Maya... he'd love to go clubbing again.

They had decided on lizard-lips after considering all sorts of alternatives. A mouth shaped of soft leather, bellows and a long pipe – it was to be Tom's job to work the bellows to provide breath for Estethius's brain to speak, and tongue that had had to be borrowed at midnight from a recently buried corpse, and suitably be-spelled and re-animated completed that part of the device... but that was only a small part.

The lager part seemed to be making sure that it didn't end up killing them all and destroying Ambyria. Tom was quite keen on that part. And quite nervous in the midnight hour as the wild thunderstorm raged outside and the great bolts of lightning struck the copper rods and made the huge glass magnetromes in the laboratory shudder with pulses of violet fury, until the switch was pulled and the galvanic energy stored in them poured into the brain and its apparatus.

It did not explode as Tom worked the bellows.

Instead, it shrieked in triumph: "Life! Life, at last! Mwahhhaa haa! I triumph! Now you will pay my price, fools. Now is the hour at last! Mwhaha...uh." The maniacal laughter was cut short. "Where is my body? That fool of boy must have wired it wrong! I will summons the demon..."

"You'll do nothing of the kind," snapped Emerelda. "The vat your brain is suspended in is connected to a thaumatic field indicator. The slightest trace of magic... and, well, I won't tell you. But you won't like it."

"Who are you?" demanded the brain. "Who dares to do this to me? You will suffer... woman."

"I'm here to ask you questions, Estethius. Not answer yours. You have a mouth to speak, and an ear to hear with. That is all. Now, on pain of... well, pain, you will tell me about the curse. All the details. How it was done."

"Saliana?" said Estethius. "It must be you. I've done for your little king. You'll never see him again. Mwhaha haa. You thought shape-shifting would give him an advantage."

"I am not Saliana. She's been dead for many years. Everything you tried for, all your planning, all your scheming, all failed," said Emerelda.

"Except, obviously, my curse," said Estethius. "So they killed the boy. It was the one risk. Expendable idiot, killed too soon."

Master Hargarthius opened his mouth to speak, but Emerelda put her finger across his lips. Pulled the lever attached to the copper wire that led into the brain in its seething basin.

The mouth shrieked.

"And that's a warning. A start. I want answers. I can keep this up for as long as it takes," said Emerelda.

"So can I," replied Estethius's brain, the tone grim, vengeful. "My revenge has endured, has it? And it will, generation after generation. She should not have slighted me, false jade."

"Who are you talking about?" asked Emerelda

"Queen Athena. Who else? Or has she been forgotten in the mists of time? Just the suffering goes on. Mwhahaha... arghhhh!" The brain got another blast of pain.

"You will tell me how the curse was made," said Emerelda, when she'd decided that it had learned a lesson.

It hadn't. "Oh I will tell you. Simple but powerful and beyond your undoing. Once the demon brought me the tears and blood she was doomed, and every child a girl, likewise doomed. With the year and a day of agony from the birth of that child, generation unto generation... and the wantons will not be able to stop breeding."

"You attack those who did nothing to you, who were unborn at the time," she said.

"The sins of the mothers, mwhahaa," cackled Estethius's brain. "But I am generous. Meet my terms and I'll return the blood and tears that my sendling demon-prince seducer stole from her for me. I want the body of your finest knight – better than that fool-of-a-boy's feeble little body, if there is a princess I will have her for my bride, and the Kingdom of Ambyria for my reward. Then I will return the vial of blood and tears. You will never find them without me. No torture, no privation, no means fair or foul will get it from me, ever. And now, I raise my will, I command the demon king Aspore..."

As the needle on the thaumometer moved, the fail-safes cut in, breaking the connection to the mouth, and the ear. The brain plopped back down into the basin, bobbing silent, malevolent. Probably thinking dark thoughts full of rage and revenge and triumph...

Briefly, before it was lifted out by Master Hargarthius, with his largest tongs and put back into its jar of hypo-amniotic suspension fluid, and the heavy lid jammed down. "Well. That was not exactly a success," said the Master, gloomily. "He hasn't changed much. And I'm glad to have it proved to me that he planned to take my body. I was quite fond of my body back then."

Back in the kitchen, which everyone, well, the cat in particular, had decided was a good place to discuss anything, and which both Master Hargarthius and Emerelda had done their best to proof against spying ears. It might, or might not be successful, but at least it was warmer than the tower-top and less crowded and smelly than the garderobe would be. The witch was particularly crabby. "I dislike hurting things, but I think I can make an exception," she said.

"Hmph. It won't help," said Master Hargarthius. "Ask the skull of Mrs Drellson."

"Oh he thrived on pain," cackled the skull. "Even his own. It seemed to please him."

"Er. Could we try some kind of reward? Sort of fish and stick," Tom was not fond of carrots and couldn't see why anyone would be.

"He's not going to negotiate either," said Master Hargarthius. "I remember that all too well."

"Could we give him what he wants... and then kill him?" asked Tom to whom Ambyria and knights meant little, and the Princess a lot. It was rather like letting a mouse that wanted you away from its hole think you'd gone...

"He was the foremost magician of the age. Not easy to kill. And anyway, Duke Karst and the other nobles would never agree. The status quo works for them, even if finding a suitable husband for the royal princesses is difficult, when your offspring will be cursed," said the witch with a sigh. "A lot of work for nothing much. We're still no wiser, and no better off. And this level of magic will have attracted some attention, I daresay."

"Well, we are wiser," said Master Hargarthius. "I now know the curse-spell he's referring to. It's in a rather obscure grimoire from

Partkticia, on the bottom shelf in the study... If we had the tears and the blood, and the princess I could break it."

"Why didn't you say so?" demanded the witch.

"Because we have no idea where to look. And if Estethius hid them... we won't find them."

"We will question the demon," said Emerelda.

"That is worth trying," admitted Master Hargarthius. "I did not recognise him when he came back here. Better get him a pickle, boy." So Tom did, and they trooped up to the Master's study, to where the demon Prince had been moved, to keep him well away from the sphere of Estethius's influence.

It seemed that Hargarthius was not the only one not to recognise what Prince Hariselden had become. The witch stared incredulously at the Demon – who said "Pieces and lurve, man... woman... cats... cool-cats."

"What have you done to him?" asked Emerelda.

"Hmph. Nothing. Well, nothing deliberate. But it seems that pickles...make his mind channel something in another dimension. He seems content, as long as we keep him supplied with pickles."

"It's outa this world!" said the demon in swirl of pink smoke as he devoured the pickle. The pansies were doing a multi-colored conga-line and then a limbo-dance around the base of the handle.

"I don't think it is right," said the witch, shaking her head.

"Hmph. Magicians capture and summons demons who are imprisoned, constrained, used... and that only happens because their very reason for being is a wish to destroy all human life and torture our souls... which, more often than not they manage one magician at time, and you're upset because this one is happy?"

"Yes, but this one seems... well, it's... it's unnatural."

"We want to find the blood and tears," said Tom speaking when he probably should have been silent. "I don't mind how natural the demon is."

"I'm a denatured chile. I was spawned, spawned to be vile..." yelled the demon cheerfully.

"You don't know anything about blood and tears."

"Blood, sweat and tears, yeah. I know. I know, uh huh, uh that's the way... the child is the father of the man..."

"In other words, he doesn't know."

Questioning the demon was exhausting, and confusing. But at last the witch was convinced she had the story: he didn't know what Estethius had finally done with them. He'd collected the blood and the tears. With trickery the witch had something of a description of the containers, which were absolutely not golden... or in other words, were. Were huge and plain, or in other words, weren't. It was enough to make Tom's head hurt, even if the smell from the pot hadn't been making his eyes water and his nose run.

To Tom's relief, they returned to the kitchen, and left the demon contentedly to his pot-dreams, so that they could talk about what they'd learned.

"Two small golden containers, with lids, ornate," said the witch.

"Or at least that's what they looked like the last time the demon saw them," said Hargarthius. "And I know I haven't found or seen such things." He grimaced. "If they were gold I would have sold them in the early years. They might well have been stolen when I let the knights into the tower, by the back door. There was some looting. I've looked for his treasury. For years, I looked. I don't think it is to be found."

"Nevermore," said the raven, gloomily.

"The treasury... where was it?" asked Tom, who had done a fair amount of exploring. The tower was extensive, confusing, but not infinite.

"It went away. It was next to the broom cupboard."

"So things move around in this tower," said the witch, leading, coaxing... she did it well.

"Yes, I think it was magically evolved from a much smaller structure. The broom cupboard is a fixture, though."

"Nasty place," said Tom.

"Yes," agreed Master Hargarthius. "Estethius shut me in it once. He used to call it 'the netherworld'. It isn't, however. I thought it a likely place. It's just a small cupboard. The pantry is more alarming. Magical rules are entirely different in there. The milk arrives magically at the back of it. And sometimes there are new cellars and dungeons. I learned how to make it jumble itself up faster, quite accidentally, a few years ago. I still don't understand how or what happens, though."

"When I was young gel," said the skull of Mrs Drellson, "my gramma told me that when the first people come to these mountains, there was a haunted old building here. No one would go near it... Long, long before Master Estethius. He just moved into it and it grew. I remember it growing while I was working here. Nineteen below stairs staff we had, and needed them all. There were always extra dungeons and cellars." The skull managed a disapproving sniff. "It'd shrunk when Master Hargarthius called me to service here again, with only one boy! But it is growing again. But this time there are more rooms."

She sounded pleased about that. To Tom it just sounded like more cleaning.

"I saw another study once. I should have gone into it, but I thought there might be someone in there," he admitted. "I haven't found it again."

"It sounds as if the search may well be harder than I imagined. And I imagined it would be hard, as the actress said to the bishop," said the witch.

Tom was not familiar with actresses or bishops, but they had it right. "I would have found it by now if it was easy and not hidden. Mrs Drellson makes me clean everything," he said, with a sigh.

"I am sure it is well hidden," said the witch. "Fortunately, I have an excellent gold-divining spell. It's um, more effective and cheaper than turning base metal into gold."

Master Hargarthius raised his eyebrows. "Ah. Alchemy at its best. I am sure I wasn't the only one who wondered at your success."

She chuckled. "You'd be amazed how often the find is in some fellow's pouch or pocket. And that I could find, without magic. Although," she looked at Hargarthius's robe, and then at Tom's, and winked at Tom, "It might be easier to dig it up than to get them to spend any of it."

"Hmph. The cost of magical supplies is ruinous," said Master Hargarthius. "Anyway, apply the spell. Maybe you can find Estethius's treasury for me, too.

"And I might even tell you if I do," she said twinkling her eyelashes at him. "If you were really nice to me, that is."

Master Hargarthius drew breath to go 'Hmph' again, and then shook his head, and managed a reluctant laugh. "No wonder you were called the wickedest witch in the West."

"You have no idea what an effort it was, or how much fun, at times. But the right answer was: 'Can I get you a glass of wine?' And my thought would be, 'What a nice man,' as I said: 'white, dry and chilled, Sweetie'."

Old Grumptious worried Tom by laughing a lot, and telling Tom to fetch her a bottle, unless she'd like two.

"One glass for now," she said. "Work first, and drinking later."

And work it was. Messy work too, to Tom's irritation. He ended up carrying his broom with him, to suck up the mess before someone stood in it and spread it around, as they worked their way slowly up from the cellars. So far they had found one gold Salabar – so deeply wedged down a crack between the stones that only the edge could be seen by reflecting a light down the crack. It was still there, despite Master Hargarthius's earnest attempts to get to it. "Must be wedged from when the tower grew," he said at long last, when the witch's foot-tapping got quite extreme.

They had found Master Hargarthius's pouch too, but that was a known place. The area around the broom-cupboard yielded to Master Hargarthius's disappointment, nothing.

And then – at a volume which made all of them – even the cat – cover their ears, came the sound of the ominous chime, followed rapidly by the panicky shrieking of the Skull of Mrs Drellson. "Alarums, Alarums! Invaders on the tower-top. Hundreds of them!"

"A flying attack! They must still have managed to listen in to us," said Master Hargarthius.

"Or decided that not knowing was too dangerous," said the witch. "Well. We'd better get to defence... I assume you have defences?"

Hargarthius nodded.

"And an escape route?"

"There's a hidden door. It leads out to the midden. It's actually quite some distance from the tower."

"Right. It's night out there. I'll help you. We'll send the... cat, and the boy out. They see in the dark well enough, and I'll help you fight, at least a delaying action."

"It's my tower," said Master Hargarthius grimly. "And I suspected... Go boy. Keep the cat close."

The cat hissed arching its back, the hair on its back standing up.

"I don't have time for this," said the witch. "Go girl. You know how to get to the other place from the gate in my demesnes. Go boy. Take her."

So Tom picked up the cat and ran.

He'd also suspected... but there were things a cat and famulus did not meddle with. "You're the Princess, aren't you?" he said, as he ran, towards the hidden door.

Her only reply was a yowl of alarm – which had nothing to do with what he said, but a great deal to do with the burly, armed knights marching down the passage – and him with nothing more than a broom and a cat.

He skidded to a stop and turned and fled – they plainly had found or known the secret door too. In the kitchen he nearly ran into the skull. "Knights!" he panted. "At the back door!"

The skull of Mrs Drellson sighed. "They've released something upstairs that is devouring magic, boy. That's all that holds the tower together. And me. I should have told Old Grumptious that Master Estethius hid the tears and blood in the pantry."

"Why didn't you?" panted Tom, hauling the heavy table up to bar the door.

The skull shook itself disapprovingly. "It was the witch. She's turned his head. He was never really good at being evil, and now she's got him eating out of her hand."

"I need somewhere safe to hide the... cat."

The raven came fluttering down the passage, bringing with it a stench of burned feathers.

It pecked at the pantry door. "Nevermore!"

Mrs Drellson's skull sniffed. "Last time you went in there, you didn't come out for ten years."

There were ominous creaks and explosions from upstairs. Shouts and the sounds of crashing against the door from the back door to the kitchen.

Tom scooped up the cat – who scratched him and hissed. He paid no mind but opened the pantry door, and... closed it completely behind him. He dropped the struggling cat, and hastily lit a salamander and the lamp.

The cheese hummed loudly. Instinctively, Tom leaned the broom against the shelf and reached out and stroked it. It seemed to expect that, now.

❧❧❧❧❦❦❦❦

Alamaya was furious. How dare Tom! She wanted to fight...

The raven had all but chased them in here, but hadn't followed.

Now they were trapped, trapped in this tiny room. Trapped with that black-waxed cheese that made her feel odd, just looking at it. The pantry couldn't be more than ten cubits long. She'd seen the back wall when Tom had opened the door.

Only... where was it now?

❧❧❧❧❦❦❦❦

The Chief Wizard had been angry at the slowness of the military... but as he was still reliant on Duke Karst, there was nothing much he could do. And, it was true, no-one was that keen on being the first mage into Estethius's old tower. They might not fear Hargarthius, but it was still Estethius's tower. A place of dark sorcery and great power... that he intended to possess for himself.

CHAPTER 17

TO GNOME IS TO LOVE ME

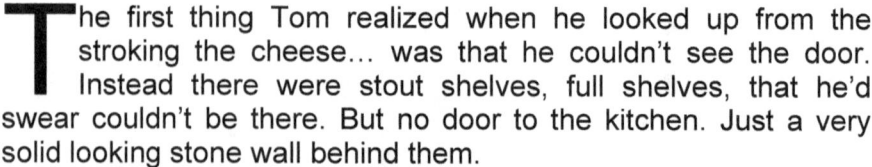

The first thing Tom realized when he looked up from the stroking the cheese... was that he couldn't see the door. Instead there were stout shelves, full shelves, that he'd swear couldn't be there. But no door to the kitchen. Just a very solid looking stone wall behind them.

He knew a moment's relief. It looked just like any other stone wall. It would surely fool the attackers... and then it came to him: that was from this side. It wasn't that no-one could get in from the kitchen. They just couldn't get out from inside.

He turned to look for the cat.

Only to see her walking off down the long stone passage that was where the back wall of the pantry ought to be. Where the jug of milk always stood.

The jug was still there, the cat was just... on the other side of it. There was a sort of strange mistiness about her. He grabbed his broom and turned to run after her calling... and the cheese made a strange sound. Any sound from it that wasn't a burring hum was strange. This was an odd 'meewlp' sort of noise. It seemed... pleading. But he couldn't let the cat-princess wonder off... so he picked up the cheese in the other hand and raced after her, past the milk-jug.

ৠৠৠৠৠৠ

Alamaya had been inspired by curiosity when she's stepped past the milk jug.

And what she found there to her was certainly curiouser and curiouser.

A part of her surprise was realizing that she was both naked and no longer a cat. This was not like her brush with Dr Mirabellus Ontogenetic Reflux Liquid, or Godmama's somewhat gentler process... this was instant. She stood up, because being on her hands and feet was not particularly comfortable, and while it was easier to look between her legs to see Tom hurrying towards her, it made seeing in front difficult. All she could see were some feet.

Standing up did not particularly improve the view. It was... spectacular, just not what she wanted to see.

ৠৠৠৠৠৠ

Tom, rushing forward, was suddenly and abruptly obliged to drop the broom and the cheese. That was because he suddenly had no hands to hold them with, and his balance required he go onto all four feet.

Added to this was the fact that he was somewhat tangled up in his robe, which had fitted him as an apprentice, but very badly as a cat. He struggled to free his forelegs, and then scrambled out from under it.

He was looking up at the delightful girl he'd gone clubbing with. Now of course she didn't have white makeup on her face, or, actually, anything else on either. Perhaps that was what they wore – or rather didn't wear – in this country of chasms, crags and gnomes. They were, from a cat's perspective, broad, large and angry looking gnomes. That could have been due to the spear the one was wielding or the battle-axe the other swung. It wasn't the milk-pail that the third, fleeing one had dropped. None of them appeared to be naked. Tom took all of this in, as he leaped to one side, to avoid being hit by the falling broom.

That was a good move. Unfortunately, it nearly landed him on top of the snow-leopard.

Fortunately the snow-leopard seemed keener on chasing gnomes than on eating a tom-cat in one bite.

᯼᯼᯼᯼

Alamaya found the sudden disappearance of Tom – who vanished into his robe, which fell to the ground with a startled yowl even more worrying than two gnome-guards and the gnome milk-maid. The snow leopard that landed on its feet next to Tom's robe bounded past her seconds later, even before she really had time to worry about it. Being human, and naked, and confronted with warlike and angry gnomes, not to mention being hit on the shins by Tom's broom were quite enough for her to deal with.

Tom made a very handsome and muscular young cat. He stalked forward, and rubbed his jaw against her legs and said "Mwrowrwow."

Alamaya had a fair idea what that meant, but she still picked up Tom's robe and put it on. And because the snow leopard was stalking back towards them, she picked up Tom's broom. It wasn't quite what she would have chosen as a weapon, but it could certainly outrun her if she tried to flee. So she took a firm grip on the solid oak shaft and said: "Shoo!" as fiercely as she could.

It didn't work.

Neither did Tom, stalking forward, fur fluffed to the maximum, hissing like half a dozen steam kettles.

The snow leopard kept coming, slow, measured, deadly... until it got to the fallen wooden milk bucket. Then it stopped, and began to lap the milk. And Tom... hair going down, advanced too. Sniffed – from a safe distance, and then went to join the snow leopard drinking. Alamaya almost felt left out. The snow leopard was both beautiful and terrifying. She felt a curious attraction to something that lethal, but not enough to make her stupid. She wondered about retreat into the pantry. The problem was... just where was it? Presumably not more than ten steps away – but yet the path she stood on wondered on, up the hillside.

Maybe she'd been moving faster than she realised. There were skid-marks on the trail. "We need to go back," she said to Tom, who had finished lapping milk with his new-found girlfriend. Huh. There wasn't as much difference between a snow-leopard and a cat as there was between humans and cats, but it did seem ambitious.

Tom stalked past her, tail in the air. The leopard did not follow. Tom walked on up the path so, with several looks back Alamaya did. The path up the ridge-line ended about a hundred yards further along at the base of a sheer cliff, where, on a rock-shelf – recognizably the same rock shelf as at the back of the pantry, sat the milk-jug.

What was behind it was rock. Impenetrable rock, at least so it seemed when she pressed on it. Tom sniffed at it. Touched it with a tentative paw, and then turned and looked at the snow leopard, which had come up silently behind them, and was lying down, watching.

Perhaps there was some form of silent communication between them, but the snow leopard stood up and began walking down the trail. Tom followed and turned his head and gave a brief 'mworw?' that plainly meant "Are you coming? Follow me." So: because there didn't seem much other alternative, Alamaya did, following the rocky path down towards the valley.

The path was steep and stony, and not kind to her bare feet. As a Princess, and even with God-mama, she hadn't spent much time barefoot. Tom's boots were far too big even if his robe was welcome. But... she had a broom. That would do away with the need for walking. She knew the correct spells.

She stopped and so did the cats. "Flying is easier than walking," she informed Tom, and, she supposed, the snow leopard. She wasn't planning to let it get on the broom, though.

As it turned out that was one of those things that she didn't have to worry about. She recited the cantrip holding out the broom to make it hover so she could alight. She drew her hands away in the prescribed manner, and the broom fell with a thump, that startled the curious Tom. He strutted away, tail in the air, pretending he had not got a fright. With a sigh and a few of God-mama's choicest words, she picked up the broom and walked. The path veered off the ridge and into the steep-cut gully, and scrambled its way down along the tiny mountain stream, across mossy rocks. On another day it would have been beautiful. Now her only thought was that the moss was at least soft underfoot, and the stepping stones kept her toes mostly out of the icy water.

Of course the cats, both big and little, walked 'with' her in the way cats always did. They weren't actually walking with her. That would have been beneath their dignity. No they just happened to be in the same area as her. They even managed to look surprised to see her there. Having been a cat herself, Alamaya understood it a little.

It was still no comfort when both of them disappeared just as she came to the gnome village, cut into the sides of the valley, with the path now becoming a cobbled road, occupied by rather a lot of small, but broad and armoured and armed gnomes. Most of them had spears. Most of those spears were pointed at her. Yes, they were gnome sized spears, but they were still sharp looking.

The language in which she was challenged was not one she recognised, but she had a translation spell...

Which did not work.

In fact it made the yelling worse, a garble of senseless sound. The spears advanced. The gnomes were smaller than she was, but only having a broom to fight them off with did not help. She was outnumbered twenty to one, too. She considered turning a few into frogs to even the numbers out... and then realized that her spells to make the broom hover hadn't worked, the translation spell had made things worse... magic didn't work quite the same way here.

And the cats had, as cats will, deserted her.

As one of the gnomes finally got his courage up, something hissed down and shattered just in front of him. The gnomes backed up, bunching their spears – not looking at her, for a change. Alamaya realized it was just a roofing slate, and that had probably been Tom's tail vanishing behind the chimney pot.

Several gnomes pointed, and even if she did not know the language, Alamaya recognised borderline panic and hysteria. Cats on the rooftops were plainly terrifying here. Spears now pointed at the roof as much as at her.

A bloodcurdling howl from the opposite side of the little row of houses broke the morale of the gnome soldiery entirely. In a scattering of dropped spears, they turned and fled.

The snow leopard stepped out from between the houses, and Tom dropped off the roof, and continued to saunter down the cobbles to the little village green.

Sometimes village greens had statues in them, for the pigeons to express local feelings about. This one had something different: It had a spiked cage, with a dejected looking person in it. The cage was little more than a fifteen foot tall ring of bars that gleamed with an oily sheen – but that seemed enough to trap the prisoner, who sat on carpet and looked at them. The person was human-sized, not gnome-size.

"Who are you?" asked Alamaya, expecting more gibberish.

The reply was however in Ambyrian. "I'm Marcenius… er, Famulus to the Wizard Hargarthius. Can you get me out of here? Please?" There was a certain hopelessness about the prisoner.

And Alamaya could see why: it could be a challenge, as the cage appeared to have no gate. "How did you get in?" she asked. Maybe a ladder would work? Or cutting or bending the bars?

"Magic. And I can't climb them. They ooze oil from the top and they're sharp. Oh, I can't tell you how good it is to hear my own language."

Looking closer Alamaya could see that they weren't so much bars as blades.

And then… she was looking at them from the wrong side.

Obviously they had stepped into some kind of magical trap, thought Tom, looking at the bars, now they were inside the cage. It did have a small stream trickling across the cobbles, and a carpet. That was all.

Tom had, on many occasions wished for the simple joys of being a cat again. When they'd come through the wrong side of the pantry, and he'd become a cat again, he found himself wanting, desperately to be human.

For starters Alamaya was now very human. Secondly, he was very much a cat, and worse, a cat that had something no cat accepts easily: responsibility. For a third thing he was beginning to work things out and had no way of telling her. It had started with the cheese, and then the broom, and then the translation spell. And now he, Alamaya and the snow leopard were stuck inside a cage with Master Hargarthius's former famulus – and, unless Tom was very much mistaken, the magic carpet.

Which the famulus could not make fly, but Tom could have. If he hadn't been a cat. If he'd known the spells.

Mind you, the blade bars were not designed to keep a cat in. If it hadn't been for that responsibility thing, Tom could have slipped away. It would have beaten listening to the Master's previous famulus whine as the gnomes started popping their heads out of their little houses. Tom would guess that throwing nasty stuff, if not rocks, would be next.

He walked over to the princess. It was necessary to climb up her to get her attention away from that sorry loser of a famulus, who was going on about how they should have been quicker to get him out, and how he hated cats. The snow leopard was looking outward, and by its posture, not pleased to be in the cage.

"Ow! You're being a pain Tom. I can't pay attention to you now."

Tom growled at her.

To his surprise the snow leopard growled too, as she was about to try and put him down. Tom jumped down and walked over to the carpet. The poor thing did not look new after being out here with the trapped famulus. It smelled, but not as much as the famulus. Tom stood there and 'mwrarled' loudly, looking at her, tapping the carpet.

"Is that a magic carpet?" asked Alamaya, eyes narrowing.

"Yes. But it doesn't work here," said Marcenius, miserably. "Magic doesn't work here, or it doesn't work properly. It's dangerous. I turned myself into a toad once."

"Toads could escape."

"Yes, but they caught me and put me into a bucket until I got better," said Marcenius miserably. "And being a toad was horrible. I ate flies."

ꛥꛥꛥꛥꛥ

Tom was busy turning the carpet over with his claws as she watched. She shook herself. He was not just a cat, any more than she'd been 'just a cat'. But it was all too easy to forget that and to judge on external form. He was telling her something. So she helped and was rewarded by an appreciative loud purr.

"What are you doing?" asked Marcenius. "I don't want that side on the dirt."

"When you turned into a toad," she asked, ignoring his carpet-desires and going on with the job, "Just what were you trying to do?"

He stepped forward to interfere, got a burring growl from the snow leopard, and instead answered the question. "Turn them into toads, of course. I was quite good at it."

"Right. I get it, Tom."

"My name is Marcenius, not Tom."

"That's fairly obvious. The cat is called Tom. Now, we'd all better sit on the carpet."

"Upside down?"

"Yes, idiot. Quick, before any more gnomes – or their wizards realize what we're doing." The snow leopard was quicker on the uptake than this boy. It had got onto the carpet and sat down.

"Uh. You mean you can make it fly? We can't take that monster with us. Leave him for the gnomes. They're terrified of it."

"Shut up, get on and say the flying spell," said Alamaya, impatiently, wondering if she should try the broom. On the other hand there wouldn't be room for all of them on that.

"But..." Marcenius protested.

"Do as you're told or I'll set the leopard on you," hissed Alamaya.

That worked. And so did the flying carpet, rising slowly. Slower than Alamaya liked. The gnomes came running out, and were pointing and yelling. One of them, she noticed, was wearing the typical 'this is my job' advertising garb of a wizard – moons and stars and a sequinned hat. She wished she had something to throw at them. Or a spell that wouldn't turn her into a frog instead of them.

"Make it fly faster!" she yelled.

He prattled out a spell... which slowed them to snail-crawl. The gnome in the wizard outfit was waving his arms around in a way that spoke of either a magic-ritual or some kind of fit. Alamaya didn't wait to find out which. If magic worked in inverse... She risked the de-frogging spell, and the gnome wizard's next magical word turned into 'ribbit' and his next gesture was a hop, as they, with glacial slowness, continued to rise.

"Tell the carpet to slow down, you fool," said Alamaya.

Either he had never been too bright or his stay in the cage in gnomeland had weakened his wits. "But we're already going very slowly. I can walk this fast," protested Marcenius.

That was true, and the only redeeming feature being that they were rising steadily. They were now about four times the height of the top of the gnome roofs. Alamaya resisted the desire to slap – or better still, from the cattish side of her nature, scratch the idiot. "Spells work in inverse. So a go slower command is a go faster command. The carpet is upside-down and thinks it is going down."

"Oh. But I never learned a go slower command."

So they had to put up with a slow flight, but at least it was an upward one, away from the gnome village.

The downside of that, well, the two downsides, was that it grew steadily colder, and that Marcenius, having had no-one but gnomes to talk to for many months, was making up for it. He told her about trying to find his way out of the pantry and failing. He told her about blundering into gnome-land and failing to get back into the pantry. He told her what a brilliant famulus he had been. He told how the girls in the village were all over him, as the carpet drifted like a slow cloud over the riven landscape of deep valleys and knife-edged ridges.

Tom simply moved in and snuggled onto her lap, purred and went to sleep. He was at least warm. But even that was not enough. Eventually, the shivering was getting too much, and the only content soul on the carpet was the snow leopard. "We'd better go down," said Alamaya.

"That'll be spell for up," said Marcenius.

"No, the spell for down. The carpet is upside-down already. I suppose you don't know that either?"

But he did, and set them down on a rocky knoll just above one of the myriad streams of Gnome-land. It was plain that rained a lot here, and indeed, the clouds were massing on the horizon.

Alamaya was catlike enough to view getting wet as very unpleasant, although it might help the smell of Marcenius. It was understandable, but did he have to stand so close? "So. Where do we go now?" she asked. It was Tom she was asking, but Marcenius assumed it was him.

"We could fly on to search for other people, or to find a nice place for you and me to settle down. I don't think there are any other people here. I learned enough gnome-language over time. They'd only ever seen one other giant like me. But he didn't look like us. He had black hair and an eagle nose. They found my nose very puzzling. They had him captive years ago, but he got away."

Alamaya's natural hair color was jet black, and she did have a distinctly aquiline nose. She'd always envied those pert button noses, but the Royal house of Corvin had beaks. Neither looking for a place to 'settle down' with this idiot, nor going in search of other people (although that had to be better), were any part of her plans. She had a life to get back to, God-mama to rescue, or failing that, avenge.

And she didn't want Tom as a lifelong cat either.

Fortunately he seemed to feel the same way about it, including sticking his claws into Marcenius's leg.

Marcenius tried to kick Tom.

"Don't you dare kick my cat!" snapped Alamaya. "Or I'll set the leopard on you."

"It scratched me," complained Marcenius. "Look, we'll have to get on. There might just be the two of us."

"Then there would shortly be just one of us."

"Mwrowr!" announced Tom, loudly getting onto the carpet, and sitting down. He turned his head to the snow leopard and addressed it with a questioning "Mwow." And the big cat got up and joined him. The cats sat on the mat, and waited. They waited in the fashion of cats, with that peculiar combination of the infinite patience of waiting to ambush prey, and mild exasperation with human slowness to do what was expected of them.

Alamaya joined the two cats. "Well, come on."

"But I thought we could sit together in the sun for a bit," said Marcenius.

"Fat chance. Now let's get this thing flying."

"But I'm still cold."

"That is true for me too, but I don't want to be wet as well," she said pointing at the clouds.

Marcenius looked gloomily at the clouds. "You shouldn't have come to Gnome-land then. It rains all the time here."

"It wasn't exactly my plan. Now, get on and let's fly. I'd leave you here except there's no room on my broomstick for the leopard. Tom seems to have taken a fancy to her." She skritched behind Tom's ears as she said this, and he contentedly snuggled into her, as if he had not a worry in the world.

Maybe he didn't. That was what humans had to do, even cursed princesses.

This time Alamaya stopped Marcenius from trying 'speed up' spells. Actually the carpet was fairly zipping along towards the mountain peaks.

"Where are we going?" asked Alamaya.

"I don't know... I told it to go that way... but it's not listening."

"You idiot. The opposite direction."

"I know," he said crossly. "But it's not doing that either. It's... it's doing its own thing."

"A homer!" said Alamaya, as it dawned on her. God-mama had talked about putting the spells on her broom for getting her home after a hard night out... but had eventually decided against it. 'Too much chance of falling off the broom. It's all very well if you have a carpet to lie down on. And besides I can always find a bed.' She could. It was a way home that Alamaya needed not a bed, and she had a feeling that interdimensional spells might not work. She knew none for keeping herself in a specific dimension. "Put it down," she said.

"What? I haven't picked anything up."

"The carpet." Honestly, he was thicker than Laney's boyfriends.

"But it is flying so well. And we don't know where we want to go."

"Yes we do." She was about to say exactly where she wanted to go, when it occurred to her that he might not want to go back to his old Master. So she settled on "I know how to get us back to ordinary people. Not gnomes. Now set the carpet down."

That the carpet would still do. Thinking about it, it was probably a sensible protection of its fringes from drunk magicians who wanted to throw up or get rid of some beer. It was whether it would consider that a mere pit-stop on its way home or not, that was worrying Alamaya. She had taken landmarks carefully and worked out precisely the direction they had been flying in – the opposite direction should be 'home'.

Tom and the leopard did get off and look around but they were plainly unimpressed with the spot, and sat down on the carpet again.

It appeared that the carpet was suitably deceived, and soon they were flying off back the way they'd come. Down the precise line over the same landmarks... Away from the mountains, and unfortunately, towards the clouds. The clouds were boiling up and over a cliff-edge. Whatever lay below was hidden in the cloud-mass pushing and shoving its way to get a chance to rain on the gnomes and their mountains.

The carpet was heading straight towards them. She could see the streamers of rain from here. And she could see what else was riding the updraft. So could the cats. Cats catch birds. But this bird was big enough to catch cats. Or flying carpets.

They'd seen it, and it had seen them, and was closing on them, flapping its enormous wings to gain height. Marcenius panicked. Alamaya had been listening and watching his spell-casting on the carpet. That was the down spell...

Which took them up to meet it.

꧁꧂

Emerelda, facing the menace in Hargarthius's tower, resigned herself to the fact that her reign as the wickedest witch in the west was probably over. She recognised the tide of shimmering, fuzzy looking grey goo seeping down the stairs. She also recognised the sound of armoured men breaking down a door, below. She could only hope Alamaya escaped in time, because the chances of her being spared – even as the princess, let alone as a cat, were not good.

Hargarthius flung a sizzling thunderbolt at the goo.

Had it been almost anything else it would have vaporised. He had an enormous level of power, even if his control was awful. As it was... the goo expanded slightly and the thunderbolt vanished. "Don't. You'll only make it come down faster. It is a gel-matrix of thaumato-absorbent nanny-whatsits. It absorbs magic. And I believe it is rather like being trapped in pork jelly, if you get into it."

"How do we stop it?"

"Mechanically, not magically, I am afraid. If we can get to the magic workers sending it, we could deal with them."

"Can we levitate...?" he asked.

She shook her head. "It will reach up for magic. In fact we'd better retreat now. If we can hold it out long enough I can set up a hyper-dimensional transfer gate. If not, well we'll be trapped in it, it'll set, rather like gelatine, and they can come and haul us out at their leisure."

"Back to my bed-chamber then," he said. "It has a very tight-fitting door."

"And it is suitable place to make a last stand with me," said the witch, with a shadow of her normal sense of humor.

🦋🦋🦋🦋🦋🦋🦋

On the roof of what would always be Estethius's Tower, to Chief Wizard Kolumnus, his team of wizards struggled.

"We need relief!" complained Targonius.

Kolumnus ignored him. Targonius was capable enough, but he had joined the Royal Council of Mages to avoid work. Kolumnus had to admit to himself that the tower must have huge amounts of magic. It was a little draining.

CHAPTER 18

BETWEEN A ROC AND A HARD PLACE

The vast eagle-like Roc swooped at them – amazingly fast, shrieking a challenge, with its talons reaching. Alamaya ducked, knowing even as she did it, that it was too little, too late.

Or it would have been, had the snow-leopard not lunged up to meet it. There was a tumbling chaos of wings and claws...

It was difficult to say which had which – the gigantic Roc had the snow leopard in one talon – but the snow leopard was clawing and biting.

"Turn around! After them!" yelled Alamaya.

"No. Must get away!" panted Marcenius frantically spell-chanting.

The carpet turned sharply in pursuit of the bird. Had she had time to think of it, Alamaya would have realized that in his fear Marcenius had forgotten to reverse the spell. Alamaya was too busy belabouring the head of the Roc with the broomstick to think. It tried to bite her, and Tom, somehow on her shoulder, jumped and clawed at the huge golden eyes. It let go of the leopard, which landed with a bloody thump on the carpet. The roc was blindly flapping, ripping at the carpet, and trying to bite, when it occurred finally to Alamaya that reversing turning it into a frog would be easier to fight.

The green frog wasn't very good at flying.

At least the carpet, even with the new rips, did keep doing that, although it was losing height, spiralling into the clouds.

Down, down and then down some more.

As she was trying to haul the wounded, bleeding, snow leopard properly onto the carpet, she caught, through the cloud, a glimpse of the cliff they were descending rapidly down. They weren't quite falling, but it was certainly very fast.

It was an enormous cliff, which she could have worked out without seeing it, because the air got thicker and warmer as they went lower. But Alamaya was too busy ripping pieces off Tom's robe to try and staunch the bleeding snow leopard's wounds to pay any attention. They came to a bumpy landing on the scree-slope next to the cliff.

Finally looking up from her task, Alamaya realized they'd landed in the nether-hells – or something rather like it. It was hot, the air thick... and the place dripped and oozed – even the scree-rocks were covered in hanging excrescences like faintly glowing snot. It had to be faintly glowing – the heavy cloud made it as dim as twilight down here. The air was full of the leathery flapping of something flying away and odd slithery sounds came from between the rocks... and Tom leaped off the carpet, stuck his nose in the air and bounded off across the rocks, leaving her to cope with the injured snow leopard. The leopard raised her head and licked the tears from Alamaya's face as she fought to staunch the blood. The leopard wept too. She was bleeding herself, but that didn't matter. "Help me," she yelled at Marcenius.

He unwound from a panicked ball, looked around – as Tom came back, meowing urgently. Tom weighed a fraction of what the injured snow leopard did, but to her surprise, he grabbed the snow leopard by the scruff of the neck and was trying to pull. For a moment, Alamaya wondered what he was doing, whether she should push him away – and then she got it. "Help me carry her!" she snapped at the hapless Marcenius. "Take that end of the carpet."

"Uh. Where to? We've got to get out of here," squawked Marcenius.

"Tom has found a place," said Alamaya, keeping her patience with difficulty. "Take that side of the carpet."

"The beast is dying. Just leave it. We have to find somewhere safe…"

"Pick it up or I'll turn you into a green frog too," snarled Alamaya, so he did.

They staggered after Tom who kept turning around and mewing at them. And there it was… an un-natural square cut hole in the cliff-wall. The cat turned and looked at them and stepped into it. A flapping leathery thing – all talons, teeth and lederhosen-with-wings flew out, shrieking. Alamaya ducked, barely in time, dropping her end of the carpet to fend it off with the broom which had been lying on the carpet.

Marcenius screamed and ran, still holding his end of the carpet. The snow leopard slid off. Alamaya looked for Tom inside the opening.

She could dimly see a figure there. A human. "Help me, for Zoryanthus's sake!" She didn't think about what a human was doing there or if they would help, she just grabbed the snow-leopard's front end and hauled into the opening.

And then could not pull any more.

Because she was a cat.

ଔଔଔଔଔ୧୧୧୧୧

Tom had smelled the broom closet even as they were descending the cliff. To think he'd ever been unhappy about the lavender-and-bleach reek of Long-haired Star (with 98% un-natural ingredients) containing beach, Aunt Chlorine and all sorts of other nasty things, tested on animals and toxic. Original abrasive cleaning powder! It co-mingled uneasily with the ConifirSoul, and had always smelled like it should be the gateway to the underworld, not the way out of it. Now, not even fish could smell as good.

He'd followed his nose – found the broom closet, and at least the Princess had been quick to catch on.

Things had gone slightly wrong when he'd stepped inside the closet. It wasn't as wide as the pantry, and turning human had knocked him into a bucket, with a mop and a cloth balanced on the end of the handle —and flung the dry, leathery smelly cloth from its roost to where it assumed its true nature. But looking back into the dimness as he struggled to his feet, Tom saw Alamaya swat it away and pull the injured snow leopard forward. He would have helped, but he knew, out there he'd be a cat.

And in here she was a cat.

And in here the injured snow leopard became a wounded cheese.

A very puzzled cat, who plainly expected him to answer the questions, and to get them out of here. Now. So, Tom, who was now naked, retrieved what was left of his robe, and tried his door opening spell.

The door cracked open — and the netherworld behind them closed, making this place even darker with just a crack of light out there.

Unfortunately what was outside the door into the tower began to ooze in.

And unfortunately the princess-cat was impatient. She put her front foot out claw at the door. Which immediately became a hand.

By the time Tom had managed to pull the door closed as much as possible, she was entirely human and showing him she could swear as well as the witch could. "That hurt! Um... could I have, some of that robe? What happened to the snow leopard?"

Tom bit his lip while he shrugged himself out of the remains of his robe, and handed it to her. He unwrapped the cheese from the other pieces of his robe. "It always was the cheese. It was... just different in that place." He stroked the cheese instinctively, and got a faint burring purr.

"Well we're not leaving it in here. Come on, we have to get out."

"We have to deal with that stuff," Tom pointed to the puddle. "It's pressing against the door. Nearly head-high, I guess, and that makes it hard to push open and it's oozing in here."

"What is it?" asked Alamaya.

"I dunno. Magical muck," said Tom who was used to cleaning magical muck up. He tied a piece of his torn robe around his waist — more to give him time to think than anything else. "We can try the ConifirSoul on it. That works on most things, and doesn't smell as bad as the Long-haired Star. There's a carboy of concentrate there on the shelf behind you."

Alamaya grabbed it and poured some onto the grey goo. It hissed and retreated. "Yes! If we can splash some out of this crack... Help me push," she said, determinedly.

"Um. Let me get my broom going. In my, er, your pocket, there should be a little vial with a couple of neeps eyes in it."

She fished it it out, handed it to Tom. "Why don't you put the cheese in your pocket?" he asked. It was a practical thing to do, seeing as he no longer had any pockets.

She wrinkled her nose. You could smell the cheese even above the pine-tar. "It's cheese. I mean..."

"It saved your life back there. And it's... sort of a friend."

"So it did. And I owe it my loyalty even if it does smell funny!" So she took it and put it in the pocket of the robe, as Tom stuck the neep's eye on with spit and activated the super-hooom-broom. The twigs writhed and reached and hit the patch where the goo had been...

The super-hooom broom made an odd whining noise. For a moment Tom was afraid the muck had killed it. But then it sucked even harder.

"Quick, some ConifirSoul," he yelled.

Whether it was the ConifirSoul or the sheer power of super-hooom, the broom was forcing its way out into the hallway. Alamaya leaned against the door next to him and poured some ConifirSoul onto her hand and flicked it out of the gap.

With a hissing and a furious hoooming they pushed out into the hall. Tom cleared gelatinous goo, as Alamaya flicked ConifirSoul. "Where to?" He shouted.

"The laboratory? The study? I don't know," shouted Alamaya, back at him.

By lack of decision they made their way towards the lab. "Master could be in there," shouted Tom.

But he was not. The place was awash with the gelatinous goo... and it seemed very close-walled. It was a small crowded room now, no space between the benches. The broom closet had seemed smaller too.

"It's shrinking," said Alamaya looking at the walls and roof.

"Like, you're telling me, dude," said a voice from the chamber pot. "Who called the fuzz?" asked the demon, peering out at them.

"Hariselden! What's happened?" shouted Tom above the noise of the super-hoom.

"Uncool stuff," said the demon actually sounding disapproving. "Like the fuzz didn't roll in and didn't break up the party."

He wasn't even bothering to lie subtly.

"Don't you know where the witch and Master Hargarthius are?" asked Tom.

"Like, dude, of course. They're sitting next to you."

As they plainly weren't, that answered the question.

"And this stuff?" asked Alamaya above the hooom –roar.

"It's a magical mystery tour. Just... put a spell on you. It makes you magic, chick."

"And you?" she asked.

"Oh yeah cat, it'd kill me."

Alamaya began drawing the seven circles in chalk on the newly cleared bench-top.

"Don't waste your time cat-chick," said the demon... climbing out of the pot. "The binding spells are spells too. That stuff dissolved them."

"So... what are you still doing here?" asked Alamaya. "I mean don't you have demon principalities to return to?"

The demon sighed smokily. Looked around as if he was scared he might be overheard. "Look. It sucks down there. Orders, orders, orders, giving them, taking them, step outta line and you're toast. Hierarchy is everything. And you know how hard it is to lie about everything? Here I got a nice little pad, deflower any flowers I feel like, good vibes, and no one checks to see if I am lying according to the current narrative..."

"So, will you help us to free God-mama and Master Hargarthius? Take this war to our enemies?" asked the Princess, sounding every inch of a Princess.

"Man, I wanna make lurve not war," said the demon putting his feet up.

"I could get you some pickles," said Tom, finally shutting the super-hooom down, as he'd run out of furry gray goo to hooom up, and it was threatening to clean the ceiling again. "For some help."

"Now that idea I really dig, cat," said the demon Prince.

Tom decided that probably meant 'yes'.

"We'll go and get them," he announced.

"If we have enough Conifirsoul," said Alamaya.

Tom smiled. "There's several full carboys in the cupboard here. And, hang on, there's that atomizer – it'll spray it. We could dilute it a bit."

Even diluted, the conifirsoul was as tough on grey goo as it was grime and dirt. And the high shelf provided fresh neeps' eyes.

So they went out of the laboratory and into the passage again.

The goo hadn't returned, and they were able to press on down to the kitchen... which was now not very far. As they got to the pantry door, and Tom shut the super-hooom broom down, Alamaya actually managed a laugh. "Back here... on this side of the door. We're cats, Tom. We always need to be on the other side of any closed door."

"But there always might be something better on the other side," said Tom, with perfect cat logic, opening the pantry door.

The raven flew out of there, with a cry of 'Nevermore', before the knight staggered out. Raised his sword, and dropped it to frantically pull at his visor.

Tom just kept repeating the spell, and sending in more mice. He opened the visor, and seven mice ran out... and then a green frog hopped off as the suit of armour fell over.

"It seems iron stops frog spells, but not mice spells," said Alamaya. "Look at the goo, Tom – it has come running." And indeed, it had, tendril of the furry slime flowed towards them.

Alamaya sprayed it, Tom got the hooom broom activated, and pushed it back. "Right. Let's get the pickles and get back to the laboratory."

"Do you think I should put the cheese back on its shelf? It's... it's gone very quiet."

"I suppose I could give it some milk," said Tom doubtfully. "I don't know much about healing cheese."

Alamaya stuck her hand into the pocket of what had once been Tom's robe... And pulled out... not a cheese... but two tiny golden vials, dented and damaged.

"Nevermore! Nevermore! Nevermore!" shrieked the raven triumphantly, flying around the pair of them, like something demented. Perhaps it was. It had plainly been trapped in the pantry for some time."

"I'll get the pickles," said Tom, rather sadly. He'd... got used to the cheese. And he'd recognised the faintest of hints of it about the snow leopard. Worked out that somehow, in gnome-land – where all the spells were reversed it must be what the cheese actually was. But Master Hargarthius had said that spells in the pantry – gnome-man's land – the place that was somewhere between here and elsewhere, were different again. No matter. He was glad to have found the vials, but rather missed the cheese... and the snow-leopard. That was an ally worth having, and rather feminine and graceful too.

Several jars in the pantry had been broken, more of a mess for a famulus to clean. Tom sighed. He collected an intact jar of pickled... chili peppers, He had no idea what those were or how they got there, but they'd have to do. When he came out again, he found the Raven sitting on Alamaya's shoulder.

So, armed with the jar of pickles and a raven they made their way back up the broad stairs and long passageway to the laboratory.

Alamaya shook her head. "Am I losing my mind, Tom? It's a long way now. It couldn't have been fifteen paces before. And the passage is wider."

Tom shrugged. Buildings changed. Or at least this one did. "The tower must be changing again. Growing."

Indeed, the laboratory was now the size of a ballroom.

"Hey man. Getting pretty spaced out in here," announced the bull-headed Demon Prince Hariselden, from a hammock in the corner. He was being waited on, hand and foot as it were, by half a dozen pink sylphs clad in skimpy pansy dresses. One of them was polishing his foot-talons, another brushing his long luxuriant hair, one kneeling with a silver platter, set with a filigree basket of red grapes, and a crystal champagne flute into which one was pouring bubbly pink liquid, one peeling grapes, and the final one languidly wielding a peacock feather fan.

Tom immediately worried that the raven, who detested demons, and this one in particular, might get into what could only be a losing fight. But the demon might have been invisible for all the attention it got. Instead the raven flew off to the corner, about some business of his own. "What's going on?" asked Tom, not thinking of trickery questions, then realizing he should have.

But he got a straight answer none-the-less. "Like, that stuff was sucking the magic out of this place... and now it is pouring back. But more than came out. High energy stuff, cat. There are sparks jumping out of the walls. The magicians outside are getting really scared and preparing to come down in force. They're busy putting on nano-proof waders. " He looked at the jar and intoned eagerly: "Magic shiltz you carry..."

"No. Pickles. You offered to help us if we brought pickles," said Tom

"The significance of the pickle!" said Hariseldon, gleefully. He snatched up the jar with an impossibly long arm and cracked it – and then poured half of it down his throat, pickle juice and all. Then he tossed a pickle each to the pink pansy sylphs... And his appearance changed too... a wolfish man with a mane of wild hair and billowing black-and pink smoke, flashing with of chrome and a thunderous roaring he yelled: "I like smokin' lightin'… heaving metal chunder!" And he made his words true as he raced out of the laboratory, followed by spinning, dancing shrieking pansy maenads.

"Do you think they can defeat the mages?" asked Alamaya, after they left.

Tom shrugged. "I don't know. I doubt it, but it buys us time."

"Time to do what?" she asked.

"Time to do what this famulus always does," said Tom. "Clean up the mess. Find Old Grumptious."

"Old Grumptious?"

"Master Hargarthius," explained Tom. "And the Witch Emerelda."

Alamaya gave him an enchanting gurgle of laughter. "Most of the time, knowing my God-mama, I'd say 'try in bed'. But now…?"

"The study. Or a captive," said Tom. He avoided even thinking 'Or dead.' Instead he called out. "Hey, Raven. We're going out."

In reply they got a noisy gargling noise from the far corner.

"Weird bird," said Alamaya. "What's it doing?"

"Eating something in one of those jars. Probably something it shouldn't," said Tom, with an accepting shrug, born of long experience with the raven. "Come on, let's go."

"I'll just fill the atomiser," said Alamaya, and did.

They went forth with the super-hooom broom and the mist of Conifirsoul to do battle against the grey goo in the halls of a tower that literally seemed to be growing behind them. It was also magnificently clean, even if it reeked of a devastated pine forest. In the distance, Tom could hear metallic booming music and a lot of screaming.

ৠৠৠৠৠ

"Hmph," said Master Hargarthius, looking around in the moonlit darkness, attempting to untangle himself from the Witch Emerelda. "I have dedicated a fair part of my life to researching other dimensions. I… was expecting something bigger."

"As the actress said to the bishop. I think we have ended up, unless I am much mistaken, inside a smart car," said the witch.

"What are you doing in my car?" asked a nervous female voice, from the near darkness beneath them.

"Yes," said another male voice, breathily. "We'll call the

cops."

"We can't call the cops, Johnny," said the woman. "Dylan would…"

"We're just leaving," Emerelda informed the dismayed couple. "As soon as I work out where the door is. Ah." The light came on and she could see that they were occupying very little space on top of a plump blond and a balding man, suitably dressed for the sport they'd plainly been engaged in. "In flagrante delicto."

Hargarthius struggled out of the door. He offered her a hand, untangling her limbs and making her way out, with a brief contact with the horn, that caused palpitations beneath her. It was plainly a popular – at least at night – little side road for couples wanting a bit of un-interrupted peace and quiet. "So," said the magician, looking around. "You know this flagrante delicto place well?"

"I've been there before, if not in this precise locality," admitted Emerelda.

"Charming place. The rain so is lovely and warm. And the swamp lights on those distant poles are fascinating. I wonder how they get the demons to hold it so still? So, what do we do now?"

"Well I don't think those two would appreciate being asked for a lift. So I think we walk towards the lights." The lights turned out to be from an approaching vehicle.

"A horseless chariot! I have always wanted to examine one," exclaimed the magician. "Why has it got those decorative blue and red lights on the roof? How do they color the swamp gas like that, and make it flare with such regularity?"

"You can ask the officer when he stops."

The policeman wound down his window and peered at them in the side mounted light. He blinked. Perhaps he wasn't used to seeing a red haired woman of somewhat fuller figure wearing her black-sequined gown walking in the rain with a straggly white-bearded man, his robe embroidered with stars and moons, and a tall pointed hat on his head, on his patrols. Still his: "What in hell are you doing out here in your bathrobe, grandad? And can't you afford a better class of working girl at your age?" was probably not the best choice of words any law-enforcement officer has ever made.

As Emerelda drove them back towards the lights of

civilization she did her best to explain that, really, the officer was quite correct in thinking the translation spell was disrespectful bad language. She wasn't sure how well newts heard or understood, but at least they didn't use firearms very well. She was mildly amused at being taken for a working girl. She'd retired years ago.

They left the police cruiser in town with its windows open to keep the newt damp until it recovered, and flew off on someone's yard-broom, which at least meant they could fly above the clouds to the home she maintained here. It was a fairly normal apartment, but Hargarthius enjoyed the lights, and the water-features in the bathroom. He was rather sorry to leave it, when she told him she had the spell ready for the interdimensional transfer.

They arrived – as she'd planned, some distance from Hargarthius's Tower, next to a little copse on a hillock.

Even so, looking at it from the edge of the copse, they were still not far from the army encamped around it. "I'd guess that the entire might of Ambyria is massed against us," said Hargarthius.

"Yes. I think that would be very accurate," said Emerelda. "Mind you, it seems a lot of effort, considering the size of your Tower." She pointed. It was a small, squat building now. At this distance they could barely see it, and it was almost dwarfed by the pavilions of Ambyria's kinghood, and indeed the siege-engines that had been brought along. It was not at all what it had been when she'd arrived there to see if she could find Esthetius's brain.

He sighed. "It was largely a magical construct. They're sucking the magic out of it." He grimaced. "It wasn't much of a place, but it was all I had. Well, I suppose we had better disguise ourselves and go in search of that boy and your 'cat'."

She looked at the remains of his tower. At the army assembled around it, and knew that she still had to go in. It was not likely that she'd succeed in finding Alamaya, or that she would escape undetected. That would probably mean getting killed. "Why are you going, Hargarthius?" she asked quietly.

"Hmph. I suppose because I have to," he answered retreating into his grumpiness.

"You could walk away. There are other countries, and

you're still an able magician. There's not much left there," she said.

"Hmph. I can't just leave the famulus. He was more of a cat than a boy. Annoying, under your feet, but I ended up... well, being used to him, more than most of the boys that were ever in service there. He caught mice well. He was more useful than most boys. More useful than princesses, for that matter," he said loftily.

"I've a duty to that one, and she's a Tindrell and a Corvin."

"Well, that's your business," said Hargarthius. "The house of Corvin seems to have been a disaster for Ambyria for the nearly forty years. Do nothing but primp about court, get married and die."

It was true enough, but she felt obliged to defend the girl. "That's a bit harsh, seeing as they're cursed to do that."

"The girls could have stayed unmarried. Her mother was a weak figurehead, interested in clothes and pleasing herself, and by all accounts this one seems the same."

That was not unfair either, Emerelda admitted to herself. "Give her a chance. She's been cosseted to death. And at least Alamaya has shown a bit of rebellion and, I believe fought off foes with your boy. The Corvins were great rulers once. First in war, first in hardship, honourable to the death. And being a cat has probably taught her a few things."

He pointed at the army's tents. "And that lot probably would eat a cat. Which is another reason to rescue them, if we can. It was a risky disguise, Emerelda."

The old curmudgeon was fond of the boy, in his odd way, although he'd never admit it, realized the witch, but all she said was: "She did it to herself, by accident. Well, a sort of accident. With ontogenetic reflux liquid."

"Dangerous stuff," said the magician.

"You're telling me. I ended up with a minotaur, not a handsome young stud," admitted Emerelda. "Anyway, I suppose we will need to be quite careful about changing our shape or appearance. I imagine the Chief Wizard will have his little sycophants looking for us trying to escape, so they'll expect magical disguises. I have some make-up in my purse, but clothes I should have thought of."

"They may be confused by us going the wrong way, rather like those two," said Master Hargarthius, pointing. Approaching the copse were two people, walking with studied insouciance – one was young woman who had, by appearances, recently been a milkmaid, before taking up the new and more lucrative profession of washer-woman, doing some scrubbing for the army. The other a man-at-arms, a sergeant, by the looks of him. It was their intention to reach the privacy of woods, to spend some time with nature.

As newts they were able to get very close to it, and had no need of their clothes, which were non-magical and at least roughly the right size for Hargarthius and Emerelda.

"The beard has to go," Emerelda informed the magician, taking a pair of scissors out of her shoulder-bag.

He clutched onto it. "Absolutely NO. What's a magician without a beard?"

"Less recognisable? Look, let me just trim it."

That, he very reluctantly let her do. As she cut it an inch off his chin, she reflected that it would teach him a lesson. At his age he ought to know better than to trust a woman with scissors.

"You look a lot younger," she said, soothingly, as he felt for his absent beard. It was true too, even if that was merely sixty instead of ninety.

"A magician is not supposed to look young," he protested. "I spent years cultivating that beard. I used to have to dye it white."

"Well," she said, reaching into her purse. "Now I'm planning to dye it black. And then I will add a bit of makeup to ease those wrinkles."

"Knowledge lines," he muttered. But he didn't stop her.

A little later a sergeant-at-arms, and a washer-woman possibly of flexible virtue – because she was definitely bulging out of that blouse – set off toward the army encampment. The spear on the scowling black-bearded sergeant's shoulder probably wouldn't stand close scrutiny – It was a real spear-head on the end, and the runes on the staff were somewhat disguised with dirt. Her shoulder-bag wouldn't stand examination either, for that matter, but then, why would anyone be looking. As they walked closer, something very odd began to happen.

The tower – which was barely twenty feet high, perhaps three squat levels… started to grow.

It did not grow in direct proportion, but rather with a bulge around the middle. But it was now at least forty foot tall, looking rather like a very pregnant woman with a thin short leg, a huge bulging midsection... and a tiny little upper story...

It did make approaching the army and the tower a lot easier. Everyone was now looking at that, not at arbitrary sergeants and washerwomen. There was a lot of shouting and chaos going on, as is typical of most military campaigns, at that well-known usual stage, when the plans go awry. You'd think soldiers would be used to it by now, thought Emerelda.

And then a strange and terrible sound echoed across the camp. Well, strange and terrible for Ambyria. About normal for a bunch of bikers.

Emerelda realized there was something noticeable about her and Hargarthius – most of the washerwomen, camp-followers, sellers of useful bric-a-brac to take home (because even if there wasn't any loot, mama or the girlfriend or both would be expecting something) quite a few soldiers, and a lot of horses, were going the other way, as fast as possible.

The sound of demonic full-volume song came booming out of the tower.

"Like a true denatured chili'
We were burn,
Burn to the Vi...illie!"

It echoed out over the hills and valleys, and the tower continued to grow – still perched on its narrow little stalk – but growing wider and taller.

Order began to sound out of chaos, with trumpets and marshals and heralds – some of whom were yelling "All mages to the Chief Wizard. All mages to the Chief Wizard."

"What do we do now?" asked Hargarthius. "I hope my tower doesn't fall over."

"I suppose," said Emerelda, "We could go to the Chief Wizard. I'd guess that's the Demon Prince loose in your tower."

"Undoubtedly. I'd guess that my famulus must, therefore, also be in there. The binding spells on the demon where placed by him," said Hargarthius, sounding hopeful.

She hated to shatter those hopes, but the truth might serve better: "The grey goo may well have freed him."

"Well then I hope Prince Hariselden devours the Chief Wizard before they bind him." He sighed. "But he shouldn't be too much trouble for any one of half a dozen mages that Kolumnus has on his staff."

"It seems like they're having trouble or they wouldn't be calling for help," said Emerelda.

"Sergeant-at-arms. You're supposed to be massing the footmen for the attack on the lower door," shouted someone who was doing his best attempt at trying to be in control.

"But officer," said Emerelda. "He is supposed to be guarding me. On orders from Duke Karst himself."

"Oh," Then he took in her appearance. "Who are you?" A considerable amount of doubt, mixed with caution was voiced in that question.

"Oh, this is a disguise. I'm one of the Chief Wizard's staff. I'm going to him now, as soon as I get to my broom." She pointed to several brooms and a carpet lofting towards the now very high tower-top. "We were incognito, watching, in case the occupants attempted to flee magically. No word of anyone getting out?"

"No, Ma'am," said the officer, respectfully. "The orders were to wait until the magical gel solidified. We did lose one knight before we had to pull back... I'd better get on. Sergeant, report to your post as soon as you're done."

Hargarthius managed to say: "Sir." Instead of simply turning the man into a newt.

"Now all we need is a broom," said Emerelda.

"A carpet," said the Magician firmly. "I can manage a levitation spell without any fancy factory installed spell-work in the weave. Of course it is different getting it to go far."

In spite of the circumstances it was enough to bring a twitch of humor to the Wickedest Witch's lips. Male mages didn't ride brooms. It was too phallic, apparently. Well, respectable witches didn't ride ever carpets either. Emerelda had never found them as comfortable as a broom, or a swan or even a hippogriff. "You rode on a broom with me in that other dimension," she pointed out slyly.

"Hmph. That was there, not outside my own tower, which seems to be growing out of hand."

It was. It was a good two hundred feet tall by now, and the stone-work looked new. And it was still balanced on a narrow, short little stalk.

Fortunately, the nearest knight's pavilion provided both a birch-broom and a small carpet to satisfy both of them.

CHAPTER 19

UP, UP, ONTO THE RING OF FIRE

They made a good cleaning team, reflected Tom, as he and Alamaya followed in the demon's wake, with the building growing steadily behind them.

They found the skull just short of what Tom hoped would be the Master's study – the ever-changing geography of the house was confusing. He couldn't even follow his nose because it all smelled of conifirsoul. It was definitely a skull, but Tom was honestly not sure if it had belonged to Mrs Drellson or not.

It was now merely a dry skull, lying there.

"It's probably the one that haunted your kitchen," said Alamaya, with a shudder.

"Mrs Drellson. The housekeeper. I knew her well. She was only mostly bad," said Tom, regretfully. It seemed everything familiar was getting destroyed. First the Tower, then the cheese, and now

Mrs Drellson.

"Ugh."

"She didn't worry you when you were a cat," said Tom.

"I seemed to be missing a part of me then."

"Anyway, she was defending the tower. Us."

"Oh. Yes. That is different, you know. Loyalty calls for loyalty. We'd better put her somewhere safe, until she can be buried with honor," said Alamaya, and she picked the skull up.

She wasn't being in the least sarcastic. Tom had taken to sarcasm. It was natural cat behaviour. Maybe going through the insecurity of gnomeland had changed the Princess. She was... different somehow. He didn't mind honouring the skull, but he'd rather have had it spitting green lightning and telling them to work faster and harder, and to scrub the cracks between the stones properly. That might not be nice, but would at least be familiar. But all he said was: "I think that's the study."

It was, but it too had been afflicted by the magic being drawn out. It was merely a small untidy room full of books and fuzzy grey goo. The eerie vastness of it was lost. Even the books were just books. The poor flying carpet was rolled up on the edges of the little room - and very dull. The room – as they hooomed and ConiferSouled it, was growing and changing – but it didn't reveal a magician or a witch.

"I'm going to need some more ConifirSoul," yelled Alamaya above the hooom. "And do you see much point in getting all of the goo out? We should just go on."

"No point in leaving it behind us. It might creep out and get us. Besides, if Mrs Drellson's skull taught me anything it's that there is no point in doing half jobs," answered Tom, going on sucking. "Just give me another minute and we can go back to the lab. Master Hargarthius kept ordering more ConifirSoul. There must be eighteen bottles of it back in the lab."

"We could try your master's bedroom first. This is my God-mama we're talking about, and it is the next room," said Alamaya.

It was. It was also empty, although getting the door open was difficult. The cracks proved to be jammed – from the inside – with torn sheet.

"I guess this was where they went to. But unless the goo devoured them and didn't even leave bones..." Alamaya left that hanging.

"It left the skull," pointed out Tom.

That cheered her up. "Then they escaped. Magic I suppose."

"What now?" asked Tom. "We're beaten without them."

"We do not admit defeat," said Alamaya lifting her chin. "The skull of Mrs Drellson would have us finish the job, so we will. As soon as we have more ConifirSoul."

So they walked the now immense distance to the lab.

"Did you close the door?" asked Alamaya as they got there.

"No. I left it open so the raven could get out."

"Well, it's closed now," she said, opening it and stepping through before he could advise caution.

But there proved no need for that caution. The laboratory was high-roofed and huge now, but silent. There was no sign of trouble, or even of the raven.

"I wonder how he got out?" asked Tom.

"Maybe there's a new window. Where would be a good place to put the skull?"

"Pick a spot," said Tom, looking around, warily walking about, to check the extent of the new larger area for a magician to fill with debris, foul smokes, and flying glass.

"Next to my royal grandmother, I think," said Alamaya walking to the Raven's favorite perch, the bust of Athena. Then she said... "Eugh. Tom. Come and have a look at this."

So Tom did. As a semi-feral young cat he'd seen a few lamb carcasses that the crows had been busy with, and been hungry enough to scavenge some of the remains. He knew the look of dagger-beak marks in soft tissue... like a brain.

Estethius's brain had been dragged out of its vat. The raven had devoured the frontal lobes and a fair bit of the rest.

They weren't going to be asking any more questions of the evil magician. Not without necromancy, or re-animating raven droppings.

"So that's what he was eating," said Alamaya.

"It might have eaten him too," said Tom, warily. "Because he's not in here, and he never ever closed a door behind him."

"Birds don't," said Alamaya.

"Any more than cats do," said Tom. "Mrs Drellson's skull and Old Grumptious, they were forever lecturing me about it. Except for the pantry door. That they always said to leave open."

"And did we ever find out why! So, what do we do now?" she asked.

"Well, talking of the pantry, and if we're going to die or whatever... the goo is obviously still shutting off the top of the tower, so we might as well go get some food and not die hungry.

And I'd love a drink of milk."

Alamaya blinked. "So would I. And I'm not fond of milk. Well, I didn't used to be. I only drank some as a cat because I was thirsty. Now even thinking about it is making my mouth water a bit."

So they went down the long passages toward the kitchen. Which had become kitchens, large, lofty, with multiple fire-places and spits hung with strange black implements.

The grey goo was a small puddle by the far door.

The pantry door was still there. Unfortunately so was a large, and largely naked knight, fumbling though his armour.

Emerelda rapidly became aware, as they headed towards the tower, that once again they were heading in the wrong direction to be unobtrusive. Witches, magicians, warlocks, wizards – the magical establishment of Ambyria – were all deserting the tower. Some on wobbly brooms, and some on burning carpets. And some were just jumping, which wasn't going to end well, unless they had very good ground-softening spells.

One of them would be all right, because he hit Hargarthius's slow-rising carpet.

Moments later, before she had a chance to see what happened to her co-conspirator, she wished for ground-softening spells herself. She should have thought of the speed of travel blowing her hood back. The blast from the Chief Wizard blew the bristles off her broom and sent it spiralling out of control.

Fortunately, the tower expanded just then and let her make a crash-landing onto a scene of chaos. Unfortunately, it was still stone and a hard landing, even if cushioned by a large gelatinous blob of magic-devouring furry grey goo. Half the roof was on fire – or at least dancing with wild hoops of flame, and the air reverberating with:

"The ghost pepper went down, down, down, And the flames burned higher!"

Emerelda struggled to her feet as, on the far parapet, Hargarthius pulled himself up. His carpet had been sluggish, and bombed by a second person – but the lower line might have been a safer approach.

He was trading spells with four mages... while busy rising on a carpet with a burning fringe.

And then she lost sight of him in the wall of fire that surrounded her. She tried to raise a defensive spell... and failed.

She realized she was splattered with sticky goo from her landing. She ripped the stolen cloaked and hooded washerwoman's clothing off, and used it wipe the muck away. The stuff was terribly magically draining. She stood there in the remains of her underclothes, as maniacal burning agonized-shrieking pansy maenads whirled around her in a circle of fire. She just couldn't muster the energy for the magic she needed...

And then a swooping broomstick came over the flame wall.

Hargarthius's control was erratic, possibly because he was flying one handed – the other wielding his staff from which he sprayed a shower of ice crystals. Or possibly because he was a rotten flyer. It didn't really matter. He was there and she gratefully sat on the shaft behind him and they made a wobbling ascent.

"I thought you didn't approve of broomstick-flying for men?" she said, holding on tight.

"They're faster than carpets. And someone had left one on the parapet. I lost the carpet to some fat wizard. Anyway, I think one has to move with the times," said the magician loftily.

"Where are the times going?" she asked.

"The other end of the tower. The broom is struggling to fly. And I have an out-of-hand demon to deal with."

At least he had the tact, wisdom or mere luck not to say anything about weight, reflected Emerelda. And she had the tact not to mention the fact that he knew broom-flying spells.

They swayed and lurched toward the roof...

And out of the flames stepped the handsome figure of the demon prince: "Did you think I would leave you frying, when there's room on my broom for two!" crooned Hariseldon. Then he sniffed. "Oh man. That's so emotional. I'm a demon. We're not set up to deal with this kind of thing. It's like, un-demonic to cry."

Hargarthius was quick enough to realise there was no need to try binding. Instead he asked the demon, almost politely: "Just what is going on here? What made the tower grow?"

"Like those cool cats sucked the magic eating stuff into the inverse-universe, so instead of drawing magic out of everything it touched, it was drawing it out of those mages and their spell-gel. Only, see, only way back here is through the portal and that's like closed, man. So it all went into the place between, where this place is. Where it grows from. And all that power poured into this place. Like, you should see what it did to the pansies. Hot babes, man!"

"Do you understand any of that?" Hargarthius asked Emerelda.

"Other than I think he means your Tom and my God-daughter – the cool cats, I gather – did it, no, not really." She wondered whether she was strong enough to constrain the demon, let alone battle with it, because it was plainly free. If the other mages felt as exhausted as she did, no wonder they fled and failed.

The demon prince yawned – a terrifying sight – had it not been accompanied by: "Sorry. Man. I'm tired. I think I'll just have a little lie down and catch some rays, and chill with a bit of their burnin' luurve." The pansies were burning lethargically. An agile witch could have jumped over the ring of flames around them, now.

Hargarthius tugged what was left of his beard. "Demons do not like sunlight," he said.

Hariseldon shook his head – suddenly wearing a broad-brimmed hat – at them. "Dude, that is like *so* yesterday. Now sunshine almost always makes me say hi." And he wondered placidly away, ignoring them, spreading himself out and changing into a vast daisy, surrounded by wilting pansies, their painted faces turned worshipfully inwards.

"And now?" asked Hargarthius, quietly speaking to Emerelda.

"And now I think we go downstairs, before we have to deal with him, and find out what your famulus and my God-daughter have been up to," said Emerelda. "I think the tower-top is safe enough for now."

So they made their way down the wide stair, avoiding the occasional sad furry lumps of magic devouring gel.

The magician sniffed. "ConifirSol. That boy has been cleaning again. He likes the stuff. The way he goes through it, I'd swear he drinks it. Still, that is better than my last famulus. He drank everything."

It did indeed smell rather strong in the new vast halls of the tower. Emerelda was wishing it slightly less vast, with the amount of bruising her crash-landing had given to her derriere. "Where do think they might be?"

"Hmph. Probably in the kitchen," said Hargarthius. "The boy has a relentless appetite."

ஒ௸௸௸ஒஒஒஒ

The knight had plainly been in search – besides of more clothing, which right now for him seemed to consist of two dish-towels – for weapons to defend himself. He had a long, thin dagger in hand as he stared at them "Princess Alamaya!" he exclaimed, just as she was getting ready to turn him back into a green frog. It seemed that his brush with the grey goo had cured that.

"Yes," said Alamaya, relaxing slightly. She recognized him as one of the royal guard. She was, oddly, for the first time in her life mildly irritated by his lack of respect. Perhaps being out of Borbungsburg castle had made her more aware of these things. It wasn't that the guards and knights and courtiers didn't go through the forms and appearances of respect, normally. But their posture and tone were just not what they were when dealing with Duke Karst. Suddenly, that really annoyed her. She was the Corvin! The last surviving member of the royal house. "Why do you not bow, Sirrah?" she asked.

His answer was a lunge with the misericorde in his hand. "A Borbung!" he shouted.

Alamaya barely avoided being skewered. The blade sliced across her side, as she dived sideways, and rolled... against the wall. Standing over her he prepared to strike again, his face a vicious mask of hatred and triumph. "We knew you were here, bitch. Now I will kill you. A-Borbung!"

Only his lunge plunged the dagger into Tom, basically as Tom thrust between them and hit him with the broom.

ஒ௸௸௸ஒஒஒஒ

Tom knew the sensible cat-thing was to set his broom to drubbing the knight, and to run. Conjuring a mouse wasn't going to do much.

Only he wasn't prepared to be sensible and catlike.

The shock of being stabbed numbed the pain. Briefly.

It disordered his senses quite a lot. He saw both Alamaya and somehow, the snow-leopard blurring into and out of each other, and heard her voice rather like a roar, cry as she sprang up and grabbed his broom: "You will die for that, traitor. I swear by the raven. By my ancestors' noble name..."

"Spell..." said Tom weakly.

And someone came running at a loping trot. A short, spare, hook-nosed man, with ragged salt-and-pepper hair. He was barefoot, in badly-fitting, too-big clothes... with a sword. "I'll deal with him, granddaughter. You see to the boy."

♨♨♨♨♨⚵⚵⚵⚵

Alamaya recognised the shade she had summonsed.

King Uther's portrait still hung in the halls of Borbungsburg Castle, even if he had vanished. It wouldn't have mattered. He looked like every other Corvin noble: Hook-nosed, dark haired, sharp eyed. She might have wondered why her grandfather's ghost was wearing such odd clothes but she was too busy kneeling next to Tom, pressing him down as he tried to stand up.

He coughed some bloody spittle, possibly from biting his tongue. "Need... need to go. 'way. Alone."

"Shut up and lie still," she said, knowing all too well the cat instinct to crawl away and die.

"Hurts..."

The stab wound in his chest bled. Alamaya forced herself to be calm, to hold back the tide of rage at the man who had stabbed him and her grief, and to simply prop his head on her knee. "I'm going to try and stop the bleeding and get help." He was dying and she knew it and was terrified by it. But now was not the time to allow fear or sadness to take over.

♨♨♨♨♨⚵⚵⚵⚵

Emerelda heard the shout of: "A Borbung!" echoing up the stairs and started running. So did Hargarthius.

They both arrived out of breath, gasping in the kitchen.

Too late.

Too late for the Borbung knight anyway.

King Uther looked at them. "What took you so long?" he asked, his bloody sword in hand.

"God-mama! I need help!" called Alamaya, very much in human form now, and dressed in the famulus's robe, or part of it. Tom wore a kilt of the rest, and some blood. Emerelda was relieved that it seemed to be coming out of him, not the girl.

Emerelda was no magical healer, but she'd seen a few wounds in her time. She also knew which side of the body the heart was on. There was a fair chance that he'd missed getting that stabbed, but there were still arteries to be cut. He might just recover – people did. He might have a chest cavity filling with blood. Or he might not. It was hard to tell, and medicine lagged far behind in this world. "We'll get him to a healer, dear. They have some good physicians back in America. The Tindrell cousins have connections."

"Hmph. You're not allowed to die, boy. There's still a mess to be cleaned up here." Emerelda was surprised to see a tear trickling down Hargarthius's cheek.

"Master?" said Tom, weakly. "Is that you?" He blinked his eyes to try and focus on the black-bearded face.

"Yes. It was very undignified to have my beard cut and dyed, but necessary. Now you are to recover speedily or I may change my mind about promoting you from famulus to apprentice."

"Apprentice...?" asked Tom.

"Hmph. Yes. Time I passed my skills on. All these stairs will kill me. Come now Emerelda. Prepare that interdimensional transfer."

"I hope I have the strength. That gel took it out of me, even briefly."

"You must. You MUST. He got stabbed to save my life," said Alamaya. "Or I must try. I'm not very good at it yet. Of course I can activate a return-spell if you've got one."

"You can talk me through it," said Hargarthius.

King Uther intervened. "You will do that, Emerelda. This is a Royal command. Instruct Old Grumptious here. He's a powerful, if self-taught magician."

"What did you call me?" said Hargarthius drawing himself up.

Uther simply stared at him. "Get on with it. They can't get in the lower door. It's got a portcullis now. I had just been to check on it when this Borbung tried to kill my Grand-daughter. I'll go and have a look from the tower-top to see what is happening out there. The boy was good to me. Fed me and talked to me."

"You?" asked Hargarthius.

The king looked down his long nose and said: "Nevermore. Do you know what it is like to have only one

useless word to communicate with? Now get on with it. But I was trapped in that form until I killed Estethius, to fulfil my oath. Now get on with it before I notch your other ear." And he walked off.

❦❦❦❦❦❦❦

Chief Wizard Kolumnus closed his eyes. He had a blinding headache, and felt magically as weak as a new-born kitten. The Demon Prince and his maenad entourage had played their weapon against him and his mages. They'd stayed safe in the bound of the gel, and bombarded the roof-top with deafening sound, and flame. Added to the fact that somehow the spell was going wrong, drawing magical power out of those setting it in motion, and the disconcerting fact that the tower was getting taller by the second had made some of his staff, and those he'd co-opted, desert. Some of them.

Others had died instead.

And then that red-haired bitch had counterattacked. Well. She'd got her comeuppance at least.

But he still had an army, and he still had Duke Karst.

And he still had a final defensive trap. The Wickedest Witch was burned to a crisp. If Hargarthius died, well, he could deal with whatever else remained. He would take control over this well of power… as he always intended.

Then they'd learn a lesson Ambyria would never forget.

CHAPTER 20

IN WHICH WE ARE NOT AMUSED

—————▶•◀—————

om found his second visit to the world of clubbing rather different, and less pleasant. He'd had to leave even his trusty broom behind or he could have used it on the fellow who stuck needles into him. That was why witches used dolls for that. The dolls didn't complain, or try to bite. Alamaya stopped him doing more than that. They allowed her to remain with him, on account of him being foreign.

The clubbing world was strange. They didn't seem to get that *they* were foreign, and he was a cat.

But he was also a cat who was feeling somewhat better and no longer needing to hide away.

They sent him for a Cat scan. They were very puzzled by his tail. The next time he went through their magic iron donut he put it down. Obviously the tail invisibility spell Alamaya had put on it didn't work too well on the device. Well. It was a Cat scan after all.

"You've been very lucky, Mr Tindrell," said the young man that Alamaya addressed as 'Doctor'. "Managed to miss your lung and any major blood vessels. It was plainly a very narrow-bladed knife. An inch either way, would have had you in in trouble."

"So can I go back to the tower now?" asked Tom. Misericords had to be narrow to stick in through chinks in the armour.

"I think we need to keep you in for observation tonight."

Tom wasn't too sure he liked being watched, but it did come with supper. Fish. And when he asked, milk.

✨✨✨✨✨✨✨

Emerelda had to admit that she didn't really like giving away hard-learned secrets, but that under the circumstances it was justified.

"It's less hard than I expected," said Hargarthius. "I can't get down to the cellars yet, so wine is not available but can I offer you some beer?" he asked.

"In the absence of wine that will do nicely," said Emerelda. "It's easier to access that place than most of the other dimensions, simply because it so very close. Things leak across. Look at the demon for instance..."

"I'd rather not look at the demon," said King Uther, returning from the upper stories of the tower. "Not after he seduced my late wife. Yes, I know, he was just doing his job, and he saved my grand-daughter. But I still don't have to like him. You can draw me a mug too, while you're at it. There is quite a lot of chaos out there, and I think it will be a good half hour before they can organise a battering ram. And the roof is overpopulated by a demon prince and his entourage sleeping it off in the sun. I closed the portcullis and a heavy iron door on my way down, just in case.

"I didn't know I had those," admitted Hargarthius.

"You didn't. They're new. The tower probably decided it needed them. I noticed it changed over the years. It's alive, you know, grows to fit what is inside it. Ah. My thanks." He took the tankard of beer. Drank. "You have no idea how nice it is to drink properly, instead of taking a beak-full and tipping it down your throat."

"Erhm. My liege," said Master Hargarthius awkwardly. "I apologise that I may have treated you with some disrespect in the past... I wasn't aware... I would have done my best to lift the spell."

"Think nothing of it," said King Uther with kingly grace. "Besides, you were generally not unpleasant. You fed me, and I don't think that you, or anyone, could have broken the enchantment. I was a party to it, in my folly. And a spell enacted with the will of the bespelled is hard to break. I had to kill Estethius, and I had to do so as a raven. That was my oath. Besides, I was spying on you."

"Spying on me?" Hargarthius shook his head. "But what was I doing wrong?"

"Nothing. But I didn't know that. I assumed at first that you might actually be Estethius. Once I had decided that no, you were simply too un-skilled at magic, and teaching yourself, well I decided you must be hiding him, somehow. I was very ready to kill you. But my ten years trapped among the gnomes had taught me a lot about patience and something about cunning."

"Gnomes are not mythical then?" asked Emerelda. The beer wasn't bad, really.

"No, unfortunately not," said King Uther with a grimace. "After I managed to fly in here – the Enchantress Saliana had transformed me into a raven so I could fulfil the prophecy and have the raven kill Estethius, I found him in the pantry. I was... too hasty. He managed to knock me down with his staff and flee, closing the pantry door. When that door is closed... well, another opens, into Gnomandy. Unfortunately, there, spells are reversed."

"Unfortunately?"

"Rather so. I was a man, stark naked, and trapped in a foreign country. I walked into their little village. They stuck out for bait in a roc trap in the gnome village. I learned the language, tried to talk my way free, all the while working to escape. It took me the better part of a year to escape, digging by night, hiding my tunnel with cobbles and rubbish they threw at me. First with my fingers, then with scraps of stone, then with a bone using the stream to wash my dug dirt away. Then it took me another nine years of living as fugitive monster and bandit – a giant to them – to trace a rumor of how I might get back. I had to climb down the cliff and fight monsters and search... I could not believe how fast my grand-daughter and the boy made it back from that place. I thought I might have to organize a military intervention. Still, it was safer for them, than here. Desperate times called for desperate measures."

"Er. How did they get there?"

"They hid from the knights who had come in the hidden back door. I suspect it was not as hidden as you had thought. One of them chased me – as a raven – into the pantry. I managed to stop him going into Gnomandy, which turned out just as well. He broke quite a few jars. I thought that cheese might get him, but it didn't. Anyway, I was bracing myself to going back through Gnomandy to the broom-cupboard, when the boy and my grand-daughter opened the door. I was expecting the Chief Wizard Kolumnus, but it was them. They were back and had found the golden vials. So I went ahead and killed Estethius, as he no longer had anything we needed, which freed me from my geas. Thirty-seven years too late, of course."

"You killed Estethius?"

"Yes, thoroughly. I ate his brain to be sure." The King rubbed his stomach. "Fortunately ravens are not squeamish, but it has given me indigestion. And now that I have my body back, the Corvin honor is redeemed, I expect you two to break that curse." He looked down his nose at them. "And it seems I will have to reclaim my kingdom, because we have an infestation of Borbungs."

"What happened to the royal 'we'?" asked Emerelda dryly.

"I think I left it in Gnomandy," said the King with a belch. "Pardon. I've been a raven for a long time, and they're not known for the delicacy of their court manners."

"I don't know how bad the infestation is, but it is going to be… interesting, convincing them that King Uther has returned after… nearly forty years, looking not much older. Maybe ten years or so," said Hargarthius.

"That'll be the time in Gnomandy," said King Uther. "I didn't seem to age as a raven. That was about all it had going for it."

Emerelda looked at her empty tankard again, hopefully. She sighed. The amount of training one had to put into men, these days. "Your grand-daughter, King Uther, is your key. Alamaya is recognised, and accepted. There might be a few Borbung supporters among the nobility, but not that many. Most of the noble houses still bind to the Corvins. With her at your side, I think most of the nobility would also be loyal and recognize you. She's… I would guess, not keen to rule. She was trying very hard to escape it."

"She was as regal as any queen, facing down that Borbung!" said Uther. "I was proud of her. I thought it would be safer for her in this other world, Emerelda. But we may have to get her back."

"She seems to have grasped loyalty at last, if only to a cat. Well, he's boy too."

"How long must he be with the leeches in this foreign world?" asked Hargathius. "And will they cure him? He's the best famulus I've ever had, even if he does get underfoot, and ask far too many questions. And use a lot of ConifirSoul. I must admit I don't like the smell"

"The grey goo didn't like it either," said King Uther. "That and that broom of his. He stuck a neep's eye on it, and it sucked like... like a pack of lampreys, but far more powerfully.

"A neep's eye! What will that boy do next?" asked Hargarthius.

"I don't know," said Emerelda. "But we might as well use the technique to get rid of the remaining gel. That way we can get down to the cellars and find some wine."

So they did. They also found a former bouncer, who was singing religious songs, having been a newt and then not a newt, and buried up to his neck in grey furry jelly. As Emerelda was tired of cleaning and her bruise was sore, they took him upstairs to the kitchen, gave him a mug of beer and set him to cooking supper.

He had more talent for that, than for being a newt.

Tom was glad to be 'discharged'. He was slightly disappointed to discover that he was not magically proof against being charged. "That would have been useful," he said, as they climbed into the taxi. "Seeing as we... well I, have to go and rescue Old Grumptious. I mean he's a curmudgeon who nearly squashed me, but he'll probably forget he's being attacked because he just thought of a new line of research."

"God-mama is just about as bad," admitted Alamaya. "But... uh, there is my Grandfather... well, he looked like the picture of him in the hall of ancestors."

"The raven. Huh. Well, he never got distracted. Except by food. Where is this horseless carriage taking us?"

"It's one of my return-spells. God-mama prepared them for me.

You remember. You used one."

"Yes, but that dropped me outside the tower... There's an army camped there."

"Oh. I had thought of suitable clothes, but not of that." She'd brought a small case in with her in the morning, and Tom had wondered when he put them on. But he was no expert in clubbing-world attire. The people in the 'hospital' place had stared, rather a lot. She looked like a Princess, but that was what she was. Yes, the taxi-driver had said: "Off to a fancy-dress, are you? Or is it a Frozen party?" but they always said strange things. The last one had accused him of being Count Dracula.

She pursed her lips. "Hmm. Well. I suppose we'll just have to go ahead then.

"What?" asked Tom, puzzled.

She shrugged. "They're supposed to be rescuing me. The army and Chief Wizard and the Royal Council of Mages are mine. I am... I mean We are the heir to the Noble House of Corvin. They obey our orders."

"Not me. I'm just a cat-famulus. Might be an apprentice."

"Not you. Me!"

"But you said 'we' and 'our'. I heard you."

"That's the Royal 'we'," she said loftily.

"Oh. I could get the driver to stop and you could find a bush somewhere," said Tom, sympathetically.

"Tch. Not that. It's just that I mean... well, I'm two people."

"Me too. Well, I'm a cat and a boy. It's quite confusing, really."

"Well, then I'm three people. A cat, a person and the Royal Princess. So I... we speak in the plural. And WE are going to give this army its marching orders."

"We are?" Tom wasn't very sure about giving orders. He didn't much like taking them, and those knights had mostly been much larger than he was.

"You could just leave me to do it," she said. "I can drop you off."

"Uh. No." said Tom.

"You're as brave as a lion, Tom," she said, admiringly.

Tom wasn't. He just had the feeling that the Witch, and his Master might catch up with him, if he didn't help her get away. And... well, he ought to do it. That last part was troubling. Not cat-like at all. Stupid. More like a human.

"I did bring you a fake beard. A long straggly white one," said Alamaya, comfortingly.

※※※※※※※

They were standing on a new balcony some seventy feet above the field. Hargarthius tapped the mesh that enclosed the upper section. "I feel like I'm in a cage," he said, grumpily. "We could watch from the roof."

"It is arrow-proof," said King Uther. "I'm not so sure about the siege engines, when they get those working. At the moment they're really not trying very hard. Settling in for a siege, I'd say."

"Hmph," said Hargarthius, looking down on the ram. "That's my door they're battering on. They could damage it."

Emerelda looked up from the working she had laid out on the floor. "Do you two mind being quiet? I am trying to concentrate. Interdimensional magic-to-mobile-phone communication is tricky. It's either that or Alamaya's not answering."

"I think you'd better come and have a look at this, Emerelda!" exclaimed Hargarthius.

So she stood up and did.

A yellow cab was bouncing its way across the field of battle... well, carving its way through the fleeing besiegers toward the front door. Horses found the yellow apparition threatening. It seems that the footmen didn't feel much better about it.

"We'd better get down there in a hurry. We may need to sortie to the rescue..."

"An army of three. Unless we call the leaper away from cooking breakfast," said King Uther. "I hate to ask, but do you think you could manage the illusion of slightly more regal clothing? People do judge by appearances."

Hargarthius pushed back his sleeves, and picked up his staff. "Then there'll be a fair number of newts judging by appearances," he said, crossly.

Emerelda smiled inwardly as they hurried down the stairs. Hargarthius's appearance had certainly altered his behaviour, so maybe he judged himself by it. Anyway, she was somewhat magically recovered by today. She obliged King Uther. There was a finite amount of Newtering that any magician could manage at one time, so an army would over-run them eventually – but did any soldier wish to find out if that amount had been reached?

The magician hauled at the lever to open the great door and portcullis.

It opened in time for King Uther to hear his grand-daughter pronounce – in a voice which might well have frozen boiling lava solid: "We are NOT amused." Unlike King Uther, Emerelda knew who her God-daughter was imitating. It was very effective, even on the sweating men who had just dropped their ram and seized weapons. Possibly the fact that one of them was now a very sweaty frog might have helped. "Have you not been taught how to bow?"

It was quite amusing to see Alamaya dressing the part, down to the tiara and a long-trained gown, sparking with diamonds... well. Something like diamonds anyway, in appearance. She was accompanied by white bearded mage with a silver and ebony staff, in a hooded royal-blue robe. He looked a lot less certain of himself than she did.

※※※※※※※

The Knight who had been directing the rammers had got control of his horse. He raised visor. And then brought his sword up in a smart salute. "Your Royal Highness!"

Alamaya was glad that she recognised him. She gave him the slightest inclination of her head. "What is going on here, Sir Bonavius?"

"Er. We're laying siege to the evil magician Hargarthius's tower. He's er. Kidnapped you. Um. With the Wicked Witch Emerelda."

"We are not kidnapped, Sir Bonavius," she said loftily. "And we do not think you should speak thus of our Godmother."

"Yes, Your Highness. If I can escort you to Duke Karst..."

"You can have him brought here," said King Uther in gravelly voice, or at least a voice that suggested crushing. "He has a great deal of explaining to do."

The knight stared at him. So did Tom. He didn't look much like a raven now. Except he did. He wore black, adorned with gold. He had a feathered cloak over his shoulders, trimmed with ermine. And he was wearing a crown.

Alamaya curtseyed. "Grandfather!"

King Uther walked out and kissed her, very formally on the cheek. "Spoken like a true Corvin, girl," he said quietly. "But here comes trouble. You can get back to the tower..."

Instead of sensibly getting inside, which Tom increasingly thought was a good idea, she shook her head, and turned to face the mass of knights riding up fast, lances lowered. "Anyone got a trumpet?" asked King Uther.

"No. But this'll do," said the Witch, leaning in the window of the taxi-cab, where the driver still sat, mesmerized, and pressed the horn. The cavalcade slowed. "There's only note, but let's see if I can play the royal salute of Ambyria," she said, cheerfully, and proceeded to do her best.

It was enough to slow the van of the charge.

"Too close and I start turning horses into newts," said Master Hargarthius, hefting his staff.

The knight who had been directing the ram was quick on the uptake. "Form up! An honor guard in front of his majesty and her highness."

"That's a knight who will shortly have larger holdings," said King Uther, "And soldiers who are going up in the world."

Tom was not convinced that 'up in the world' didn't mean elevated on the point of a lance. He took a tighter grip on the shaft of this fancy-pants staff Alamaya had got for him, and winced.

"The Doctor said you're supposed to take it easy," said Alamaya, noticing.

"I'll just go and have a little lie down," muttered Tom, not moving. "If we live long enough."

The heavy galloping horses had slowed to a stop in front of them. The lead knight lifted his visor to reveal the grim face of Duke Karst. "Princess Alamaya!" He exclaimed.

"Ahem" said King Uther. "There are going to be some grim examples made if we don't get a royal salute, very soon."

One of the knights responded by spurring his horse and dropping his lance point. "A-Bor... And then dropping his lance to the ground because newts, even newts riding newts don't hold lances very well.

King Uther looked at the fallen armour, and then pointed to the nearest battering-ram footman. "You. Catch that newt. Take off your helmet and put him inside. There are going to be some very difficult questions asked when he recovers. Duke Karst. Dismount. We have various matters to discuss."

"Who are you?" demanded the Duke. But even his iron composure was...less sure of itself.

"We are your King, Duke Karst. King Uther, the second of that name, of the royal House of Corvin." He said it loudly, so the all knights could hear. Half the encampment could probably hear. He'd had a loud voice as a raven, and it hadn't got any softer or gentler because he wasn't just saying 'Nevermore'.

"You're an imposter," said Duke Karst. "King Uther would be an old man now."

Uther looked at him. "You're looking at being shortened by a head, Duke Karst. We have been under an enchantment, from which my loyal servitors have helped to free me. We do not like your doubts, but none-the-less we will prove it to you. Meldro."

The grizzled knight three along from the Duke looked startled. "Me?"

King Uther nodded. "Even after all these years we recognized you, Melchius Meldro. Once a podgy squire who used his knight's sword to knock apples off the tree on the other side of the wall of the royal orchard. I was a prince of the realm, then. I came around the corner and startled your horse and you nicked the blade on the wall. I got you out of trouble for that. I helped you turn the grindstone and polish it."

The elderly knight dropped his lance with a clatter... and clutched his pommel and then dismounted.

He walked forward, drew his sword turned to face his companions. He touched the polished blade with a gauntleted hand. His voice was thick with emotion: "Here is the place I polished that nick out."

Then he turned again and dropped to one knee. "Your Majesty! Welcome back. Zoranythus be thanked that I should live to see you restored! Ambyria rejoices, Your Majesty!"

Several other Knights had dismounted. "Someone could have told him the story," said Duke Karst, loudly. "But I will treat with you, test your assertions with our Chief Wizard. Knights Kelvinius and Porbittius, escort her Highness to the rear, and you... gentlemen may accompany us to the Chief Wizard and his staff. He has magical ways of divining the truth."

One of things about being a cat was one was more aware of things going on around you than most humans were. Tom had noticed the improbably long flowers dangling down the wall. Hundred foot long pansies are more noticeable than normal sized pansies.

"If we suddenly had an army... there might be pickles," he said, loudly.

"What?" Several people looked at him, people like Duke Karst, that he'd rather didn't. But the flowers vanished. And a trumpet sounded behind him, and the sound of drums and other instruments. And marching feet. Many marching feet.

"Dam Busters March," said Emerelda, cheerfully. "Our troops. I think you're being told you're in a pickle, Karst. I'd dismount before you're dismounted."

Of course nothing ever ended tidily. That was a famulus's job, to clean up the mess, and right now Tom was feeling a bit fragile for it. Anyway, he was an apprentice now. The new famulus, once a bouncer in a Goth club, was very lucky the skull of Mrs Drellson had not been resurrected to instruct him. Or not yet, anyway.

First there were more important matters to deal with. A curse. And a Chief Wizard and his surviving cronies.

"First the curse," said King Uther. "It's blighted my line. I want it gone, Hargarthius."

He'd been good at getting his own way as a raven. He was even better at it as king. "It's a simple matter, your Majesty. The tears sapped the courage and nobility of your line, the blood tied it into the breeding, making your heirs all female, all unable to rule, and all dead within a year of childbirth."

"I just need it remedied, not explained."

"Well it is part of the same thing. The tears and blood need to mingle, freely given and freely accepted, the spell read."

"I don't see the golden vials doing any volunteering in the giving or accepting," said King Uther. "Get on with it. The golden vials."

Alamaya still had the vials.

What they didn't have was anything in them.

The King, the witch, and the magician looked in horror at the rip the Roc's claw had left down the side of both vials.

Eventually, Tom broke the silence.

"Excuse me," he said warily.

"Hmph," said Master Hargarthius. "What is it, boy? We've important matters to ponder. Go take the demon a pickle or something."

Tom pressed on. "Does have to be here and now that the two mingled?" he asked.

"Well, it can't be later," said Emerelda, sadly. "It was a pity you didn't know sooner. When the injury happened."

"Well. I think it did. You see... the vials were disguised as the cheese... but Estethius must have done that spell IN the pantry. Things work differently there. And when I took the cheese into... what did you call the place? Gnomandy, it became the snow-leopard. It was strong and brave and noble... it got injured risking its life for all of us. And Alamaya was crying, and bleeding trying to save it. And the leopard was crying and bleeding too. And... um she hasn't been quite the same since."

"I had noticed that," said Emerelda.

Alamaya shrugged. "I didn't want to be a princess, let alone the Queen of Ambyria, before. Then things happened. Tom nearly died. I grew up," said Alamaya. "I am a Corvin, whether I like it or not."

Emerelda chuckled. "Seeing as you told me you wanted to just stay in the other-world, and just be a party-girl, and never come back to Ambyria... I think Tom may be right. It's odd about the cheese, though."

"Revenge," said Master Hargarthius. "Estethius always hated cheese – so he made the finest part of the line of Corvin into something he hated. I suspect... now, that the curse *could* only be broken in Gnomandy – where the tears and blood were in a form that expressed the nature of what they were magical symbols of. It is part of you, now, Princess."

Alamaya looked at herself. "I rather like the idea of being part snow-leopard. I am not so sure about being part cheese," she said with a small smile.

"I was fond of the cheese," said Tom, rather sadly. "I used to feed it milk and stroke it. It used to purr at me."

The Princess patted his arm. "You know, you might be right, Tom. I've decided I really like milk, and I didn't used to."

Emerelda decided to lead the discussion on before the two of them got busy with the subject of stroking and purring. She was, in herself, fairly certain the curse had been broken. "Well. There are tests I can do. But now I think we'd better go and deal with that last sore: the Chief Wizard – before he runs off and is hard to find. I think, Tom, you should lie down for a bit and rest that wound. No, Alamaya. You do not need to help him to lie down. But you do need to stay here. You'd be a prize worth capturing, and you need to learn more magic. Uther, I think we'd better have a few troops." She refused to call him by a title, after all, in hierarchy terms they were equals, but her subjects were harder to command, which is why she seldom did. It suited both sides

She had expected the Chief Wizard to have fled. His acolytes had. But he was sitting in a kind of throne, in the middle of his pavilion.

"I suppose you think you've won," he said as they entered the tent. "I was waiting. I knew you'd come. It's a pity you didn't burn, Emerelda. But this will be worse in some ways."

"He reminds me of my old master when he didn't get his

way," said Hargarthius.

"I always admired Estethius. Why he picked a dead loss like you for a famulus I will never know. I begged him for the position," said Kolumnus bitterly. "And now you will both die. You are in bespelled quicksand. It will draw you down to your death. And by all means try your worst spells against me, before I leave. I have put a great deal of research into my ethereal shield," he sneered.

Emerelda's feet were already sinking, trapping her.

But she had her trusty shoulder bag with her. It was an alternate universe fashion accessory that she really liked. She had thought that it and its contents might be useful for the problems they faced on returning here.

So she took her Smith and Wesson .357 Magnum out of her bag, calmly, and put three rounds through his body-mass just as her instructor had taught her, and two more through his head. The throne kept his body more-or-less-upright, and she was proud of her grouping. Kolumnus, however, was too dead to appreciate it, and his brain was too scattered for a jar.

The noise was enough to call soldiers.

And one thing about camps and soldiers, was that they had ropes to haul her out of the quicksand.

It was quite un-necessary for Hargarthius to have stripped his robe off, laid his staff on it and used it to spread his weight and get out of the quicksand by leaving his boots in it. How like a man, she thought. He had to prove he could escape all by himself, even if he only had socks to wear afterwards.

EPILOGUE

Being an apprentice, Tom discovered was entirely different from being a mere famulus. It meant you got to share the washing up. Tom wasn't ready to trust the bouncer to a hoom-broom, but at least he was quite a good cook. Tom hadn't realised he wasn't, as he hadn't much experience of what good cooking ought to taste like, and disembodied re-animated skulls don't do much food-tasting.

He was also expected to spend time reading. Of course, that was extra time that he had to find somewhere.

Some things had, however, returned to normal. The demon had returned to his chamber-pot in the lab. When Tom asked him why – as he was no longer bound, the demon had given a smoky shrug. "The pansies dig the place. And it's easier than providing my own pickles."

Tom wasn't sure that was the whole answer, but it was all he was getting from Hariselden.

Emerelda, King Uther, and Alamaya had all left for Borbungsburg castle, along with the army. "Why don't you change the name?" Tom asked, ever curious.

King Uther had looked puzzled. "Why? The Borbungs built it. I can't go back in history and build it instead. And it must gall them every time they think of a Corvin on the throne there. Besides, everyone with any intelligence would know it a lie, a claim to have built something we did not."

They were due to go to the castle soon. Tom heard a great deal about it from Alamaya, who had introduced him to a magical messaging system called Txt. It was a gr8 help with spelling, if not with spells. Being human was hard on cat. But there were times he had to admit it was better. And in three days they'd be taking the new carpet, and repaired trunk to the castle. King Uther had decided to make Hargarthius the new Chief Wizard. "But I have no desire to be that. I don't believe in organized magic. Even less than I believe in government being involved in magic," the Master had protested.

"Exactly. That's how we knew you were the ideal candidate. After nearly thirty years of watching you, we know you'd be terrible at it," King Uther informed him, regally.

Human politics were difficult to understand, and in Tom's opinion, needlessly complicated. He had a catlike impatience with the Master not doing precisely what Tom wanted right now, which was to go there.

In the meanwhile he at least had the thought of Alamaya's farewell to comfort him. Her theory was, now that King Uther was doing the serious business of being King, being courted by all the court ladies from half the kingdoms around, in between executing Borbung sympathisers and going about the normal declaring of war and signing of peace and the other hack-slash-and-mutilate of good government, that the two them could slip off to go clubbing sometimes, just as soon as they both could get away. He was looking forward to it. A lot.

About the Author

Dave Freer is the author or co-author of more than 20 novels. SLOW TRAIN TO ARCTURUS was a Wall Street Journal sf bestseller. Various other books have also been on the Locus bestseller lists. His CHANGELING'S ISLAND was shortlisted in the Dragon Awards for the best Fantasy Novel and for best Young Adult Novel.

He lives on a remote island off the coast of Australia, with his wife, dog, cats, pigs and chickens. You can get the full bio and links to his other sites from his Amazon Author Page. For a complete list of his work and stories which are available nowhere else, see davefreer.com.

www.ingramcontent.com/pod-product-compliance
Lightning Source LLC
Chambersburg PA
CBHW072050170626
46813CB00004B/1293